# CALL TO ARMS

---

## DIVISION SERIES #2

ANGUS MCLEAN

Published 2015 by Smoking Gun Publications

ISBN 978 0 473 56085 0

# ALSO BY ANGUS MCLEAN

**Chase Investigations Series**

*Old Friends*

*Honey Trap*

*Sleeping Dogs*

*Tangled Webs*

*Dirty Deeds*

*Red Mist*

*Fallen Angel*

*Holy Orders*

*Deal Breaker*

**The Division Series**

*Smoke and Mirrors*

*Call to Arms*

*The Shadow Dancers*

*The Berlin Conspiracy*

*No Second Chance*

**Nicki Cooper Mystery Series**

*The Country Club Caper*

**Early Warning Series**

*Martial Law*

*Getting Home*

*Stand Fast*

# CALL TO ARMS

## BY ANGUS MCLEAN

# PROLOGUE

The heist went down on a Tuesday morning.

It was March, the tail end of summer, verging on autumn. Being Wellington that meant it was windy and cold. People died and lives were irreparably changed forever.

The armoured truck rolled out of the Australasian Corporate Bank's secure car park on Featherston Street at exactly 0950 hours with three uniformed guards and $20 million in gold bullion on board.

Their destination was the Reserve Bank three blocks away on The Terrace and only a handful of staff from either bank knew of the bullion movement.

It was past rush hour and the planned journey of less than a kilometre was projected to take less than four minutes, even with the road works on Brandon Street.

In the driver's seat of the armoured truck sat Rex Mueller, a former coal miner who had been with the security company for a decade. He was a grizzled man in his early fifties with a beer gut and a copy of Best Bets permanently hanging from his back pocket. Beside him sat Sanjay Pillay, a skinny thirty year old Indian who was on his first bullion transfer assignment.

Mueller guided the truck out into the traffic and chopped up a couple of gears, checking his mirrors all around as he did so. Moving so much gold always made him nervous, even though he knew they basically melted into the background. The truck was plain white with the markings of a cleaning company and all the guards wore plain overalls. Aside from their origin and destination, to the casual observer there was no indication of their true purpose.

But despite that Mueller couldn't shake the nagging feeling in his gut. He'd woken that morning with a sick feeling and it had stayed with him right up until now. He'd had the same feeling down in the mines sometimes, and he trusted his instincts.

But the show had to go on, and he tried to push it aside.

Besides, they had the cops watching their backs, so what could go wrong, right?

Mueller took a deep breath through his nose and tried to shake the feeling. He focussed on the road ahead and cast a quick glance at Pillay, pleased to see he was watching his side diligently.

'Alright back there, Steveo?' he asked through the intercom.

The guard in the back came straight back. 'All good so far, bokkie.'

Mueller smiled to himself. Steveo was a country boy from down the line-he'd learned that anywhere in this country was "down the line" from wherever you happened to be-and had adopted Mueller as his mentor. He loved to rib the older man, especially adopting Afrikaans words to use, but was a good guard who put in the hours.

'Stop checking out those ninjas and watch our back,' Mueller told him, referring to the two special tactics cops in the back with Steveo.

'Roger that, baas.'

Mueller snorted and eased back from a Toyota hatchback in front of him that was dicking around. He could see an old lady's grey perm over the top of the driver's seat and cursed elderly drivers.

He still couldn't shake that impending sense of doom.

As the armoured truck turned into Brandon Street behind the red Toyota hatchback, Jonah Jones keyed his walkie talkie.

'Brandon now. Ten seconds.'

'Gotcha,' came a reply from one unit, followed a moment later by a second acknowledgement.

Jonah undid the seatbelt and hefted the Ruger Mini 14 with the folded stock in the foot well. He glanced at the driver of the grey Mitsubishi Pajero beside him and their eyes met. Both men nodded.

'It's go time,' Jonah said.

In the plain blue DAF van two car lengths behind the armoured truck, the driver indicated a right turn and watched the truck take the corner into Brandon Street. The people mover between them followed and the DAF driver was close behind. His name was Chris Greening and he was a member of the Special Tactics Group. Like the man beside him he wore a plain grey jacket over his kit. The four guys in the back were fully kitted out in their black gear, but as the newest addition to the squad Greening didn't get to play this time round.

As he started to move round the corner on the green arrow he caught a flicker of movement from his left and heard his passenger shout.

'Fuck, watch out!'

A medium sized cargo truck blew through the intersection and smashed straight into the left side of the DAF. Glass exploded and the sound of impact was deafening as the van was lifted and thrown into the oncoming lane. The truck didn't slow but instead shoved the van harder, overbalancing it and throwing it onto its right side.

Greening's head slammed against the window and the world spun around him. Shouts and thuds sounded from the boys in the back as they were tossed round like rag dolls.

At the same time as the van was taken out a city bus pulled out from the curb in front of the armoured truck.

Mueller cursed and hit the brakes, at the same time as he heard shouts from the back of the truck.

The STG operators were shouting at him to move, having heard an emergency call over their secure radio. Steveo joined in, banging on the partition between the cab and the rear and bellowing at him to move.

'There's a fucken bus in the way, man!' Mueller shouted back in frustration, leaning on the horn.

'Oh no, mate...' Pillay started to say, and Mueller saw the threat immediately.

The bus door opened and two men stepped out. One carried an assault rifle of some sort and Mueller's jaw dropped when he saw what the second man carried-an RPG7 rocket launcher. Both men wore normal street clothes but with body armour over the top and topped off with balaclavas and gloves.

They were only ten metres away, staring straight into the cab of the armoured truck, when the one with the launcher raised it to show them. He pointed at it and then at them.

The message was clear.

IN THE BACK of the stricken DAF, Sergeant Brad Travis pushed one of his colleagues off him and reached for the back doors. The boys were all shouting and someone was moaning, obviously injured, and he keyed his radio.

'Zero-Alpha, One-one.'

The squad commander came back immediately. 'Zero-Alpha.'

'We've been T-boned and incapacitated, corner Featherston...'

The rest of his transmission was drowned out by the crackle of automatic weapons fire and rounds started pinging through the sheet metal of the van. Brad threw himself at the doors, wrenching the handle and exploding out into the sunlight in a black-clad 120kg fury.

He hit the ground and rolled, snatching at the Heckler and Koch MP5 on its sling, sweeping the safety to auto fire as he came up and swivelled, scanning for threats. The sound of gunfire was dulled by his ear protectors but with two gunmen just metres away it was still loud.

One was side on to him, pumping rounds from a semi-automatic shotgun into the bottom of the van, obviously hoping to get the boys in the back. The second was up near the front of the van and had an assault rifle of some kind-Brad couldn't quite see him clearly.

The guy closest to him started to turn, the barrel of the shotgun coming with him. He wore body armour over normal street clothes, with a balaclava over his head and gloves covering his hands. The guy started to shout something and Brad cut him off.

The MP5 came up and he triggered a burst, catching the guy straight in the side and spinning him front on. The shotgun went off again and blew the exhaust pipe off the bottom of the DAF. Brad's second burst was three rounds which stitched the guy from the collar bone to the left eye, blowing brains and blood out in a fine mist. He dropped like a puppet with cut strings.

The second guy popped into view now, an AK variant in his hands seeking out whoever had just taken out his mate.

Rounds arced over Brad's head as he ducked back behind the van, bellowing at the boys to get moving. Through the open door he could see one of them was down in the back, but the other two were scrambling for the back door.

He keyed his radio. 'Ten-ten, ten-ten, automatic weapons. Contact contact!"

The AK continued firing, blowing out the windscreen, rounds zipping through the van and flying all around. Whoever was using it seemed to have some training from the trigger control they were exercising; this wasn't a gang-style spray and walk away.

Brad kept low and moved right, grabbing Matt by the vest and yanking him out of the van.

'Jase is down,' Matt panted, referring to the front seat passenger. 'I think he's hit.'

Craig joined them, his SMG at the ready and fire in his eyes. He was an older guy and Brad's top man on the squad.

'One guy at the front,' he said tersely, 'got an AK or similar.' He sniffed habitually. 'Jase is down, so's Kel. Not sure about Greeno.'

Brad scowled. 'Matt, chuck a stunny at the front and we move in three. Double banger. You guys go left, I'll go right. Take that fucker out.'

The boys nodded and Matt readied a flash bang. Brad counted off on his fingers and on three Matt lobbed the grenade over the van towards the attacker.

It exploded with a thunderous boom and a blinding flash of magnesium and the three operators moved.

The second detonation erupted and they burst clear of the van, seeking targets. The gunman had ducked back to the side of the road where a station wagon was parked and waited for them, his Norinco Type 84 at the shoulder. He averted his eyes from the flashes he knew would come, and when he saw the first black clad cop emerge on his right, he opened up.

Craig's right leg was blown out from beneath him and he went down with a thump. Matt turned towards the shooter and blasted a long burst that took chunks off the front of the station wagon. Brad was also cutting loose from the other side of the van but the shooter had already moved, keeping low as he circled to the rear of the wagon. He plucked a fragmentation grenade from a belt pouch and pulled the pin. Releasing the spoon he counted to two and lobbed it overhead.

Matt was dragging Craig backwards by his vest, his MP5 up and ready when he saw the grenade sail towards them.

'Grenade!'

He back pedalled faster and triggered a short burst towards the shooter, hoping they could make it back to cover but knowing they wouldn't.

The grenade detonated and peppered the area with shrapnel. Craig took more hits and Matt fell backwards, his lower body being protected by his colleague but his arms and hands all taking hits.

Brad let out a growl and glanced round the front of the van. Rounds punched through the steel roof just over his head and he ducked back, swearing angrily.

He keyed his radio.

'One-one, grenade deployed, we need help here! We've got at least two casualties.'

He risked another glance and got more rounds in return, more accurate this time.

'Fuck!'

For now, he was pinned down.

THE FRONT DOORS of the armoured truck were open and Mueller and Pillay lay on the road face down with the gunner carrying the assault rifle standing over them. The gunman with the RPG stood facing the rear of the truck, the launcher on his shoulder and aimed straight at the three men in the back.

'I know you can hear me,' the rocket man shouted. 'Open the doors and come out. If you don't, you all die. Do it now.'

The doors slowly opened and the Maori guard in plain overalls showed himself, hands in the air.

Movement came from the Pajero at the curb, and two more men alighted, clad like their colleagues. One carried a Mini 14 with the stock folded, the other a WW2-era M3 "grease gun." They stood to the side of the rocket, weapons trained on the rear of the truck.

It was only thirty five seconds since the incident started.

'Don't shoot,' Steveo called out, his voice wavering and his eyes wide. 'I'm unarmed.'

'Open the doors,' the rocket man ordered. 'Do it!'

Steveo pushed the doors open wider, knees bent as he started to step down. From behind him came a shout. 'Down!'

Steveo threw himself forward and down. The two operators in the back darted forward now, MP5s raised and a flash bang arcing out towards the attackers.

The rocket man stepped away and the two gunners with him came forward. The man with the submachine gun closed his eyes and pinned the trigger back. The M3 snarled and spat fat .45 rounds into the doorway, nailing both operators.

The flash bang went off deafeningly loud but the sub-gunner held the trigger down until he felt it rattle to a stop.

The operator on the left dropped with a round through the groin, bright arterial blood spurting out in a long jet. The second cop got off a burst that caught the sub-gunner in the chest of his ballistic vest and knocked him flat. He leaped from the back of the truck and spun to address the threat from his right, but too late.

Jonah Jones unleashed the Ruger and hosed him down with .223 rounds, punching bullets through the cop's right arm and shoulder and neck. The cop involuntarily triggered another burst as he fell, and Jonah stepped forward, putting another burst into him as he lay prone and dying on the road.

He then turned to the unarmed guard who lay at his feet. Steveo looked up at him, hands raised.

'Please don't kill me,' he pleaded, 'please don't kill me.'

Jonah put a round through his head and stepped back. The man with the M3 picked himself off the road with a chuckle, fingering the damage to his armour.

BRAD REGROUPED with Matt and Craig at the rear of the van. Craig was holding a dressing to the bullet entry wound in his right calf, while Matt quickly applied another to the exit wound at the back of it, where most of the blood was coming from.

The older man was spouting an endless stream of curses and seemed in good spirits.

The street was chaos, civilian vehicles haphazardly stopped every-where and people running for cover. Brad saw one young guy standing on the footpath, brazenly holding his phone up for a selfie with the carnage as his background.

'Get back!' Brad shouted, waving him away. The young guy ignored him, and even grinned while he continued filming. 'Get under cover!'

The young guy shifted positions, recording Brad as he moved towards him.

'Get behind cover dickhead!'

Still the guy didn't move. Brad exposed himself to fire as he dashed forward onto the footpath, slapping the phone away and snarling as he hustled the young guy into a doorway and shoved him to the ground.

'Stay the fuck out of the way or I'll shoot you myself, you fucken clown.'

He raced back to his colleagues and changed magazines, knowing he only had one spare now plus his sidearm. If this shit went on much longer he'd be out of ammo. Just as he started to speak he heard another vehicle arrive.

A white Ford Transit pulled up near the damaged cargo truck, which was now idling and leaking engine fluids onto the road. The rear doors of the Transit van opened and they could see the barrel of a machine gun pointing towards them now. It looked like an old M60 and Brad felt his mouth go dry.

It began to chatter as Matt and Brad both went flat, covering Craig. Heavy bullets slammed into the Police van, physically rocking it with the impacts. The gunner moved from behind the station wagon, pausing only long enough to empty his magazine into the van before jumping into the front passenger's seat.

The van stayed where it was, engine running, and Brad realised they were waiting for something.

Sirens were sounding and he hoped the cavalry was on the way. He keyed his radio again.

'One-one, we have a machine gun in a white Transit, taking fire. We have another casualty. We need eyes in the sky and an SFP at Waring and Taylor Streets, copy?'

The proposed Safe Forward Point was two blocks away; plenty of space for back up to assemble and move forward.

The boss came back. 'Zero-Alpha, working on it, struggling to get a chopper. Stand by for further.'

'We need it now,' Brad snapped back, 'it's a fucken war zone down here.'

He ducked as rounds pierced the van around him, and glanced at Matt who was still trying to dress Craig's wounds.

'Fuck this. It's time for offense.'

THE BUS MOVED BACK to the curb and the M3 gunner jumped into the cab of the armoured truck. The rocket man got behind the wheel of the Pajero and slipped it into gear. Jonah Jones paused before joining him, and raked the cars on the far side of the road with the Mini-14, emptying the magazine as he blew out windows and sent rubber-neckers diving for cover. He ejected the mag, slapped in another thirty rounds and put bursts into the vehicles on the near side of the road.

Satisfied with his work, he took the passenger seat of the Pajero and keyed his walkie talkie.

'Let's go.'

The bus driver paused to collect the guns from the two STG oper-ators before climbing into the front of the armoured truck and both vehicles calmly moved off towards The Terrace.

As they got to the intersection, they went to turn left but suddenly the Pajero stopped. Barely eighty metres away was a marked Police car, with two cops hurrying to arm themselves from the gun cabinet in the boot.

The driver got out with his RPG and raised it to his shoulder. A watching civilian shouted a warning and the cops looked up, just in time to see a rocket propelled grenade streaking towards them. They both dived to the side and it took the car out in a ball of flame, the explosion setting off car alarms all around them. Flaming debris rained down and a mushroom cloud of smoke rose to the sky. The rocket man climbed back into the Pajero and followed the armoured truck towards the motorway.

BRAD HEARD the machine gun open up again as he crab walked around the side of the van. Pieces blew off the van and bullets chipped the walls of the building behind him. The gun fell silent and the engine revved. He took a last deep breath and dashed forward.

The white Transit was moving off, the back doors still open, going straight ahead down Featherston Street.

Brad raced into the road, the MP5 at the shoulder as he triggered short bursts at the rear gunner. The risk of collateral damage was huge from all the rounds flying around the place, and he was willing every round onto the target as he fired. The slide locked back before he knew it and he did a rapid magazine change on the move, slapping his last one into place and chambering a fresh round. The gunner cut loose again but the barrel was jumpy, sending the rounds wide and high. Brad methodically pumped the trigger, seeing a second guy in the back of the van step up beside the machine gunner, who was lying prone.

He could see his rounds impacting in the back of the Transit, sparking and ricocheting, and he saw the second guy drop as he took a hit. The mag went dry and he dropped the MP5 on its sling, snatching the Glock 17 from his thigh holster instead.

The Transit was accelerating away across the intersection, maybe forty metres away now. Brad kept moving forward as he kept the Glock up in a two-handed aim, squeezing off shots at the machine gunner, who was still firing short bursts.

Seventeen squeezes later the slide locked open and he automatically dropped the mag out and slammed his spare into place, the Glock never moving off line. The Transit was fifty metres away now and about to move out of sight behind the stationary traffic.

The machine gunner raised himself off the floor, reaching for another belt of ammo and Brad squeezed off two shots, knowing this was it.

The first round took the gunner in the left armpit as he reached up and across, punching straight through and into his neck. The second round blasted through his left ear into his skull. He slumped across the machine gun.

The Transit continued on and Brad came to a stop, lowering his gun.

He turned and looked around him. He could see bodies further up Brandon Street, three lying in pools of blood and two others starting to move.

Pedestrians and motorists were everywhere. Bullet casings littered the road, sparkling in the sun. Gun smoke hung in the air.

He glanced down and saw blood on his pants. He didn't know if it was his or not.

He keyed his radio and gave an update to the boss back at the station. Sirens came closer and he could hear the roar of engines approaching. A couple of patrol cars flew past, chasing the Transit. Still no chopper upstairs though.

Brad unstrapped his helmet and yanked it off, feeling the fresh air on his sweaty face.

'Fuck,' he muttered.

# 1

Jack Travis saw the visitor well before he got to his front door and pushed himself up from the dining table, putting down his pen and picking up his coffee mug.

The blue Hyundai Sonata bumped down the gravel farm driveway from the road, approaching the weatherboard bungalow slowly and pulling up near the open detached garage. A forest green Holden Colorado double cab ute was parked inside, splashed with mud.

A Honda quad bike stood nearby. A border collie barked and ran from the porch, wagging his tail excitedly and watching as the visitor alighted from the vehicle.

He was a medium sized man with sandy hair and an unremarkable face, dressed casually in chinos and a black Kathmandu jacket. When he walked he had a slight but noticeable limp, and he carried himself stiffly.

Jed Ingoe-known as Jedi- had been the Regimental Sergeant Major of 1NZSAS Group until he lost part of his leg in an IED incident in Afghanistan. Invalided from the Army, he had traded being one of the hardest men to ever wear the sand beret to being the Operations Officer for Division 5 of the Security Intelligence Service.

Known as The Division, it was the most covert unit of the security service. The former Special Forces operators it employed carried out the dirty work of the Government, the blackest of the black operations. The stuff that needed to be done to keep the playing fields level-within reason-between the good guys and those that sought to disrupt peace.

Ingoe never did anything without reason, and so it was today that he came cold calling on Jack Travis. He turned his gaze from the rolling farmland to the paddocks closer to the house. A couple contained heifer calves and chooks pecked around another near a coop. He saw that the ground dropped away from the other side of the house to a pond where a few ducks swam lazily. A small creek ran through the property and fed the pond.

Beside the house was a large vegetable garden behind a trellis fence, a smaller herb garden adjacent to it. Citrus and other fruit trees grew on the other side of the house and a grape vine had spread itself along a fence. The house was on tank water and he could see a couple of solar panels on the roof.

Ingoe turned back to the house itself, which was in need of a fresh coat of paint. A pair of muddy gumboots stood by the door, which was open. An oilskin coat hung on a hook above the boots.

A man stood in the doorway. He was six foot and strongly built, a few years younger than Ingoe. Receding dark hair going to grey and clipped very short, unshaven and with an outdoorsman's complexion. He wore faded jeans and his checked flannel shirt was hanging out. A steaming cup of coffee was in one hand, the other tucked in his pocket. He was watching Ingoe.

Ingoe's stoic expression creased into a smile and he moved forward, hand extended.

'Good to see you, Jack.'

'You too.' Travis gave his hand a short, hard pump. He smiled and moved inside. 'Come in, I've just made a pot.'

Ingoe followed him in through an open living area into a large farm-style kitchen. Classic rock was coming from a stereo in the lounge. Ingoe wasn't too up with the play with the genre-if it wasn't about cowboys and lost love and life on the range, he didn't want to know. Travis took another mug from a cupboard and filled it from the machine on the bench. He gave it to Ingoe and gestured for him to take a seat at the breakfast bar.

Ingoe did so and took a sip. It was black and strong. French doors opened from the dining area onto a wide deck that overlooked the rolling green farmland. Ingoe admired the view for a moment. 'Machine coffee,' he commented. 'You going all Ponsonby on us, Jack?'

Travis smiled again. 'Just like good coffee.' He flicked a nod towards his visitor's leg. 'How's the leg?'

Ingoe shrugged. 'It is what it is. I get by.' He took another sip and put his mug down. 'Living off the grid yet?'

'Working on it.' Travis used a remote to turn down the stereo. 'It's everybody's dream isn't it?'

Ingoe changed tack. 'Been back long?' Travis gave him a sharp look and Ingoe grinned.

'A month. I had six months in Iraq and two in Syria.'

'Residential?' He was referring to residential security, a common role in trouble spots for former operators on the Circuit.

'Some, plus escorting some news crews.' Travis gave a small grin. 'Interesting times.'

Ingoe nodded, warming his hands on the mug. 'Seen the news?'

'Yep.' Travis gestured towards the morning's paper spread out on the dining table. A laptop stood open beside it, with a notepad and pen. The pad had brief notes jotted down.

Ingoe nodded. 'Big news.'

'Bad news. Sounds organised.'

'Very.'

'How many dead?'

Ingoe paused, considering his response. 'More than what the media say.'

'They've said a security guard, three cops and two civilians dead, plus one baddie. And five cops and four more civvies wounded.' Travis watched him, assessing his reply.

'That's true. Probably two more casualties for the bad guys though, we think one dead if not both.'

Travis let out a low whistle. 'That's some serious fire fight. And in downtown Wellington too.'

'And about twenty million bucks worth of gold bullion taken.'

Travis whistled again. 'They had a machine gun and grenades and an RPG?'

'Yep.'

Travis sipped his own coffee before crossing to the pantry and taking out a biscuit barrel. Ingoe took one and examined it with a wry grin.

'Anzac biscuits?'

'Made with my own hand.' Travis took a bite of one and they both chewed in silence for a minute. 'So this isn't a social call then.'

Ingoe put his biscuit on the benchtop. 'No,' he said carefully. 'All that ordnance came from somewhere, and the bullion is going some-where too.'

'Sounds like a job for the cops, not our...your outfit.'

Ingoe tilted his head slightly. 'In theory. There's an international angle to it though.'

'And? You don't need me. The Boss made it pretty clear I wouldn't be coming back.'

Ingoe met his gaze. 'The cops involved. They were STG.'

Travis paused. Ingoe continued.

'One of them took out three of the bad guys.' Ingoe met his gaze calmly. 'Your nephew.'

Travis felt a kick in his chest and put his mug down. 'Brad.'

INGOE'S HYUNDAI was disappearing out onto the winding road to make his way from Onewhero back across the river towards Tuakau. Travis stood on the deck and watched it go, emptying his mug, his brow furrowed.

He turned back inside and glanced at the notes he'd been making when his former boss had arrived. The robbery and subsequent shootout was headline news worldwide and he had followed it closely over the last several hours. Experience had told him it was more than a bunch of hoods robbing a cash-in-transit van, as had been told to the media.

Experience. From joining the Army as a boy to eighteen years in the Group, ending up as a Squadron Sergeant Major-Warrant Officer Class 2, and next in line for the RSM position after Ingoe's tragedy. Next in line, that was, until his run in with an obnoxious Air Force pilot. The pilot had objected to being taken to task over his recklessness and Travis had objected to a twenty six year old officer trying to put him in his place.

The result was a broken nose for the pilot and a pending court martial for Travis. It could have been dealt with had the pilot not been the son of a senior Cabinet Minister. His exit without charges had been arranged quickly and Travis found himself out in the cold, thrown into work on the Circuit with former comrades from all arms of the forces round the world.

The last year had been a journey of intense self-discovery for the tough former SSM, and he had planned on taking some time out to get his property operating how he wanted it to be. His remark to Ingoe about living off the grid wasn't too far from the truth; the attraction was strong, although he was realistic enough to know that to be completely self-sufficient was a big ask and very time consuming.

He had heifers and chickens, sufficient fruit and vegetables all year round, and a good trade arrangement with neighbours who ran sheep and pigs. Seasonal hunting helped keep the freezers full.

But as he watched the Hyundai disappear from sight down the winding country road, Travis knew without a doubt that he was about to step back into the fold.

He'd let his nephew down before; he wouldn't do it again.

## 2

————————

The Division's base was in Upper Queen Street in an otherwise innocuous seeming building.

Government employees came and went downstairs, but two floors were reserved for the operators and support staff.

Travis was on time for his meeting with the Director, and was met in the reception area by a pair of heavies in suits. He was put through a metal detector, an electronic fingerprint scanner, checked for recording and transmitting devices and eventually allowed to sign in. His photo was taken and he was issued a Visitor's Pass.

Ingoe took him up in the elevator to a different reception area lined with floor to ceiling shelves of heavy tomes. An older lady manned the desk there and checked his Visitor's Pass before pushing an intercom button to alert the Director.

'Thanks Trixie,' Ingoe said, and Travis was amused to note that Trixie gave Ingoe a lingering smile as she buzzed open a side door. Ingoe led the way into a long conference room. Three people were waiting at the polished table.

The first was a chubby man somewhere around sixty, with a bland Government-issue face and an understated charcoal suit. He had the air of authority about him, a full head of grey hair and shrewd blue eyes which sized Travis up as he entered the room. He had spook written all over him. The Director.

The second person was anything but bland. She was taller than average for a woman and athletic looking, maybe mid-thirties. Her chestnut hair was thick and wavy and fell to the shoulders of her sharp navy blue suit. She had intelligent hazel eyes behind dark rimmed glasses and her skin was tanned and clear of makeup aside from subtle lipstick. Travis felt her eyes on him as he let the door swing shut behind him. Maybe a lawyer?

The third person he sensed before even laying eyes on him. Brad Travis stood by the window, his big mitts in the pockets of his jeans. His sandy hair was messy and he was unshaven and scowling. He was in his late twenties. He wore a black T shirt that accentuated the bulging muscles in his torso and arms. He didn't smile when Travis made eye contact, just nodded.

Travis nodded back and shook the Director's extended hand.

'Thanks for coming in, Sergeant-Major,' the man said, with what might have been a smile. His hand was surprisingly hard and Travis mentally reassessed him. 'It's very important to us that you are here, for reasons that will become apparent very soon, I am sure.'

'No problem,' Travis murmured, 'and it's Jack.' He turned to the woman.

'Susie,' she said. Her hand was firm and dry and she made solid eye contact, assessing him close up. Not a lawyer, he decided. Probably another spook. He caught the whiff of scent, something alluring and warm and probably very expensive.

'And of course no introductions are needed for Brad,' the older man continued, gesturing to the six foot four monster at the window.

Travis stepped forward and extended his hand. Brad enveloped it in a crushing grip, holding for longer than was necessary and staring intently into his uncle's eyes as he did so. He had green eyes that were hot and defensive. Travis extracted his hand and took a seat beside Ingoe.

The Director sat opposite them, Susie at his side. Each had a leather compendium open before them. The Director gestured for Brad to sit as well but he shook his head and stayed where he was.

'I'm fine thanks,' he rasped.

The Director eyed him for a moment before relenting and turning back to Travis and Ingoe.

'Obviously everything said in here stays here. This meeting never happened and we have never met. Any breach of that trust will be treated extremely seriously, is that clear?'

Travis nodded his assent.

'As you are aware, Wellington's Police Special Tactics Group was involved in the bullion robbery and shootout yesterday. Sergeant Travis was one of those involved. It was the largest shooting incident the New Zealand Police have ever been involved in and left three officers dead plus two civilians and one of the security guards. Further to that five other officers and four civilians were wounded, three critically-one of the officers and two of the civilians.'

He let that sit for a moment before continuing.

'One of the robbers was confirmed dead at the scene. Two more of the robbers were shot and we believe at least one of them is dead, if not both. They escaped along with the rest of the gang, and no bodies have turned up.'

The Director looked to his colleague beside him and she took the lead.

'The robber whose body was recovered has been identified as an Auckland-based criminal, a member of the Southern Bandits outlaw motorcycle gang. Raymond Baillie, known as Little Ray. A patched member with various convictions, including previous robberies, firearms offences and Class A drug dealing. On parole for the last year from a seven year stretch.' She paused, watching Travis. 'My area of focus recently has been home grown terrorists, including the usual jihadists but as part of an investigation into them, these guys have floated to the surface.'

She hit a button on a remote and screens slid up from the table top in front of each of them. A montage of photos appeared, each being either a mugshot of a hardened criminal or a surveillance type photo of a patched gang member. They wore gang regalia with the Southern Bandits patch.

'Over the years they have been one of a number of gangs working in the methamphetamine trade, running brothels and gambling rings, and the usual stand overs and aggravated robberies and other violence that comes with their business. They have made millions and are traditionally hard to pin down.'

'Obviously Little Ray abided by his parole conditions,' Brad growled.

The Director looked at him sharply. 'That's something that the Corrections Department will have to answer. It's not something we are concerned with.'

He looked back to Susie and gave her a nod to continue.

'Intel tells us that the jihadists are actively fund raising in this country, via all the usual routes of fraud, donations from sympathiser's etcetera.' Susie's eyes took on a gleam now as she got to the guts of her narrative. 'More recently we've had intel that the Southern Bandits have lined up a big job that will potentially earn them millions.'

'And so it was,' the Director commented. Susie sat back and he took the lead again. 'The bullion being transferred was almost 400 kilograms, close to twenty million dollars' worth. It was a fairly standard job as far as bullion transfers go.' He caught the questioning look on Travis' face. 'They happen more often than you would think.'

'Do Stidge always do the escorts?' Travis asked, using one of the nicknames for STG-the other one was Super Tough Guys, but it didn't seem appropriate to use right now.

'For jobs that big, yeah,' Ingoe replied.

Travis nodded and the Director watched him intently.

'What's on your mind then, Sergeant-Major?'

'Well,' Travis said carefully, 'I'm just wondering why I'm actually here.' He ticked points off on his fingers. 'I'm in neither the spooks, the cops nor the Group. I'm not involved in any way at all. I don't know who did it aside from what you've just told me.'

He cocked an eyebrow at the Director and waited. The Director looked to Ingoe, who rolled his chair out from the table and turned to face Travis.

'You know Brad was the shooter. Unfortunately his face is all over the media now, so keeping him as unnamed Officer A isn't an option anymore.'

Travis nodded. He'd seen it-the front page of the morning Herald was a close up of his nephew holding his ballistic helmet in one hand and his Glock in the other, standing in the middle of an intersection surrounded by smashed cars and glaring at whoever had taken the photo on their cell phone. There was also footage on the internet of some of the action, including the clip from the kid who Brad had braved fire to drag to safety. The little punk had sold his soul to the media devil and there was Brad, forever immortalised on the 'net swearing at the kid and threatening to shoot him.

'Brad was interviewed last night about his involvement,' Ingoe continued. 'It usually takes a few days for that to happen, but he wanted to get it done and we helped facilitate that.'

'I've got nothing to hide,' Brad stated firmly. 'I just did my job.'

'And nobody is disputing that,' Ingoe replied evenly, 'but obviously there is a lot of work to be done before you can be officially cleared from any liability in that. The civilians who were wounded don't appear, at this stage, to have been wounded by Police fire. Two were injured by the patrol car explosion, one crashed their car into a wall trying to get away and the other one appears to have been hit by shrapnel in Brandon Street, which Brad never fired into.'

'What about the dead?' Brad enquired softly, and Travis immediately realised this was also news to him.

Ingoe glanced at the Director, silently handing the baton back to him.

'The post mortem of the first one was started first thing this morning. The second is underway now. The first one was clearly killed by the robbers-she had multiple hits from 7.62mm rounds. None of her injuries were caused by 9mm rounds.'

Brad let out an audible breath and Travis felt his own tension drop a notch. He didn't realise he'd been holding his breath too.

'She was in the building behind you,' the Director continued, 'so it would seem that the rounds have gone through a window or wall and got her.'

Brad nodded silently, absorbing the information. It was one less thing to worry about.

'The second person was killed near the intersection of Featherston and Brandon Streets,' the Director said carefully. 'Hopefully we'll get a result back soon as to the cause on that one.'

Brad nodded again, his face sombre. Silence hung for a few moments before Travis spoke.

'So, back to my point then; why am I here?'

The Director glanced at Ingoe then Susie, before speaking.

'We obviously have an interest in this matter and will be actively working it. Unfortunately at the moment we have a couple of other operations underway which have taken our resources elsewhere.'

'So you need an operator to come on board,' Travis finished.

The older man nodded and folded his hands together on the table in front of him. 'We do, and the pond we fish from is very small.'

'Sergeant Travis is being seconded to us for this operation,' Susie continued. 'It's not a one-man job though, and he specifically asked for you to come on board.'

Travis glanced over, but his nephew's face gave nothing away. He looked back to the woman across from him.

'No problem,' he said coolly. 'What's the plan?'

THE PLAN, as it turned out, was for Travis and Brad to kick their heels while the spooks got things organised.

The Director sat behind his wide mahogany desk. It was spotlessly clean. Ingoe and Susie sat opposite him. He folded his hands and fixed his gaze on the Operations Officer.

'So, Jed,' he said, 'is he the right man for the job?'

Ingoe inclined his head slightly. 'I wouldn't vouch for him if he wasn't, sir.'

'I respect that, and you know I don't question your recommendations; I've never had cause to.' The Director seemed to be choosing his words carefully. 'I have no issue with his credentials as I understand them to be, for a Special Forces role.' He puckered his brow. 'I also recall his name from some jobs assisting the Service previously, although of course I never met him myself.'

Ingoe nodded. If he was offended by the questioning he didn't show it. 'He did some escort jobs,' he said.

'Is he suitable for an intelligence type role?' the Director clarified. 'You know what we want; does he fit the bill?'

Ingoe replied without pause, going from memory. 'Yes. He was Regular Army first and got a tour to Bosnia. He's got eighteen years in the Group behind him. He did every operational deployment possible in that time-Bougainville, Kuwait, East Timor, the Solomons. Multiple tours in Afghanistan. He did a couple of long-looks and went to Iraq and Africa.' Ingoe gave a minimal shrug. 'Operationally he's done everything going, and some.'

'Long-look?' Susie queried.

'An attachment to another unit,' Ingoe explained. 'Going for a long look. He was with Two-Two and Delta.'

'Two-Two? You mean 22 SAS?'

'The Brits, yeah. And Delta is...'

'American, I know.' She gave a hint of a smile. 'I don't know all your acronyms, that's all.'

Ingoe nodded again and continued. 'And as you mentioned, sir, he did some escort jobs with the Service in various locations, which requires some finesse. He's more than a blunt instrument, if that's what you're concerned about sir.'

The Director nodded, a low chuckle sounding in his throat. 'On the head, Jed, on the head. If you say he's okay, then he's okay. My apologies for even asking.'

Ingoe had nothing else to say so that's what he said. Susie cleared her throat gently, catching the Director's attention.

'Something else, Susie?' he queried.

'Just, ahh...I couldn't help but notice...' She flushed slightly, unsure how best to put it.

'The tension?' the Director asked, nodding studiously. 'Yes, it was pretty clear. Jed?'

'Old water, sir,' Ingoe replied. 'Just some family stuff. I'm sure they'll sort it out between themselves.'

THEY WAITED in the conference room and a tray of morning tea was rolled in. They watched silently while the receptionist, Trixie, unloaded a platter of savouries and sandwiches plus matching pots of coffee and tea. She gave them a smile and wheeled the trolley out again, closing the door behind her.

Brad went straight to the coffee pot and poured himself a cup, chugging it straight down in one go before refilling it. He grabbed a handful of savouries and stepped back over to the window.

'It's okay, I'll get mine,' Travis said. He poured himself a coffee and took a tiny chicken and cream cheese sandwich.

They ate in silence for a full minute before Brad turned and reached for the sandwich platter. Travis moved it smoothly out of reach and waited. Their eyes locked. Brad squinted angrily and reached again. Travis moved it further away.

Brad straightened to his full height. 'Don't be a fuckwit,' he growled. 'Just give me the plate.'

'Show some manners,' Travis told him.

Brad cocked his head and sneered. 'Seriously, Jack?' He reached a huge mitt out and waggled his fingers. 'Give me the plate.'

Travis put it down and took a sandwich from it. He took a bite. The platter was still out of reach. He said nothing but held the younger man's gaze. The silence was heavy.

Brad eventually sighed and stepped forward, reaching out again. Travis moved the platter further away and held his ground. Brad stepped into his personal space. Travis didn't move. They were toe to toe.

'Don't try now to be the man you never were before,' Brad rasped, the muscles in his jaw and neck tight.

Travis could his hot breath on his face. 'I accept my previous shortcomings,' he said evenly, 'and I accept I should have been there for you but wasn't.' He held his nephew's gaze. 'And I'm sorry about what happened to your Mum,' he said, softer now. 'But you asked me to be here, so get over yourself and let's get on with it.'

Neither of them spoke for several moments. Finally Travis saw a shift in the younger man's face and he slid the platter forward. Brad reached for it and Travis stepped away, creating space and breaking the moment.

Brad took three sandwiches and wolfed them in one hit. He washed them down with more coffee then put his cup down and looked at his uncle. He extended his mitt.

'Thanks for coming,' he said quietly. 'And I'm sorry for being a tool.'

Travis shook his hand. 'It's been a pretty rugged day for you.'

Brad shook his head. 'No excuses.' He took another savoury off the other platter and inhaled it.

'You got worms?' Travis asked.

Brad snorted. 'Na, caught the red eye this morning and hardly ate. Spent most of the night with the Fitters and Turners.' He saw Travis' quizzical look. 'Professional Conduct. The fit-up squad.'

Travis nodded. From his own dealings with the MPs, he knew what that was like. He sipped his coffee. It was good enough and strong enough. He was about to speak when the door opened and Ingoe stuck his head in.

'This way,' he said, holding the door open.

Travis looked at Brad. 'Go time,' he said.

**3**

———————

Thick eye fillets were sizzling on the barbeque grill, the smell wafting into the house through the open French doors. The late afternoon sun was dropping over the horizon and the air had cooled to a comfortable 20.

Travis stood back from the grill, a pair of tongs in one hand and an ice cold Krombacher pilsner in the other. He took a draught and put the bottle down. Droplets ran down the outside of the glass. He watched the neighbour's sheep grazing in their paddock, and saw a flock of birds rise suddenly from the wood at the back of his property, disturbed by an unseen intruder. He continued to watch and a few moments later saw his dog lope out of the trees and make his way towards home.

Most of the day had been spent being briefed and making arrangements. It had taken the media just the blink of an eye to identify Brad as the shooter and besiege his flat in Johnsonville. The Director had made it clear he could not return home, at least in the short term, and plans had to be put in place for that. He had accepted-somewhat reluctantly, Travis thought-the offer of a bed at the farm, and an underling had been sent out to buy a new wardrobe for him, since he'd arrived with simply an overnight bag.

On returning home Travis had given him a quick tour of the property, shown him to the spare bedroom and left him to it. The younger man had quickly found the weights and boxing bag in the garage and set to them for a hard workout while Travis checked on the animals and prepared dinner.

He turned at the sound of footsteps behind him. Brad helped himself to a Corona from the fridge and joined him on the deck. He cast an eye over the countryside and inhaled the cooking smells, then picked up the Krombacher bottle from the side tray of the barbecue and examined it.

'German,' he said and set it down. 'Fancy.'

Travis shrugged. 'They make good beer.' He tilted his glass to clink his nephew's bottle. 'It's good to see you, considering the circumstances.'

Brad gave a brief nod. 'Considering.' He waved his bottle at the paddocks beyond. 'Why here? Onewhero's nearly the arse end of the world.'

'It's a good community. It's affordable, and close enough but far enough away.' Travis supped his beer and jabbed one of the steaks with his tongs. 'I've got seven acres. The old couple next door look after it while I'm away; I bought it from them. Plus, I'm going for self-sufficiency.'

'I noticed. Not a bad thing.'

Travis turned both steaks. 'So what took you to Wellington? A girl?'

'The job. Promotion.' Brad leaned his hip against the deck railing. 'STG's only small, you've gotta be prepared to move for promotion. I'd been on the squad up here for a while and was ready. A job came up down there six months ago.' He gave a short, barking laugh. 'No, not a girl. It's always the job.'

Travis smiled. Brad cocked an eyebrow at him.

'What about you? I don't see any feminine touches inside.'

'Tried it once,' Travis replied. 'I was okay at it when I was around.' He shrugged. 'Wasn't around much though.'

They ate at the dining table; baked jacket potatoes, well-cooked steaks, and a large bowl of salad. Brad had another Corona and demolished his dinner in short order. He was pre-occupied with his thoughts when his cell rang. It was Ingoe. He listened for a minute, grunting occasionally before ringing off. He put the phone down and took a long draught of his beer.

'The second civvie who was killed,' he said. 'It wasn't my round. He only took one hit and it was a ricochet from Tony's gun.' He shook his head angrily and scratched at the Corona label with his thumb-nails. He looked like he wanted to throttle the bottle. 'The poor bastard.'

Tony was one of the operators who'd been in the back of the armoured truck and had then been executed by the robbers. Brad had been through recruit training with him and knew him well. He'd been married with a young daughter.

Travis stayed silent. He knew what it was like to lose comrades; two of the boys had been killed in the 'Stan while he was there. It was not pleasant but was a fact of life in their trade. He knew that Brad had to find his own way to reconcile it all in his own head. The fact that the funerals for the three cops were to be held over the next few days, and Brad would be unable to attend due to the operation, made it that much harder to deal with.

'Fuck it,' the big man said eventually. 'Nothing I can do about it now.' He drained his bottle. 'Except get the pricks who did it.'

Travis leaned forward with his elbows on the table. 'We will,' he said softly. 'We'll do that.'

Jonah Jones looked around the other men, taking his time to meet each man's eye before moving on. The room they stood in was deep in the bowels of the Southern Bandits' pad, formerly a commercial property in Takanini, south Auckland. It had been extensively remod-elled over the years since the gang extorted it from a struggling busi-ness and moved in, and now boasted all-round defence via high corrugated iron fences, barbed wire, spotlights and a guard tower on the roof.

Some members lived on the premises and used some of the rooms as barracks, while other rooms were used for business, meetings, or recreation. The room they stood in was the clubhouse, fully decked out with a bar, pool tables and dart boards, juke box and bar-leaners. Memorabilia adorned the walls-various patches taken from other gangs, photos, pictures of naked women, Harley Davidson and other bike-related posters, and a bloodied Police hat taken some years ago from a cop who Jones himself had beaten to a pulp after being stopped for riding his hog with no helmet.

On the bar leaner to Jones' right was a stack of cash bundles. Beside it stood Kruger, the gang's Sergeant-at-Arms. He was a man mountain, six and a half feet tall and nearly 150kg. He had a blonde Mohawk and goatee, and was missing his top two front teeth. His huge arms were completely covered in tattoos and his chest was covered by a single tat of the side by side barrels of a smoking shotgun draped with barbed wire and roses, the rocker above it reading Live to Ride, and the one below it reading 1%, referring to the old adage that only one percent of bikers are trouble.

Kruger had a stainless AutoMag .44 Magnum stuck in the front of his jeans as he normally did.

'Tomorrow we bury our brothers,' Jones said, still looking from man to man. 'They served us well and died on their feet. Fuck 'em and let God sort 'em out.'

The assembled men let out murmurs of agreement.

'Bandits forever.' Jones raised his fist and jabbed the air. 'Forever Bandits.'

'Bandits forever,' roared the men, led by Kruger, 'forever Bandits!'

'We did what we set out to do,' Jones continued. 'And we brought home the fucken bacon. Our client is very pleased with us and has promised there's more where this came from.'

That wasn't entirely true; the client had been pissed that they'd lost three men in the robbery and had killed three cops. It brought too much heat to what was already a headline-grabber. He hadn't exactly said it, but Jones had no doubt they would not be used by him again.

But for now, the gang didn't need to know. That was between him, Kruger and the client.

'He paid up immediately, and what we have here is the cut I promised to all of you for taking part.'

In front of him were nine other men, the most trusted members of the gang; the hard core. All of them had taken part directly in the robbery. Jones took the first wad of cash off the table and tossed it to the man on the far right. It was the rocketeer. He caught the bundle and grinned.

The next bundle went to the bus driver, then the Pajero driver and the getaway van driver. And on it went, until each man had their bundle of cash. Tito, the half-Mexican who had stood beside Jones with the M3 and mowed down one of the STG operators in cold blood, fingered his wad of cash and looked up, waving it at Jones.

"Hey ese, what the fuck? How much is this?'

Jones eyed him calmly. Kruger shifted his feet and glowered.

'Ten grand,' Jones said evenly.

'Whaddabout my forty, man?' Tito complained. 'I killed a fucken pig, man, and I get this bullshit? What the fuck?'

'You'll get your other thirty, so calm the fuck down,' Jones told him. 'I ain't rippin' you off; I'm savin' you. What's the first thing you'd do with forty k, Tito?'

Tito laughed. 'I'd get me some brutal pussy and bang that shit till it breaks, am I right?' He nudged the man beside him and laughed. The other man didn't laugh.

'Exactly,' Jones agreed, 'and you'd get drunk and pick a fight and probably rape some slut and you'd get locked up. And the pigs would wanna know where the fuck a wetback like you got forty grand in cash.' He stepped forward and locked eyes with the gangster. 'Am I right?'

'Aye, pro'ly,' Tito agreed.

'So you get some now, some later-your next instalments will be in a week. Then you don't fuck it up for all of us.' Jones stepped back to the leaner again. 'The pigs'll already know who Little Ray is, and they'll know we're probably involved. So for now, our op-sec has to be a hundy, get it?'

There were nods all around. The only man who didn't nod was the lean man on the far left, standing away from the rest of the men. He wore a baseball cap and a denim jacket. He was the one who'd introduced terms like "op-sec" to the gang. His name was Johnny Mitchell and he was a former US Navy SEAL. He was the man who'd shot it out with Brad at the van, using a Norinco assault rifle.

All he wanted to do was get his money and get the fuck out of Dodge; he'd had enough of these meth'd up chest beaters.

'So.' Jones looked around from man to man again. 'Any more complaints?'

There were none. Jones looked to Kruger and gave him a tilt of the chin. The mountain moved forward, gesturing to Tito to come forward. The Mexican dragged his heels but did so, tucking the wad of cash into his back pocket. He knew what was coming. It was strictly against gang rules to disrespect the President and he had to pay his dues.

The first hit was a huge swinging right hook that knocked Tito clean off his feet and sent him crashing into the men behind him. He was pushed forward again and took a swinging left, sending him the other way. Again he was pushed forward and the assault continued. After half a minute Tito lay curled up on the floor, bleeding from his mouth and nose and both eyes rapidly closing. A loose tooth lay on the hardwood floor and his breathing was ragged. He was pretty sure he'd busted a rib.

Kruger straightened up and shook his hands out, breathing hard. He stepped back. His job as enforcer was done.

Jonah Jones stepped forward and stood over the fallen man. Tito painfully craned his neck to look up through his battered, bloodied eyes.

'Don't ever question me again, boy,' the President said as he unzipped his fly.

Tito held still as a stream of warm piss flowed down his face, soon joined by several others as the rest of the men joined in, showing their solidarity to their leader.

Johnny Mitchell watched in silent disgust. He turned to go but was stopped by Kruger's bulk blocking the way.

'Join in.' Kruger told him. His voice was surprisingly high-pitched, the result of years of steroid abuse. He jerked his head towards the huddle. A couple of the men were looking over, sensing trouble.

'Naw, I'm good.' Mitchell tried to brush past, not wanting to fight this gargantuan creature, but Kruger stopped him again, this time with a giant paw on the shoulder.

Mitchell looked down at the hand and then up at the Mohawk'd gangster. His eyes were like flint and Kruger felt a chill run down his spine. He didn't know what to make of the smaller Yank, but he was one scary motherfucker. Kruger moved his hand and instead clapped Mitchell on the shoulder as if they were buddies. He let out a roar of laughter and jabbed the air with his other hand.

'Bandits forever, forever bandits!'

The men joined in, chanting their war cry, and Mitchell left them to it. He had better things to do.

## 4

Brad had slept heavily but woke up tired.

His head had been spinning, not helped by several beers and a whiskey nightcap, a turmoil of thoughts and emotions keeping his brain stimulated.

He shuffled to the kitchen and downed two large glasses of water. Feeling slightly better he wandered about the lounge, checking out Jack's CD and DVD collection. He wasn't surprised to find it was mostly classic rock accompanied by war and action movies, with some frat-pack comedies thrown in for balance.

He heard feet pounding on the drive and looked out to see Travis slowing to a walk, hands on his hips as he sucked in air, the dog with him going straight to a bowl on the front porch to slurp noisily.

Travis stretched and cooled down outside, stripping off his sweat stained T shirt and wiping his face with it. Brad appeared in the doorway, a glass of water in his hand.

'How long?' he asked, squinting against the morning sun.

'Fifty nine,' Travis replied, refilling the dog's bowl. Most of the water seemed to have hit the ground. He anticipated the next question. 'Eleven, mostly hills.'

Brad nodded approvingly. 'S'pose I should earn my keep and get some breakfast ready.'

They ate on the deck-homemade muesli and fruit, toast and coffee. Brad found a tube of Berocca in the pantry and downed one. While Jack showered, Brad wandered into his uncle's office and studied the photos there. Many were of his military days, he and his comrades in various places in various poses-the jungle, bush, desert, in the back of a Hercules, on board Pinzies and quad bikes, usually carrying weapons.

There was a citation on one wall, awarding Staff Sergeant Jack Travis the New Zealand Gallantry Decoration for bravery. The citation detailed an incident in Afghanistan and Brad was absorbed in it when he sensed a presence behind him.

He turned and saw Travis, freshly dressed, his hair wet.

'Pretty heavy,' Brad rasped.

Travis smiled. 'Funny thing is, it wasn't actually the hairiest moment we had. For some reason a couple of us got gongs out of it.' He shrugged. 'Bosses.'

As Brad followed him out of the office another photo caught his eye, this one framed and sitting on the desk by a file tray. He paused and picked it up. It was years old and showed a girl of about fourteen and a boy of about seven. They were in togs and standing on a beach, the water round their ankles and their arms round each other, big grins on their faces.

Brad immediately recognised his mother.

'That was about two years before you came along,' Travis said behind him.

Brad nodded silently. His mother looked happy in the photo and he was glad. Not much had gone right for her after that. He glanced up and saw Jack staring at the photo, sadness in his eyes.

'She was my best friend,' Travis said softly. He turned abruptly and left the room.

THE DIRECTOR'S door opened and Susie Quinn entered. She moved with purpose and the excitement in her face was clear to see.

He put his fountain pen down and looked up expectantly.

'Sir, SIG have come back to us on the origin of the weapons.' She was referring to the Police's Special Investigations Group, who handled terrorist and other sensitive matters.

'And?' He had his suspicions but she clearly wanted to break the news. He waited patiently.

'They believe they were part of the haul allegedly taken in a substantial burglary reported by a collector in Canterbury four years ago.' Her eyes were sparking with excitement. 'He had nearly two hundred firearms apparently stolen. The cops never believed it and he eventually got two years jail for selling the guns.' The Director remembered the case well. Several of the guns had turned up in the hands of criminals since, all associated with organised crime and drugs, including at least a couple of murders.

'The collector, Malcolm Cook, is out now and living back in Canterbury. He's never squealed on who he sold the guns to and has done his time.' She checked the notes in her hand. 'They've gone through all the CCTV and have matched some of the weapons; a Ruger Mini-14 with a folding stock, an RPG-7 rocket launcher, and an M3 submachine gun. They also say that an M60 machine gun was part of his missing collection, and that matches what Brad Travis and the others say about the gun in the van.'

The Director nodded, assessing the options. He considered the younger woman before him for a moment. She was a good Intelligence Officer-very good-and was only a recent attachment to the Division. Her role was liaison between the Service proper and the Division; one of the few in the department who knew the Division even existed.

'Call Jed,' he said to her. 'I think Mr Cook needs a robust interview.' He nodded, more to himself than to her. 'It's time to let the dogs out.'

**5**

___

Malcolm Cook lived in a farmhouse on a sheep station about ten k's south of Fairlie in the MacKenzie Basin.

It was a family property that he'd lived in since he was a child, aside from his time behind bars. His wife and kids had long since abandoned him and he spent most of his time now painting water-based landscapes, watching TV and trading online. He'd managed to rebuild a fairly substantial fund, starting with the help of a bent prison guard while he was inside.

He employed a manager to run the farm for him and let the guy and his family live in the main house, while he took up residence a k away in a worker's house.

His collection of firearms was long gone, but he had obtained a small battery of weapons through various contacts. The criminals he had sold his guns to terrified him, but he was fairly confident that they would leave him alone, given it was widely known he'd kept his mouth shut.

The cops were no threat-they'd been to his place numerous times since he got out and every time he met them at the door with the phone in his hand, talking to his lawyer. They'd been again yesterday, two detectives from Christchurch. They thought they were all over it until they realised there was no way he was going to talk. He simply stood in the doorway and laughed at them until they got frustrated and drove off, threatening to be back. He didn't care; he knew there was nothing they could do to him.

He was unaware of the rented green Toyota people mover driving down the main road a couple of k's away. Unaware of it slowing to a walking pace and two men rolling out the side door, each one bearing a small pack and rifle.

The people mover carried on, making its way unhurriedly towards Fairlie. In the front passenger seat sat Jed Ingoe, a walkie talkie in his hands. He keyed the talk button.

'Boots on the ground,' he told the unseen comms operator at the other end.

'Copy that,' came the reply.

He glanced at Susie Quinn who was driving, her eyes fixed on the road ahead in the near darkness. 'I hope you've got us some good digs, Susie Q.'

She gave a smile and half glanced at him. 'Of course. And I know where to get a good burger, too.'

Ingoe grinned, his face partially illuminated by the dashboard lights. 'You do know the way to a man's heart, Suze.'

TRAVIS AND BRAD made good time with their NVGs, Travis taking the role of lead scout with Brad covering the rear.

The night vision goggles allowed them to see clearly in the pitch darkness of the rural night. Within twenty five minutes they were hunkered down in a shallow dry creek bed barely three hundred metres from Malcolm Cook's house.

The intel they had was that there were neither dogs nor electronic surveillance systems at the property, but they took their time to completely circle it and check for themselves; intel had been known to be wrong before.

After their careful recce, which took the better part of an hour, they met in the creek bed and conferred by hand signals.

The farm manager's house was lit up a kilometre away. A pair of STG snipers from Christchurch were covering that house, just in case. Cook's house itself showed light behind the curtains of the lounge and dining rooms, and the flicker of a TV.

The silence was eerie here at night. The odd animal noise in the distance, the rustle of grass and undergrowth in the wind. No noise from the two camo-clad men.

Each of them carried a suppressed Diemaco C8 assault rifle with a Sig Sauer P228 for back up, Brad's being strapped to his thigh and Travis' secured in the fixed shoulder holster of his utility vest. He also had his personal favourite in a Safariland hip holster, a stainless Colt Python .357 Magnum with a 4 inch barrel, and a K-Bar combat knife on the left hip. They moved stealthily towards the house, ten metres between them, weapons at the ready. They took up positions near the rear door and after listening carefully for a minute, Travis removed a key from his jacket pocket and carefully slid it into the lock. It was amazing what intel could be gathered when a person wasn't home, even down to getting an imprint of a door lock.

He silently turned the key and pushed the door open very slightly. Pocketing the key again, he brought his weapon back up again. He looked to his right and gave a firm nod.

They entered the house.

Malcolm Cook was totally relaxed in his favourite armchair, a half finished bowl of hokey pokey ice cream resting on his copious gut and his slippers warming his feet.

One of the Star Wars prequels was playing on his 79 inch TV. The remote sat on the coffee table to his left.

He never heard a thing until the sound was muted. He stared at the TV, confused, and reached for the remote. It wasn't there. He looked left, jumped, and dropped his ice cream with fright.

A man in full camo gear with a suppressed Diemaco in one hand stood beside, staring down at him. The remote was in his other gloved hand.

'Hi,' the man said. 'Don't do anything stupid and don't make a sound.'

Cook sensed someone else there too, and jerked his head around to see another man on his other side. He was identically clad and armed. He was a big unit and fierce looking. His Diemaco was aimed straight at Cook's face, finger on the trigger.

Cook knew two things straight away; these men were warriors, not cops.

And he was in deep shit.

FIVE MINUTES later Malcolm Cook was in his bathroom, stark naked and lying in the bath.

He was trembling already, from both cold and fear. His hands were securely bound behind with soft fabric; little chance of chafing or other injuries.

The older man stood at the end of the bath, facing him. He was clearly the boss. The bigger, younger man stood over him by his head. He had a wet black cloth hood in his hand and a bottle of water at the ready.

Cook knew exactly what was going to happen.

'We want to know about your guns,' the older man told him. We know you've told the Police nothing so far.'

'I've got rights,' Cook tried.

The man said nothing, just eyed him steadily.

'I want my lawyer.'

The man continued to say nothing, just eyed him steadily. The silence hung in the room, broken only by the wheezing of the obese naked man in the tub.

'Your lawyer can't help you now,' the man said softly. He hiked his shoulders slightly. 'Nobody can help you now.'

'This isn't right,' Cook whined. 'This is not the Third World, this is New Zealand.'

'That's right,' the man said. His voice was unnervingly calm and steady. 'A country of pioneers and adventurers. Hard working people with a sense of justice and a soft spot for the underdog. People with a sense of right and wrong.' He hefted the Diemaco in his hands. 'People who don't like seeing bad guys get away with bad stuff.'

'You're not the Police,' Cook said, his voice quavering.

'No, we're not.' The man gave a thin smile through his camo cream. 'We're much worse.'

Cook opened his mouth to shout, but stopped when he saw the man raise a finger of warning.

'Tut-tut-tut. I told you not to be silly.' He pointed at the hood and water in his colleague's hands. 'If you wanna play that game, we can play rougher. It's up to you.'

Cook knew exactly what he was referring to. The hood would be placed over his head to cover his nose and mouth, and water would be poured through it. He would have a sense of drowning and he would gag and panic. It was called water boarding and was a torture technique that was widely outlawed but still practiced.

Malcolm Cook felt his heart racing. The man facing him watched him carefully.

'Make your decision,' he said softly.

Cook made it. He gave a small nod, then a more vigorous one, wanting to make sure these men knew what he was saying. 'Either way, I'm a dead man,' he whimpered.

The big man behind him gave an animal-like growl. Cook craned his neck to look at him. He could feel the anger coming off the younger man in waves. No, not anger; *rage*. This was one dangerous man.

The older of the two men gave a slight shrug again. 'That all depends on you, Malcolm. You don't have to suffer in silence. You can be relocated and protected.'

Cook managed a snort despite his situation. 'The cops already told me that. It wouldn't matter where you moved me, they'd find me.'

The older man said nothing. Cook stared at him, holding it for as long as he could before looking away. The man could see right through him and Cook suddenly realised that, although the big man scared the shit out of him with his boiling rage, the older man was actually more dangerous. He was all controlled energy just waiting to burst out. Cook had no doubt in his mind that the man would kill him in the blink of an eye.

He looked back at the man, his mind racing. He was used to talking his way out of tight situations but nothing was coming to him.

'I don't think he'll talk,' the big man behind him rasped.

Cook craned his neck to look at him again. He was pulling a thumb drive from his pocket.

'What...what's that?' Cook quavered.

The big man looked down at him. 'Option Two,' he growled.

Cook trembled harder and looked back at the older man. The man's expression hadn't changed.

'What's Option Two?'

The man considered him for a moment. 'Option Two,' he said softly, 'is a flash drive full of objectionable material. Naked kids getting sexually abused.'

Cook felt his gut drop.

'You know, real nasty stuff. The sort of stuff that sends you back to jail when it's found being shared from your computer.'

'But it's... that's disgusting! It's not mine!'

'Yes it is,' the man told him. 'That's what will be in the papers and everyone will know about it. You'll be straight back to jail to get beaten up and butt-fucked every day.'

Cook's bladder loosened and he pissed down his legs. The man glanced down but didn't comment. Cook managed to muster some defiance.

'You're a fucken animal,' he told the man. 'Just an animal.'

The man looked straight through him. 'Look into my eyes and try to convince yourself I won't do it.'

Cook couldn't hold the stare. The man nodded to his bigger colleague.

'Do it,' he said.

Cook tried to wrench away but the big man whipped the hood over his head and pulled it back, arching Cook's back so he was even more vulnerable. He pissed himself again and tried to scream. The hood was wet and claustrophobic and he immediately felt his chest tighten and his heart race.

His screamed 'No!' was muffled by the hood. The first splash of water hit the hood and the cloth flattened across his skin.

'I'll tell you!'

Brad immediately straightened the bottle up again and eased the fat gun dealer back into a sitting position.

Travis leaned in closer. 'Who did you sell the guns to?'

Cook was still panicking, his chest heaving with shallow breaths. Brad removed the hood and stood over him.

'Breathe slow,' Travis said.

After a few moments Cook had his breathing under control, although his eyes were still bugged and he looked pale.

'Who did you sell the guns to?' Travis repeated.

Cook's tongue darted across his lips and he paused.

'Don't even consider it,' Travis warned him. He held the fat man's gaze and sensed defeat.

Cook's shoulders drooped and he muttered something to himself.

'What?' Travis leaned closer.

'Speak up,' Brad rasped. 'Use your big boys' voice.'

'I said, I don't really know.'

'Don't fuck us about!' Brad snarled, about to throw the hood on again.

'No no no!' Cook shrieked, starting to hyperventilate again. 'I mean I know but not a proper name!'

'Tell us what you've got,' Travis said coldly. 'If you fuck about, we start over.'

'All I know is his nickname. He contacted me; I never heard of him before.'

'You met him though.'

'No no, never. I just went out and when I came home it was all gone. The whole lot, cleaned out. I got paid into an overseas account.'

'Why report it to the cops then?'

'I had to; they were coming round to do a license inspection. I had to explain why the guns weren't here.' His eyes were darting from one to the other and his lips were flecked with dry spit. 'You gotta believe me!'

Travis gave him nothing, although the story had the ring of truth to it. 'What's the name?'

THE MOTEL WAS a standard outfit frequented by travellers and company reps. The furniture had seen better days and the suite was a bit pokey, but it served the purpose.

The small table in the dining area was spread with takeaway containers and bags. Ingoe was tucking into a burger, a second one racked up and ready to go. Susie had finished her chips and half a shake when her phone bleeped with an incoming text. She grabbed it and checked the screen. She squinted and looked closer.

She visibly paled and Ingoe paused with the burger halfway to his mouth, watching her.

'What is it?' he said.

She turned the phone to show him Travis' text message.

*The Pastor.*

'It's a problem,' she said.

THE CELL PHONE chirped loudly in the large kitchen. The fluffy white Persian lifted its head and scowled, decided it was no threat and went back to nibbling her Fancy Feast.

The Director's slippers slapped the tiles as he entered from the lounge, scooping the phone off the counter and fumbling for his spectacles. He was still in his work clothes but had lost the tie. The remains of a lamb curry were on the counter nearby. The strains of Bach floated in from the lounge where his wife sat catching up on the latest goings-on from Facebook.

He got the spectacles settled and peered at the phone's screen. He grunted and double checked but it still read *The Pastor*.

The Director put the phone down and drummed his fingers thoughtfully on the counter top.

'Bugger,' he finally said.

TRAVIS AND BRAD legged it back from the house to the RV point.

They waited in the cover of a small ditch, back to back to cover the arcs just in case. They were completely silent, ears pricked and eyes constantly scanning. They didn't expect trouble; Cook was safely asleep in his armchair, fully clothed again in his freshly-sanitised house. The drug he had ingested was virtually untraceable and would keep him under until daylight.

Headlights approached and a pair of clicks came through their earpieces. The green people mover slowed as it got to them, the side door sliding open. They darted together from the ditch and clambered in as the vehicle rolled on. Brad threw the door shut and they moved off.

Ingoe turned and looked at them from the front passenger seat.

'All good?' Travis asked.

The former RSM gave a curt shake of his head. 'Not so much,' he said.

Brad stiffened, his defences coming up. Travis gave him a subtle nudge with his knee in the darkness.

Ingoe looked to Travis. 'I hope your passport is up to date.'

Travis looked at him questioningly, and caught Susie's eye in the rear view mirror.

'Pack your bags,' she said, 'we're off to Thailand.'

**6**

———

The table Philip Stephenson was working on was a rickety wooden thing with a matchbook propping up one leg. Whether it balanced things out or not was debatable.

Stephenson didn't care. The lean Somali on the opposite side was transferring five mil US to Stephenson's Bermuda-based bank account. He could do it with his laptop balanced on the rotting carcass of a nun for all Stephenson cared. The electronic transfer had been sent and they were waiting for it to show in Stephenson's account, each man with his eyes fixed silently to his own laptop screen.

Stephenson refreshed his screen and there it was. He gave a brief nod and punched the power button off. Both men shut their screens down and leaned back in their seats.

Behind Stephenson his bodyguard stepped forward, scooping the laptop away into his satchel. Prasong had the normal stature for a Thai, short and whippety, but he was also rock hard. A former street criminal who Stephenson had found in a bloodied bare-knuckle MMA ring in Bangkok, Prasong had killed more men than Stephenson knew of.

His most recent had been a Somali thug just yesterday. The man had been high as a kite and tried to stand over the soft-looking white man in the floral shirt outside his hotel. Stephenson had simply stepped back and let Prasong do what needed to be done. In two seconds the Somali's neck snapped and he dropped to the ground. Two accomplices watching from nearby had started forward to intervene. Prasong had drawn a Bali-Song knife from one pocket and a Walther P38 from his belt in less than a second. The men retreated quickly and left their dead comrade where he lay.

The warlord Stephenson was doing business with, Ashkir, had laughed when he heard the tale. He had ordered his own heavies to track down the other two thugs and kill them for disrespecting his guests.

Life was cheap in the Mog, Stephenson reflected. He offered a smile to the black face opposite him.

'It is always a pleasure to do business with you, Mister McFee,' Ashkir boomed, smiling broadly as he used the name they both knew was fake. His teeth were badly stained from coffee and cigarettes. 'I look forward to seeing you again soon.'

'As always,' Stephenson smiled.

Ashkir wagged a finger at him, still grinning. 'And I also look forward to the arrival of my supplies.'

Stephenson nodded in agreement as he stood. 'They will be here by nightfall, I assure you, my friend.' He spread his hands expressively. 'Have I ever let you down before?'

Ashkir grinned, also standing. 'Clearly not, Mister McFee.' He grinned broader now. 'Because you are still alive.'

They both laughed and Stephenson felt a chill run down his back. He had absolutely no doubt that this was no idle threat. He had heard of another supplier who had ripped off the warlord, and had been flayed alive. Such things were not urban legend in Mogadishu.

They clasped hands and Stephenson glanced at the two heavies behind Ashkir. Both wore fatigue vests and black berets like extras from some crap B-movie. They also carried folding stock AK47s that had been supplied in Stephenson's previous shipment. They were eye-balling Prasong who stood impassively to the side, his eyes flat and expressionless as he gazed back at them.

Some kind of silent pissing contest between bodyguards, Stephenson thought to himself. The sooner they got the fuck out of this stinking shit hole the better. He took the satchel from Prasong and slung it over his shoulder, nudging his holstered Smith and Wesson as he did so.

A third heavy opened the door and they stepped out into an air conditioned hotel foyer, the fresh air hitting Stephenson like a cold blast after the stuffiness and body odour of the meeting room. He slipped on his sunglasses and followed the heavy and Prasong out the front door and down the broad steps to the curb where a white Land Rover waited. The smells and noise of the city were invasive after the relative quiet inside.

Prasong stood at the door while Stephenson climbed in the back seat, before jumping in the front. The driver moved off immediately, cutting off a yellow New York-style taxi. Horns blasted and a stream of abuse in Somali disappeared in their dust as the Rover sped away. The driver was a burly Rhodesian in his fifties named Terry, a grizzled mercenary who had shed blood all over the globe. He and Prasong had quickly formed an unlikely alliance under Stephenson's employ and travelled everywhere with him.

The big Rhodesian glanced at Stephenson in the rear view mirror. 'All good, boss?'

Stephenson gave a curt nod and sniffed. 'As long as the shipment gets to him by tonight we'll be tickety-boo.'

Terry nodded and squinted in the afternoon sun. 'I'll get you to the airport and chase that up with a phone call, but the boys won't let us down. They're okay.' He shrugged and gave a crooked grin. 'For black fellas, anyway.'

Stephenson nodded silently. He had absolute trust in his own crew; it was the suppliers they used that always worried him. The sooner he was winging his way back to Thailand the better he'd feel.

They had flown commercially from Aden Adde International Airport to Dubai then on to Bangkok. A short taxi hop followed to an office building in downtown where they were shown into the office of Richard Chambers, a British exile who was wanted in his homeland for financial crimes. Living under a new identity in Bangkok allowed the sixty year old with the pencil moustache to indulge in his two passions-money and trans-sexual prostitutes.

Gold rings adorned his soft fingers and diamond studs were in both earlobes. A pink shirt and white trousers completed the picture. He was tall and narrow-faced, with an incongruously round pot belly on an otherwise lean frame. He looked up as Stephenson entered the plush office with Prasong in tow. Terry took a post at the door.

'Ahh, welcome my friends, welcome,' Chambers enthused, standing from behind his walnut desk and gesturing to them to sit. Neither of them did. 'Can I offer anyone a drink?'

'No, thank you.' Stephenson's tone was abrupt and the money man's face fell. 'We won't stay.'

'Alright friend, what's up? Have I done something to offend you?' Chambers pouted and placed a hand to his chest. 'Was the arrangement with my African friend not suitable for you?'

'I'm clear,' Stephenson told him flatly. 'All paid up as of ten minutes ago.'

'Oh good, good, that's wonderful.' Chambers sat again, giving him a happy grin. 'So pleased to hear it. Debt is not a good place to be, especially with some of the clients I have.'

Stephenson scowled. He was tired and irritable and the last thing he wanted was a verbal hand job from this creep. It was a shame Chambers was such a good fund manager. If he hadn't lost so much on a stupid fucking game of baccarat none of this shit would've happened. What should've been a lucrative trip to Somalia was just enough to cover an outstanding debt that Chambers had covered for him at an exorbitant interest rate. Stephenson's profit from the five mil US had been almost completely wiped out with an electronic transfer to Chambers during the taxi ride.

'Yeah, well,' he said, 'we're all sorted.'

Chambers clapped his hands and rubbed them together theatrically. 'Thank you very much, I will of course double check but I trust you as a man of your word, Philip.'

Stephenson nodded abruptly and turned to leave. As he did so he heard Terry's cell phone bleep with an incoming text. He watched the Rhodesian punch it up and squint hard at the small screen. The grizzled man's jaw dropped and he looked up sharply.

'What is it?' Stephenson hissed, not wanting Chambers to hear. He reached Terry and guided him out the door.

'It's not good, boss,' the older man grated. 'They were hijacked. We've lost the shipment.'

Stephenson's face went white and Terry thought for a second that he was going to faint. Instead he held the door and ushered his boss out.

Chambers watched them go and tapped his steepled fingers together thoughtfully.

Stephenson was an interesting man-useful, and with an interesting background. Chambers had long been tempted to try and poach his minders from him too, although the Thai thug Prasong seemed to have a deep attachment to his boss. Besides, Chambers had his own ruthless killer at his side.

As if on cue, the internal office door opened and Johnny Mitchell entered. He was dressed in his usual uniform of jeans, floral Hawaiian shirt and baseball cap. He had been listening from the adjoining office.

'They seem concerned,' he observed drily.

Chambers smiled wolfishly. 'Don't they, though. Well done on getting that in place so quickly.'

Mitchell shrugged modestly. 'No problem. I know a few people in bad places.'

Chambers knew that was a huge understatement. Mitchell had a very impressive network of contacts around the globe. It had been surprisingly easy for him to organise for the shipment of weapons to the warlord Ashkir to go missing. There had been no hijacking as such; it was simply money changing hands and two of the escorts turning on the other two, shooting them in the back and taking the shipment. The weapons went straight to an opposing warlord, who paid over the going rate for them simply to stick it to Ashkir.

'Ashkir has no idea?' Chambers asked.

'So far as I know.' Mitchell's eyes were the palest blue Chambers had ever seen. They sparkled ever so slightly as he talked. 'I'll pass the word to Ashkir about what happened; he'll deal with the two guys.'

'And owe you a favour as a result.' Chambers chuckled gleefully. He loved this cat and mouse game. 'And we'll let him know who's got his guns?'

'Naturally.' Mitchell tossed his head towards the door that Stephenson and his men had just exited. 'What about these turkeys?'

Chambers smiled. 'Keep them on the leash. They have no idea so there's no point in popping their bubble.'

Mitchell nodded. He didn't care either way. Work was work.

'The only thing we need to be a bit cautious of is the security services. They're likely to be all over this.'

Mitchell frowned. 'It's just an armed robbery, boss. The cops'll do their thing, look at those assholes the Bandits, and that'll be that.'

Chambers shook his head. 'No, you need to remember this is New Zealand we're talking about. It's a goddamn backwater, nothing ever happens there. Certainly things like that just don't happen.' He shook his head again. 'No, they're smart enough to look past the robbery and see the bigger picture.' He smiled thinly across the room. 'That's why governments have spooks. Trust me. I used to be one of them.'

7

The foyer of the Golden Key Hotel was all glass and steel and angles, and Travis supposed it was cool and cutting edge. It wasn't his cup of tea. He felt Susie's eyes on him from behind her Gucci glasses and glanced at her. Her lips were twitching.

'Not enough sawdust on the floor for you, cowboy?' she queried.

He snorted. 'I feel like if I break something I'll have to re-mortgage my house.'

'The joys of travelling on the Government ticket,' she said quietly, leaning close enough that nobody else could hear.

Their cover was as an unmarried couple on their first trip overseas together. He was a trucking firm manager and she was his accountant. It wouldn't do for anyone to overhear a mention of working for the Government-any Government. Thailand was not deemed to be a major threat but it was a country with a chequered history and a huge organised crime influence. Coupled with endemic corruption it posed serious risks for any intelligence officer.

They had arrived the previous night and stayed at an airport hotel, before coming into the city proper this morning. As far as they could tell they hadn't aroused any suspicion.

The business couple in front of them headed for the lifts and

Susie checked in while Travis wandered back to the door and checked their tail. He hadn't noticed anything untoward on the taxi ride in from the airport but in a place like Bangkok that wasn't unusual. There were plenty of shifty people around, locals and tourists alike. He wondered idly what his nephew was up to right now. His nephew; it seemed strange. After so many years of estrangement it would take time to reconnect-if that ever actually happened. He wasn't sure Brad really wanted that.

'Come on, dreamboat,' Susie called, grinning cheekily. 'Let's go.'

Travis shot her a grin of his own and tagged along as a porter took them up to their room on the twelfth floor. He left Susie to tip the porter while he quickly checked the room-or suite, he mentally corrected himself. The bedroom had a king-size bed he figured he'd never get to use, and he couldn't immediately detect anything out of place.

Returning to the lounge he saw Susie at the plate glass windows that looked out over the city. The light breeze was ruffling her chestnut hair and pressing her red cotton sleeveless dress against her body. It was a good body, he noticed-not for the first time-with toned limbs and a firm backside beneath the thin fabric. She turned and looked at him. He hoped she hadn't caught him staring.

'All clear as far as I can tell,' he said brusquely, not worrying about talking in code. They had deliberately not booked ahead until they were in the airport terminal waiting for their luggage. Having travelled on their own passports there was always the chance that one or both of them could be on a watch list with the Thai authorities, which could easily lead to their hotel room being electronically surveilled. Last minute moves mitigated the risk as much as possible.

It concerned Travis that they were unarmed but that should be remedied soon enough.

'How's my bed looking in there?' Susie enquired, tossing her chin towards the bedroom with a smile.

'Looks great. Hope it gives you back ache.' He gestured towards the sofa. 'That looks very comfy, and almost long enough for a pygmy to stretch out on.'

Susie laughed and headed to the kitchenette. 'How about you check in with home while I call our friends?'

Travis nodded and dug out the cell phone he'd purchased at the airport. It was a pre-pay burn phone with no saved contacts. He tapped in a text to a number he'd committed to memory, giving Ingoe the hotel name and suite number, along with a code word to confirm it was him sending the text and he was not under any duress. Within a minute he received an acknowledgement back.

*Don't enjoy it too much.*

It was Ingoe's not-so-subtle way of reminding to keep it professional. Travis grinned to himself. Susie Q, as she was apparently known in the Service, was hardly his type. If she was anything like most other spooks he'd met she'd be too academic and airy fairy. Theory and policies and speculation might be fine in the briefing room with a latte at hand, but when the chips were down and lives were at stake-usually your own-Travis had always found a wide gap between spooks and operators. Hence the need for the babysitters, he guessed.

Having said that, she seemed to have relaxed somewhat since they had hit the airport to fly out. She had a sense of humour, which was always a good start. The real test, he knew, would be when things went wrong. Watching her end her own call he was hopeful that wouldn't happen.

Susie turned to him again and waggled her burn phone. 'Good to go. We're to make our way to a bar and there'll be a brush pass. We'll pick our gear up from a coat-check and go from there. All good?'

Travis nodded. 'Let's go.'

'Easy, tiger. I need to freshen up first, and we've got plenty of time. The brush-by will be at six, so if we're in place half an hour before that we've got an hour and a half.' She dimpled when she smiled. 'Just relax, kick back. It's going to be fine.'

'If everything goes to plan, I'm sure it will be,' he replied evenly. 'It's for when things turn to rat shit that we need to plan.'

Susie pouted and raised a questioning eyebrow at him. 'I'm not some rookie, you know Jack.' He noticed it was the first time she'd used his Christian name. 'I have done this before, okay?'

'Fine,' he said, irritated now. 'So what was it like when your cover got blown and you had a gun to your head?'

Anger flashed in her hazel eyes. 'Don't be so goddamn...'

'Condescending? Rude? Sorry, but we've hit the ground without catching our breath on this, and I know practically nothing about you or your capabilities in the field.' He paused, taking a breath to ease off. 'I'm not trying to be rude, but if shit goes down there's only you and me.'

'Well I don't know that much about you, either,' she countered. 'Jedi told me a bit without telling me much at all.'

Travis smiled inwardly. He knew Ingoe well enough to know how that conversation would have gone. 'What'd he say?'

Susie pouted again. 'He said "He's done eighteen years in the fucken Special Air Service, what else do you need to know?"'

Travis gave a small grin. 'What else?'

'He said you only left because you broke the wrong nose, whatever the hell that's supposed to mean.'

'And I suppose you expect me to believe you haven't read up on your own files?'

She looked at him shrewdly. 'What files?'

Travis scoffed. 'Come on Susie, everyone knows the Service keeps files on the Group. You'd be a fool not to have checked up on me, make sure I'm not a security risk.' He gave a short shake of the head. 'And you're no fool.'

'Really?' She canted her head to the side inquisitively. 'You sound like you've done your own homework.'

He ticked points off his fingers as he spoke. 'A Master's degree in forensic accounting, finished through the air force. Seven years with the RNZAF, leaving as a Flight Lieutenant-sounds like you were on the fast track to the top. Seconded to military intelligence for a while and then on to the spooks.'

'Wow,' Susie said, calmer now and obviously impressed. 'No flies on you, are there?'

'Just because I'm a grunt, doesn't mean I'm a knucklehead.'

'I never said...'

'I know,' he interjected, 'just as long as we're both clear. I don't have your skills and you don't have mine. But together we should be okay. Right?'

'Aye aye, Sarn't Major,' she smirked, giving him a mock salute. 'Now time's ticking, so I better get moving. I'm sure you can amuse yourself for a little bit.'

'If my experience of high maintenance women is anything to go by, I've got a good hour. I'm going to beat the feet.'

As he headed to the door he heard her call out behind him. 'I am *not* high maintenance!'

**8**

---

Philip Stephenson operated out of a villa just outside the port hub of Nathon on the northwest coast of Koh Samui, the second largest Thai island after the traditional tourist destination of Phuket.

He had lived there for the last couple of years, with Prasong installed as the resident security and cook. Terry lived closer to the port with a middle aged Thai madam, when they weren't fighting, which was when he came looking for a bed at the villa. Stephenson hoped things were okay upon the older man's return home-he had enough on his plate right now without sorting out domestic issues.

*Enough on his plate was a fucking understatement.* He had had no joy in getting hold of the boys he'd been using in the Mog, which was never a good sign. He'd passed that task on to Terry to sort out-right now, making sure Ashkir didn't send some badass to slot him was a higher priority. The warlord was not known for his easy going nature, and losing a shipment of weapons was severely inconvenient.

He finally got through on his sat phone and spoke briefly to one of Ashkir's assistants. When he identified himself, the man passed the phone over.

Ashkir's voice was at fever pitch when he came on the line.

'Where the fuck are my guns you fucken thief? I pay you good money and you dare to rip me off-me! Who the fuck you think you dealin' with, you little honky bitch!'

Stephenson tried to interject, keeping his tone soothing, but the warlord was having none of it. He continued screaming down the line at Stephenson for five solid minutes. The Kiwi sat and listened. Finally the Somali's tirade eased and Stephenson slipped in.

'I'm doing everything possible to recover the shipment for you, believe me. I already have some leads on it and I know-I *know*-I can get them back.' He paused, but Ashkir stayed silent. 'I just need some time.'

There was silence down the line for nearly half a minute. He could hear the warlord breathing in his ear.

'Two days. You have two days, Mr *Stephenson*.' The pretence of "Mr McFee" was gone. The message was clear. 'They arrive here safe and sound, with ten percent more, there be no problem.' He paused for effect. 'You don't keep your end of the deal...I kill you.'

'Understood.' Stephenson's mouth was dry but the flood of relief was palpable. Time was good; he could work with time.

'I keep my promises, Mr Stephenson. Don't make me come looking for you.'

'I won't,' Stephenson replied. The line died in his ear and he put the phone down.

He rubbed his face and stared out the window at the jungle beyond.

He had no doubt that Ashkir would keep his word, and not a clue how to prevent it.

IN HIS OFFICE IN MOGADISHU, Ashkir put the phone down and tapped his chin thoughtfully.

He was a tall, skinny man with coal black skin and a goatee. He was somewhere in his thirties and had never lived outside

Mogadishu. From an early age he was running with criminal gangs and had first killed before he hit puberty.

One of his fondest childhood memories was of chasing the American columns of soldiers as they tried to escape the city in 1993, after one of their Blackhawk helicopters had been shot down. Ashkir had seen the Hollywood movie of the incident several times and laughed every time he watched it. It was a very different account to how he remembered the incident.

He looked across the room to where his lieutenant sat against the wall, a folding stock AK in his lap. Kablan was his most trusted man; they had lived and fought together since they were children. Kablan's right eye was a milky white, the result of a knife fight many years ago.

'I do not trust this man, Stephenson,' Ashkir said. 'But I have given him two days.'

Kablan nodded. 'It is most generous, Ashkir. I would have given him two bullets.'

Ashkir smiled. 'You might just need to, my friend. I want you to take three of the men and go to Mr Stephenson. Make sure he either delivers on his promise, or we deliver on ours. Understand?'

Kablan nodded again. 'Of course. I will need money and clean passports.'

Ashkir waved a hand dismissively. 'You know who to see. Go now, I want you there before the deadline. At forty eight hours and one minute, Mr Stephenson is to see the error of his ways.'

Kablan stood and walked to the door, the AK hanging loosely in one hand. He was ready. He was always ready.

9

The hotel was in the China Town district, heavily populated by tourists and everything that catered for them.

Travis wended his way through the crowds, melting in with his khaki shorts, loose white shirt and sunglasses. The air was hot and heavy with the smells of cooking, exhaust fumes and body heat. Small Thais and chubby tourists of every denomination bustled everywhere, street hawkers offered all types of goods for sale and noisy tuk-tuks buzzed past constantly. He stopped to buy a map of the area and a bottle of water from a vendor, taking the time to check his tail again. He doubled back the way he'd come and cut across the road abruptly, hoping to flush out any watchers that might be lurking about.

Nobody made themselves obvious. He did a circuit of the block then extended to the next block, sussing out the local shops and restaurants. As he went he drew a mental map in his head, noting escape routes from the hotel if things went wrong and possible rendezvous points. He had been to the city before and had a passion for Thai food, which had become extremely popular back home, and before he knew it he'd wandered further than he'd intended and more than half an hour was up.

He took a few moments to reflect on what he knew so far about this phase of the job. The Pastor was a former intelligence agent named Philip Stephenson. His short career in the NZSIS had come to an inglorious end when he was caught selling secrets to a Chinese businessman with strong links to the intelligence service of his own country.

It transpired that Stephenson had a gambling problem and ended up in hock to an organised crime group. Having insufficient money to repay the debt, he instead sold his soul. He had been allowed to flee the country with no further action taken, mainly due to a threat from the Chinese authorities that a significant export deal would disappear if the matter ever came to light. The liberal Government of the day backed down and allowed the traitor to walk free, leaving a bitter taste in the mouths of many.

Susie herself had not known him, but the legend lived on. The spooks had kept tabs on him as best they could from afar, and knew his current situation was basically as a trader of anything going. He wasn't known to be a player in the intelligence scene any more, but it was pretty clear that the Director would dearly love some payback if the opportunity arose.

Travis tossed his empty water bottle into a nearby bin, only to see a beggar immediately dive in and snatch it, probably for resale. Pausing in a corner doorway to check his map, he realised he was being watched. A Thai in his late twenties was across the road, talking on a cell phone while staring straight at Travis. He looked away quickly when Travis spotted him. At the same time a younger Thai also with a cell phone to his ear jogged around the corner, breaking stride as he realised Travis was right there, then slowing to a hurried walk as he made his way past. He ducked into a doorway further up.

Travis rolled the map and kept it in his hand, stepping out into the crowds again and striding past the doorway where the younger man was pretending to be deep in conversation. He ignored the man and walked on, senses on full alert now. If they were members of any of the national intelligence agencies, they weren't very good, which meant they were probably either muggers or contractors of some sort. Either way they were a problem that he wanted gone.

He sensed the younger Thai tag in behind him and he also spotted the older one across the road trailing them in his peripheral vision. The hotel and its questionable sanctity were still a block and a half away. Up ahead he spotted a third watcher, this one another Thai in his late fifties with a paunch and the sallow skin of a heavy smoker. He was making no secret of his presence, standing near a street vendor and staring straight down the footpath in Travis' direction.

His overtness was not a good sign. It was time to go on the offensive.

Travis turned abruptly on his heel and walked briskly back the way he had come. The younger Thai was caught on the hop and had nowhere to go. Travis made a beeline for him, the younger man becoming suddenly flustered and looking everywhere but at him. He stepped to the side as if to cross the road and even looked both ways before glancing back over his shoulder for his "mark."

Travis was right on him and it was too late. Using his body to shield the action from any pedestrians behind him, Travis slammed a vicious jab to the man's kidney, causing the man to drop his cell phone and cry out in pain. Travis caught him as he started to buckle at the knees and jammed a thumb into the crevice of the man's right elbow, gripping hard and applying intense pressure to the muscles and tendons there. The man paled and his arm went limp. Travis checked his belt quickly for weapons and found a battered snub nosed revolver, which he tossed overhead onto the awning over the footpath behind him. The man started to fight back and Travis swept his legs from under him, dropping him to the ground and leaving him on the road.

He darted across the road, dodging tuk-tuks and heading straight for the other watcher. The guy was already moving away, cell phone to his ear. Travis turned and spotted the older watcher on the opposite side, moving rapidly to the fallen man who was now propping himself up against a power pole and looking in pain. The older man, who Travis presumed was the boss, caught Travis' eye and scowled ferociously.

Travis ignored him and moved after the watcher ahead of him, who wasn't wasting any time as he pushed his way through the crowds. Another guy in his twenties popped into view, dashing across the road at an angle from Travis' left, moving to intercept him.

Travis turned and ducked into a shop doorway, pushing past a couple of tourists who were trying on bead necklaces. The impeccably-presented girl behind the counter approached Travis with a wide smile. The smile disappeared quickly as Travis stepped behind the counter and through a hanging curtain into the back room. An elderly man with long whiskers looked up from a bowl of food and chattered excitedly, waving chopsticks at the white intruder. The girl was shouting at him from behind and he heard the shop door bang open again, a loud male voice joining the din.

The back door opened at a push and Travis found himself in a rear alley, surrounded by rubbish bins and pieces of junk. He slammed the door shut and pulled a bin across it before sprinting for the end of the alley, where he could see a busy street. He'd only gone a few metres when the boss of the watchers appeared at the end ahead of him, his hand going under his shirt as he shouted something in Thai.

Travis spun and went the other way, hoping he didn't catch a bullet in his back. The rubbish bin he'd moved clattered to the side as the shop's back door burst open, and the watcher he'd been following popped out, cell phone in one hand and a pistol in the other.

He saw Travis coming too late. Travis threw a hand straight into his face, the heel of his palm slamming under the man's jaw and snapping his head back. The man went down immediately, his pistol discharging into the concrete wall opposite. Travis bolted past, pumping his legs and arms hard and lining up the brick wall at the end of the alley. He hit it at speed, getting a foot part way up and pushing up, stretching out for the top of the wall. His fingers hooked over the top and he hauled himself up, scrabbling with his feet and getting a knee up to lever himself onto the top. He caught a quick glimpse of the older man running down the alley towards him, still shouting, as he rolled over the wall and dropped into a service yard.

He wasted no time getting back onto the street and mingling with the crowds. His shirt was dirty and ripped and he was sweating with the exertion. He dug the cell phone out and rang Susie's number. It rang through to voicemail and he tried again. Still no response.

He jammed the phone back into his pocket with a curse, hoping she was safe. He jumped into the nearest tuk-tuk and shoved an American twenty at the driver.

'Golden Key Hotel mate,' he panted, 'no stops, no sponsor's shops, yeah?'

The driver opened his mouth to protest and Travis waved the greenback at him. He knew it was standard practice for the drivers to divert any passengers to the business of a sponsor, who paid them for the service. He didn't have time to dick around.

The driver relented and pocketed the cash, gunning the machine out into traffic. Travis took the time to catch his breath and try Susie again. Still nothing. He flicked a quick text to her with the code they had agreed.

*A1*. We've been compromised.

He put the phone away and ran a quick physical on himself. A grazed knee and a damaged shirt was all he had to show for the escapade.

He slapped the driver on the shoulder and told him to pull over half a block short. The driver protested until a handful of greenbacks appeared in his hand. Travis left him behind and legged it to the hotel, knowing time was of the essence. He didn't have time for niceties. *Speed, Aggression, Surprise*-the other meaning of the SAS.

The other guests in the lift looked at him sideways on the way up. The porter with them looked at him suspiciously.

Jabbing the key card into the door slot, he burst into the suite and found himself face to face with the boss of the watchers. Susie stood by the window, her cell in her hand and a bemused look on her face. She looked cool and touristy in tan shorts and a sleeveless blue top. Another heavy stood near her.

Even as he reached for the man in front of him, Travis noticed nobody had a weapon drawn. Susie's warning was loud.

'Jack, no!'

He pulled back against every instinct in his body. The older man had stepped back warily. A half smile came onto his face and he put his hands up placatingly.

'It is okay, we are on your side.'

Travis glanced at Susie, who was nodding vigorously.

'This is Major Dang of the Special Branch, Royal Thai Police. They're on our side.'

'You sure?' Travis was still eyeing the two visitors carefully. 'Can they explain why they just tried to rumble me?'

Susie's brow wrinkled and she looked questioningly at the older man. He smiled and spoke in accented but flawless English.

'This is true. Please, I apologise for the incident. Perhaps we did not know who we were dealing with, and I must say I have some new men who are...perhaps overly keen?' He smiled again and held his hand to his heart. 'We meant you no harm, please believe me.'

Travis had to admit it was a convincing story.

## 10

It took some time and coffee before they were all on the same page and Travis relaxed to a degree.

It transpired that Dang was the contact Susie had been in touch with, although they had never met before. He and his men had been scoping the area of the hotel when Travis burned them. The communication had broken down on the team and the results spoke for themselves-one of the officers had a dislocated jaw and the other was very sore. Dang had not been happy with Travis for his reaction, but even less pleased with his own men. He gave the distinct impression that disciplinary action would follow. Knowing what he knew about the Thais, Travis felt for the guys involved.

Susie had missed his calls when she was in the shower, and when she picked up his message she had called Dang straight away for back up.

'And there he was,' Susie concluded, 'already on his way up to see me.'

'Lucky,' Travis observed. He was the only one still standing, not quite ready to fully relax yet. He'd wanted to frisk both men but was held back with a warning look from Susie.

'I can only apologise again,' Major Dang said with a shrug. He was no longer smiling. 'But I have apologised enough. We must move on.'

Travis gave a non-committal shrug and smiled, holding the glittering black eyes of the other man.

'I tried to identify us to you, but obviously all us Asians sound the same, huh?'

'It's all good mate,' Travis told him, 'water under the bridge. I'm pleased we've cleared the air.'

'I shall pass that on to my friend with the broken jaw,' interrupted Dang's colleague with a sneer. 'I'm sure he'll be pleased you're happy.'

Dang snapped something at him in Thai then smiled at the two Kiwis. 'Sergeant Mookjai is understandably upset about what happened. He means no offense.'

Seeing the way the lean NCO was looking at him, Travis wasn't so convinced. The man had the lumpy knuckles and scar tissue round the eyes of a street brawler.

Major Dang clapped his hands on his knees and stood. 'We must carry on, I am afraid. It has been very nice to meet you, and most...enlightening?' He smiled and gave a short bow. 'We will be in touch, as they say.'

Susie showed them out and shut the door behind them. She pointed to her ear and then to the door.

'Well I don't know about you, but I'm gagging for a drink,' Travis said. 'And I need to clean up a bit after all that palaver.'

He went to the bathroom and stripped off his shirt, having a quick wash and freshen up while Susie made idle chat with him. Returning to the lounge he dug a clean shirt out of his bag and ran a hand through his hair. He saw Susie staring at him and realised she had seen the scars on his torso-a memento from Afghanistan.

'Another time, another place,' he said briefly before covering it up. 'Let's go.'

THE BAR they'd been sent to was a twenty minute tuk-tuk ride from the hotel, beside the Chao Phraya river. They played the tourists and took their time with some counter-surveillance measures, finally arriving only fifteen minutes before the scheduled contact. They were shown to a table on the balcony where they could see the boats go by on the river and people-watch to their hearts' content. The waitress who brought them their drinks-an ice cold Chang beer for Travis and an orange coloured Thai iced tea for Susie-had a flawless complexion and a beautiful smile.

Susie saw Travis' lingering look and laughed. 'Like China dolls, aren't they.'

He grinned self-consciously. 'And probably not even half my age.'

They snacked on prawn crackers while they drank, and were halfway through their drinks when Travis spotted a short slim European man stand from his table inside and move towards the balcony. He was in his thirties and had the sort of face you would forget in seconds. He carried a copy of today's Bangkok Post, folded in half and held in his left hand.

Travis cleared his throat subtly and Susie switched on, nudging her own copy of the Post with her elbow so that it protruded out from the table. The man ignored them as he walked past to the rail of the balcony, pausing there to look out at the river and take a photo on his phone.

As the man turned to go Travis and Susie stood and gathered their things. He had to squeeze past side on with a nod and smile.

'Sorry,' Susie said, turning out of his way and slipping the Post from his hand as he went past. He scooped up her copy and carried on, and the brush pass was completed in less than a second.

Travis drained his glass and put it down, slipped on his sunnies and said 'Let's go get some dinner.'

Susie smiled and looped her arm through his, the Post tucked into her handbag. They left the bar and walked a block before Susie opened the newspaper and dug inside. A bag check ticket was there as agreed, a small padlock key taped to it.

They walked to the hotel named on the ticket, a mid-range tourist outfit where it was possible to leave your bags for a day after checking out. The high turnover of guests minimised the risk of a staff member being suspicious of a guest they didn't recognise.

Susie took the ticket inside while Travis kept watch outside. They didn't appear to have been followed. She was back in a minute with a plain blue daypack, the zip padlocked closed.

Travis took it from her and could feel some weight as he shouldered it.

'Let's go,' he said.

They found a dim sum restaurant only a couple of blocks from their hotel and took a table near the door. They ordered pork spare ribs and spring rolls to start, and while they waited Travis ducked to the toilet with the daypack. Locked in a cubicle, he opened the bag to find a large black sarong wrapped around three smaller drawstring canvas bags.

The first two bags were identical. Each contained a Sig Sauer P250 Compact chambered for .357 SIG. Each was fully loaded with a round in the chamber and holstered in a black leather Mitch Rosen holster, and was accompanied by a spare 13 round magazine and a full box of 50 rounds. The third bag contained documents-a wad of what appeared to be about five grand American and fifty thousand Thai baht, plus clean New Zealand passports for each of them. Anthony Turner and Melissa Cullen.

Travis placed one of the Sigs at the top of the bag, ready to grab, and returned to the table. Susie had cleaned up the remainder of the entrees and smiled as he sat. A large jug of iced tea sat in the centre of the table.

'I ordered for you,' she said, 'I hope a chicken cashew stir fry is okay.'

'Conservative,' he grinned, 'but safe.'

The meal was typical Thai-clean, packed with flavour and sizzling hot. They devoured it and debated over desserts before deciding against it. It felt good to be away from the hotel and, choosing their words carefully, they agreed that Major Dang and his sidekick had probably planted listening devices in their room-or if not at the time, certainly by now. They lingered over their last drinks before hitting the pavement again.

They hadn't gone far before they realised they were being followed.

PAUL WATKINS HAD WORKED at the Ministry for Foreign Affairs for five years in Wellington before getting a position with a family friend's business in Bangkok, exporting Thai artefacts, art and knick knacks to New Zealand, Aussie and the UK.

He had only been there a couple of months when he was approached by his former boss at the Ministry. He was offered the chance to be involved in the intelligence game as a courier, doing pick-ups and drop offs with agents on the ground. The embassy staff, including the resident SIS officer, were well known to the local authorities and it wasn't always safe for them to clear dead letter drops or meet with agents.

Paul loved the subterfuge of it all and it was satisfying knowing that he was actually contributing to keeping his own country safer from terrorists. Tonight's brush pass had been straight forward and all over within an hour from start to finish. After making the drop to the two agents in the bar he'd made his way back to the office and let himself in.

Everyone was gone for the day and it didn't take long to switch off the alarm, place his marker and lock up again. He knew that another agent, probably an embassy staffer, would drive past the office within the next half hour. They would see that the small cactus in the terra-cotta pot on his office windowsill had been moved from the left side to the right side, meaning that the brush pass had been completed safely.

He smiled to himself as he walked away from the office, still feeling the thrill of the adrenaline rush in his veins. The export company was what paid the bills but the spy stuff was what he lived for.

He blended into the background as he walked towards his nearby apartment, just another non-descript white face in casual clothes with a man-bag over his shoulder. He was nearly at the apartment, planning what he was going to have for dinner, when he felt a sudden prickling at the back of his neck. The feeling that he was being watched was too strong to ignore. He turned quickly but saw nothing untoward. He carried on the way he was going but couldn't shake the feeling. He dug his cell phone out and punched in his PIN, debating whether to call or not. Maybe he was just being paranoid. His handler wouldn't appreciate the security breach of being called for a non-emergency.

He reached the main street and checked the traffic. Busy as always, tuk-tuks and bikes weaving around the cars and buses. His apartment was opposite in a large block that reached for the sky. Within a minute he would be safely inside. If he still felt wary he'd make the call then. He tucked the phone away again and stepped to the edge of the road, waiting.

A bus loaded with tourists from the airport was approaching in the inside lane and he waited. The noise of traffic and the buzz of chatter and movement was loud all around him.

Just as the bus got a couple of car lengths away, Paul felt the prickle at the base of his neck again, stronger than before. He suddenly knew he was in imminent danger.

As he started to turn his head he felt hands on his elbows, hard and strong, pinning his arms to his sides. He looked into the flat cold eyes of a Thai man who pressed right up against him.

Paul was propelled forward, his feet leaving the ground as he was bodily lifted and tossed into the path of the oncoming bus. The bus driver had no chance to stop and the front grill smashed into Paul's torso, carrying him several metres before the bus slowed enough and the body slid to the roadway in a crumpled heap. He was dead before he hit the ground.

People screamed and horns honked and the Thai man melted into the crowd.

**11**

———————

'Dang's crew?' Susie wondered aloud as they trotted across a side road and headed towards the main road. They had spotted a tuk-tuk driver kerb-crawling opposite them and seeming to track them as they left the restaurant and made their way up the footpath. He wasn't touting for business and seemed to have no reason to be there.

'Maybe,' Travis muttered, 'he's pretty obvious and Dang's guys don't seem too sharp.'

'Better keep our eyes open, he won't be alone.'

They reached the main thoroughfare and turned right, keeping with the crowds of pedestrians-although, Travis noted, the crowds had thinned out between the bustle of the day shoppers and the buzz of the night time partiers. They felt exposed without a throng around them.

'Plan?' Susie asked tersely, keeping pace with him and trying to maintain a relaxed air.

'Stay alive,' he replied, and she shot him a scowl.

'Really? That's your plan? Stay alive?' she said incredulously.

He shrugged. 'Well it's not a bad plan. Simple, but effective.'

'Jesus Christ,' Susie groaned, shaking her head. 'I should've followed my sister and been a teacher. Lots of holidays, weekends off and fuck all chance of getting my tits shot off in some hell hole.'

Travis gave her surprised. 'Wow,' he said, 'descriptive.'

She opened her mouth to retort and he put his arm around her shoulders, pulling her close. 'There's another one up ahead,' he said softly, 'tuk-tuk, brown shirt with a red scarf. Third one near him on the footpath, smoking by the bar, talking on the phone.'

Susie clocked them both. 'How d'you know?'

'It's my job. Besides, both have sidearms under their shirts.'

'So, my question still stands; plan?'

'I presume you're okay with a pistol?'

She nodded. 'Of course.'

'Good. I don't see these guys being Dang's crew, which means they know who we are and aren't on our side. Stick with me, and when I run you run. We're going into the alley just ahead and once we do we're going to leg it as fast as we can. It'll either make them show their hand or we'll lose them.' He looked at her closely, inhaling her scent as he did so. 'All good?'

'Yep.' She nodded and gave him a dazzling smile, slipping her arm around his waist and squeezing. 'Probably need to lay off those dinners, big guy-you're packing on the pounds.'

'Thanks. Remember, stay close.' They were just about on the alleyway now and the men up ahead were barely forty metres away. Travis paused outside a shop to look at a rack of flowery shirts, just at the mouth of the alley. 'Nice and easy,' he said, 'I'll be right behind you. Go now.'

Susie sidled past him and into the alley. As soon as she left the footpath she sprinted. Travis gave her a couple of seconds and followed, swinging the daypack off his shoulder as he began to run. He dug out the first Sig and jammed it into his waistband, slipping the pack onto his back as he tried to catch up to Susie. She wasn't wasting any time and was several metres ahead, hair dragging in her slipstream.

He heard running feet behind them and threw a glance back-the smoker he'd spotted was after them, the smoke and phone gone now and replaced by a pistol. A tuk-tuk was entering the alley behind him. Travis focussed on getting distance, seeing Susie just about at the end of the alley now.

A van screeched to a halt across the alley in front of her and the side door slid open, revealing two Thai men. One had an SMG of some sort, the other a sawn off shotgun.

Susie skidded to a halt and started to turn, but was barely three metres from them. Both guns swung towards her. At this range they would tear her apart.

Still running full tilt, Travis swung the Sig up and thumbed the safety off. The first shot was deafeningly loud and blew out the driver's window. The shotgunner yelped with surprise and involuntarily fired his weapon, blasting a chunk out of the alley wall beside Susie.

Travis heard her shriek and fired again, a double tap this time that took the shotgunner in the chest and knocked him backwards into the van where he hung half in and half out, the sawn off still in his hands. The driver panicked and tried to escape, but bunny-hopped and stalled the van. He looked up in terror as he cranked the ignition.

The sub-gunner seemed to be more switched on and took a crouch, bringing his gun up.

'Down!' Travis bellowed, diving to the dirty floor of the alley as the SMG opened up. A long burst of rounds shredded the air above him. He saw Susie hit the deck to the side and start crawling towards him. He rolled awkwardly with the daypack on and got the Sig around, coming online when another burst of rounds pinged off the ground only inches away.

He heard a shout behind him as the two men at that end came dangerously close to a blue-on-blue with the sub-gunner. Taking advantage of the momentary confusion, Travis unleashed a second double tap towards the sub-gunner and saw the man's torso judder with the impacts of the heavy .357 SIG rounds. He fell sideways, dropping his weapon. The van roared to life and leaped forward out of sight, the wounded shotgunner slipping to the ground. The rear wheels of the van bounced over his legs as his driver escaped.

'Go!' Travis shouted, pushing up and racing towards the footpath ahead.

Susie was up and moving. A shot sounded from behind them but they ran on. The whine of an overworked tuk-tuk told them their pursuers were closing in.

Susie cut left onto the footpath and he was right behind her, ignoring the dead man-someone was already attending to him, or maybe stealing his sub-machine gun-and the screaming shotgunner as he ran past. The street was busy and bright with gaudy lights. People were flocking to the alley scene, some screaming, everyone rubber necking. They leaped out of the way as the brightly coloured tuk tuk roared out of the alley, both gunmen aboard now.

Susie glanced back and Travis slapped her on the shoulder. 'Keep going!'

She upped the pace, shoving past anyone who got in the way and jumping obstacles she could barely see on the ground. They heard the tuk-tuk racing up behind them and as it got close Travis grabbed Susie's arm and jerked her backwards. They turned and cut back the other way as the tuk-tuk reached them, the gunman in the back loosing off a pair of shots from a .45. A light above them shattered in a burst of sparks and people screamed, ducking for cover.

The tuk-tuk overshot and Travis held his fire, wary of all the civilians around. They ran instead, straight across the road behind the tuk-tuk, gaining a valuable lead as the machine struggled to turn around in the traffic. The passenger jumped out and waved his pistol at motorists to force a gap, but by that time Travis and Susie were across the road and sprinting away.

The driver shouted and gunned it after them, the passenger leaping aboard as they saw their quarry reach a rank of other tuk-tuks up ahead.

The driver of the first machine saw them coming and took off in fright, immediately crashing into a passing cyclist and sending him flying.

The second driver looked at them with a sneer and put his hand out. Travis was in no mood to negotiate.

'Gimme your wheels,' he shouted.

The driver shook his head and lifted his shirt to show the handle of a dagger tucked there. Travis slammed a fist into his face and knocked him sideways out of the tuk-tuk.

Susie jumped in the back and he fired it up, taking off with a screech of tyres. The wounded tuk-tuk driver behind them stood in the roadway, shouting and swearing until the gunmen came racing past and clipped him with a wing mirror, spinning him off to the side again.

Travis kept the revs up, weaving as best he could through the traffic, completely disoriented now. With no idea where they were he figured the best plan was simply to get distance. He hunched over the handlebars of the little machine.

'Does that make it go faster?' Susie queried from behind him.

'Aerodynamics,' he shouted back,' so you should probably keep your mouth closed.'

Her retort was lost in the sound of a shot careening off the steel body.

'Get your head down and get that gun outta the bag!' Travis shouted.

Susie ripped the zip of his bag open and searched around, hanging on for dear life as the little machine swayed and bumped. Travis braked hard and cursed, swerving around a motorist who had pulled out blindly. Susie hung onto his daypack, narrowly saving herself a spill out the side, and her fingers finally found the second Sig. She pulled it clear and shoved the holster back into the bag, taking the spare magazine that was with it and securing the bag again. The way her partner was driving he was likely to lose everything out of it.

Travis concentrated on the road ahead, which seemed to contain the entire population of the city and go forever. The enemy's tuk-tuk was staying right behind him and he guessed they were probably standard machines with similar performance abilities-the chance of outrunning one was minimal. Plus the enemy obviously had local knowledge.

In the wing mirror he could see the passenger in the back leaning out the side with a pistol in one hand and a cell phone in the other.

'Back up,' Travis muttered to himself. Sooner or later they were going to be outnumbered.

A shot boomed out from behind and shattered the taillight of the car Travis was undercutting. The car swerved left and Travis jerked the handlebars the same way to avoid a collision. He mounted the footpath and clipped a fruit stand, scattering produce everywhere. The enemy tracked him on the road, a second shot booming out and flying between them.

'Jesus fucken son of a bitch!' Susie yelled, grabbing the side for support as she slid across the hard plastic seat.

'Well said.' Up ahead Travis could see there was a small van pulled partially across the footpath, with a couple of men dismantling a stall of some sort and loading it in the back. The footpath was blocked by boxes and the top of a trestle table. 'Hold on!'

The two guys dropped their boxes and dived to the side as the tuk-tuk reached them. The front wheel hit the first box and there was a sickening lurch then a blessed lift as the wheel became airborne. The tuk-tuk leaped the obstacle and they both left their seats, slamming their heads into the plastic roof. It landed with a bone-shaking thud that threw Susie forward into Travis' back. She hit the floor in a tumble and grabbed for a hold, her feet bouncing off the ground for a few seconds until she hauled herself up again and regained her seat.

'Get your phone out and call Dang,' Travis shouted. 'We can't outrun these fuckers in this thing.'

Susie plucked the phone from her pocket and tried to get the number up. Travis cut left down a side street, getting a slight lead as the enemy's tuk-tuk overshot and had to slow to come back around.

'Any idea where we are?' Susie shouted over the noise of the roaring engine.

'Not a clue.'

She shook her head in frustration and finally got the number up on the screen from her call list.

Suddenly a white van appeared in the wing mirror, its high beams on and the front passenger leaning out the side with a shortened pump action shotgun in his hands.

'Back up's here,' Travis yelled.

'Oh, thank God,' Susie breathed.

'For them.'

'Shit shit shit!' She stabbed the talk button and turned to look behind, just as the shotgun bellowed and ripped a gash in the roof above her.

Travis swerved hard right, the tuk-tuk skidded and lifted a wheel off the ground, and Susie slid across the seat again. The phone flew from her hand and smashed on the road. Another shot followed and they heard birdshot pinging off the cab.

'Shoot them!' Travis yelled at her, throwing a full U-turn and doubling back.

The van overshot but the other tuk-tuk was right there, the back passenger leaning over and jabbing his pistol out at them. The muzzle flashed and Travis' wing mirror exploded in pieces.

Susie fired almost point blank, squeezing off three shots in quick succession before they were past and racing back towards the main road.

'Did you get him?' Travis asked, risking a look back. The van was reversing hard towards them.

'I don't know, I think I had my eyes closed,' she admitted. 'Sorry.'

'Don't worry, they need to know we mean business. Keep it up.'

Travis realised they weren't going to make the main road before the van reached them. He braked sharply and flung the little machine around in a rapid U-turn.

The van driver saw what he was doing and also braked, flicking his wheel around in a reasonable attempt at a J-turn. He got halfway round and stalled it. For the second time that night he found himself staring at the two targets, face to face.

Travis left the engine running and stepped out of the cab, his Sig coming up on line. He blasted four shots into the driver's door, seeing the man rock with the impacts as the heavy slugs punched through the thin steel. The driver slumped in his window frame and

Travis put a round through his head, spraying blood over the windscreen.

The front passenger had jumped out of his door and was hiding on the other side of the van. Travis ducked down and couldn't see his feet, indicating he was behind a wheel.

'Shit!' Travis shouted, 'I'm out! Reload!'

The ruse worked a treat. The gunman raced round the front of the van with his sawn off shotgun at the hip, expecting to find his target desperately trying to change magazines. Instead he found Travis in a crouch, the Sig in a double-handed grip.

The gunman's eyes popped open with surprise as he realised his mistake, but it was too late. Travis pumped a double tap into his chest and dropped him. He pushed up and ran forward, putting the last round into the guy's head as he twitched on the roadway.

The tuk-tuk was almost on them now, the driver having hung back while his comrades in the van took care of business.

Travis ducked behind the van again, realised he didn't have the spare magazine with him, and rammed the Sig into his waistband. He scrambled forward and snatched up the fallen sawn off shotgun, getting his hands to it as the tuk-tuk arrived only a couple of metres away.

The .45 barked again and a piece of asphalt blasted off the surface beside Travis' foot, a second shot tearing at the flap of his shirt. He lifted the stubby shotgun barrel and squeezed off a shot. The gun roared and the driver's chest was ripped open. He threw his hand up and the machine swerved, smashing into a parked car at the side of the road.

The passenger was thrown forward and cracked his head against that of the lifeless driver. His eyes were spinning when Travis got to him and yanked him out onto the ground. He kicked the old Colt out of the man's hand and pinned him to the ground with a foot on his chest. The wide barrel stared at the man's face.

'Who sent you?' Travis snarled, acutely aware that time was not on their side. The cops would be here any second.

'Huh? No Engrish!'

'Don't bullshit me, fucko. Who sent you to kill us?' He ground his foot into the man's chest, causing him to grimace. 'Tell me now or I'll blow your fucken brains out.'

'No Engrish, asshole!'

'Sounds like English to me.' Travis pumped the slide on the shotgun to chamber a fresh round. 'You got two seconds then I'll shoot you in the kneecap.'

'Fuck you!'

'I warned you.' Travis shifted position and lowered the shotgun barrel to the man's right knee.

'White man!' the gunman shrieked. 'Is white man! Pay money!'

'Who? What's his name?'

Sirens were rapidly approaching and Susie was shouting at him to get moving. They only had seconds.

'Don' know! I swear! White man like you, pay good money!'

'Come on!' Susie shouted, grabbing him by the arm. 'The cops're here, we've gotta go!'

'Fuck it!' Travis slammed the butt of the shotgun into the guy's face, smashing his teeth in and knocking him out cold. He racked the slide a couple of times before it was empty, and tossed the shotgun aside.

Seeing flashing lights up on the main road, he followed Susie at a sprint down the side street.

In seconds they had disappeared into a network of side streets and alleyways.

**12**

———

Brad had pounded the hilly roads around Onewhero for forty five minutes before arriving back at the house and hitting Jack's home gym in the shed.

He pumped weights and slammed the heavy bag for another half hour, finally calling it quits when his singlet was drenched in sweat and his muscles were screaming for rest. He emptied his water bottle and walked outside until his breathing was under control. His mind was still whirling with the recent events. He wasn't sleeping well and it was nothing to do with having killed three men-he didn't give a fuck about them, they were shit kickers better off dead, although he did wonder if he shouldn't feel something about having taken lives.

It was his buddies that were messing with his head, or more specifically, his inability to do anything for them. It was Tony's funeral today down in the Hawkes Bay in his home town, and he couldn't attend. Greeno was still in intensive care with serious head injuries, and it was touch and go whether he'd make it. If he did he was fucked anyway, leaving his wife and daughter stranded. Brad wasn't allowed to visit him in hospital or even call Sarah to show his support. As far as his STG family were concerned he'd dropped off the face of the planet. He'd had several calls on his cell but that had quickly been taken by Ingoe and passed on to his bosses.

He was angry that he was being shut out, he was angry about what had happened and how it had all gone down, and he was angry that Jack and the spook lady were on a jaunt in Thailand while he was stuck here working out, doing mandatory psych debriefs with some head doctor in the city and getting bored and frustrated.

Jack and the lady spook, he thought. Old Jack was probably up to his nuts in guts right now. As for him, he'd had a casual thing going with one of his flatmates but it was nothing more than a matter of convenience. It had been a while since anything serious.

Brad shook his head in frustration and walked inside, refilling his bottle at the kitchen tap. He downed it in a long draught, letting the overflow run down his chin onto his sweaty chest. Dropping the bottle in the sink, he looked around. It was so quiet out here he could hear his heart beating. He crossed to the stereo in the lounge and rummaged through until he found a CD to his liking. Jack had some pretty old fashioned taste but he found a Cold Chisel classic and chucked it on.

*Standing on the Outside* cranked up and it seemed to perfectly match how he felt right now.

Brad wandered aimlessly round the lounge, checking out Jack's photos on the wall unit then made his way down the hall to the office. Glancing around, he noticed a photo frame hanging by the window that he hadn't seen before. It held four photos in a vertical line.

Staring at it, Brad realised each photo was a black and white formal shot of a man in Army number ones. There was an inscription below each photo with a name, rank and serial number, followed by a pair of dates.

The top photo was Captain Sam Travis who had served during the Second World War with the original L Detachment of the Special Air Service before returning home, then a second set of dates showed that he had also been an original member of the NZ unit, serving from 1955 through until 1963.

He was followed by Warrant Officer Class 1 Pete Travis, who Brad knew to be his own grandfather, serving from 1962-81. He had retired as the Regimental Sergeant-Major.

Pete's younger brother Marty had a more chequered history, serving in the NZ unit from 1971-73 then with the Rhodesian SAS from '73-80. He moved again, transferring to the Brits from 1980-85 and ultimately retiring as a Staff Sergeant. Brad had heard he was the black sheep of the family, never settling anywhere for too long and always in trouble of some sort.

His eye fell to the last photo; Jack. His dates of service were 1996-14, and he had reached WO2 status, meaning he'd been a Squadron Sergeant-Major when he left. The next step would have been RSM, like his father before him.

Seeing the faces of the four men, all battle hardened warriors, gave Brad pause. These men were Special Forces royalty; three generations of long serving operators. He had known they were all military men but after his mother had drifted from the family, he'd had minimal contact with his relatives. Sam had died a few years ago, Pete was somewhere down the line, and Marty was overseas somewhere- Aussie, the last he'd heard.

Brad studied the four men, recognising the pride they had in their uniforms, seeing the way they held themselves. He wondered if his own path had been pre-determined. He'd enjoyed being a cop but special ops had always been his goal and he'd focussed on getting there from the day he first pulled on a blue uniform. Obviously it was in the blood of Travis men.

Turning away from the photos, he knew he had a lot to live up to. He fervently hoped that he would get to put his own skills to the test.

# 13

Anthony Turner and Melissa Cullen arrived late at a tourist hotel near the airport, lugging new bags and wearing new clothes, all of which had been bought from street vendors on their circuitous route from the scene of the shooting.

Changing cabs several times and walking different parts of the route had left them happy they weren't being followed, but they were still tense and their feeling of paranoia was running high.

Once they were safely in their suite, they followed a familiar routine; Travis physically checked the entire suite and took charge of their defences, while Susie plugged in one of the burn phones they'd bought and dialled Ingoe back in NZ.

Travis locked the door, secured the latch and placed a coffee table across the doorway. He took a post in the kitchen where he could see the adjoining buildings, and reloaded their magazines. He watched and listened to Susie's brief conversation, which consisted mostly of code words.

She disconnected and put the phone down. Her expression was one of displeasure and concern.

'He's on it,' she said curtly, 'but basically has no idea who or why.

He's coming back to me shortly, hopefully with an update and exit strategy.'

'Exit strategy?' Travis queried. 'Why? We're obviously getting somewhere.'

She looked at him like he was mad. 'Are you serious? You just killed three guys and maimed another in the middle of bloody Bangkok! We had a running gun battle on fucking tuk-tuks' for Christ's sake-two white people blowing away a bunch of locals makes it an international fucking incident, Jack. Politicians don't tend to like that sort of shit. They think it's unpleasant and pretty fucked up!'

He noticed she swore a lot when she was agitated. He figured it was probably an observation best left unsaid.

'It is unpleasant and fucked up,' he agreed instead, 'but it also happens for a reason. If we weren't putting pressure on someone then they wouldn't react like that. You don't try and kill people for no reason.' He paused. 'And it was four and two, not three and one.'

She frowned at him. 'What?'

'You said I killed three guys and maimed another. It was actually four and two.'

'Oh, what, so now we're keeping score, is that it?' She shook her head angrily, her hands planted on her hips. 'So you're in the lead because I must've missed-I tried to shoot that guy, Jack-sorry I'm not a super ninja fucking commando like you!'

'Don't be silly,' he said quietly, 'nobody's keeping score. I don't care that you didn't hit that guy; I care that you tried to. At least it stopped them shooting at us for a few seconds.'

'Like it made any fucking difference,' she retorted, still fired up. 'The bastards nearly got us, Jack. We nearly fucking died back there.' Her voice caught and she looked away. 'I thought I was going to die.' She put a hand to her mouth and her face crinkled. 'I thought I was going to get blown away by some fucking crazy bastard and not even know why.'

The tears came now and her shoulders hunched. Travis felt suddenly awkward, not knowing whether to try and console her or leave her to deal with it. He wasn't good with emotional women; there weren't too many of them in the SAS.

He was relieved when she pulled herself together, surprisingly quick but it had still seemed like a lifetime to him. She straightened up, squared her shoulders and brushed her hair back from her face. She looked him straight in the eye.

'Sorry about that, I don't usually lose it. I'd appreciate it if that stayed between us.' She sniffed and rubbed a hand over her face. 'I'm more professional than that.'

Travis shrugged. 'If what stayed between us?'

She nodded. 'Thank you.'

'It's okay though, y'know. I've known guys to piss their pants when the hammer comes down. You never know how you're going to react.'

She looked at him sceptically. 'Guys in the Group piss their pants with fear? Really?'

He gave a lopsided grin. 'Well, not us, no. I mean normal people, you know…'

The phone rang and he prowled to the window while she talked. The second conversation was longer and after a minute or so she called him over and put Ingoe on speaker.

Travis listened to the tinny voice coming from the cheap phone.

'The agent you contacted was killed tonight, Bangkok time,' Ingoe told them. 'Hit by a bus while crossing the road. Must've been just after your contact.'

Travis and Susie looked sharply at one another.

'A proper accident?' Susie asked.

'It's unclear,' Ingoe replied, 'but common sense would say no, considering what happened with you two. Best you keep on the move and stay under the radar. We don't know exactly who is responsible or why.'

'Major Dang seems an interesting character, Jedi,' Travis said. 'You dealt with him before?'

A chuckle sounded down the line. 'Yes I have, and if you're asking whether I trust him or not, the answer is "You are in one of the most corrupt countries in our region of the world." Unfortunately we don't always get to choose our playmates.'

'Are you looking at an exit strategy?' Susie asked, glancing at Travis.

There was silence for a moment. 'You're on the ground. What's your feeling on this?'

Susie looked at Travis as she replied. 'No. We're happy to continue. Let's see what shakes out in the next day or so.'

Travis nodded his assent, his respect for her going up a notch.

'That apply to both of you, Jack?'

'A-ffirm.'

'Good. I'll be in touch as soon as I know anything else. In the meantime, you want some back up over there?'

'Probably wouldn't hurt to get the ball rolling,' Travis said. 'Know anyone in the area?'

The Special Forces community was a tight knit one, and members rarely ever properly left. It wasn't uncommon for "retired" operators to be called on for a favour out of the blue. Travis knew that if anyone had a contact, it would be Ingoe. The former RSM's reply surprised him.

'I'll get young Brad geared up and on his way over. Till then, keep ya powder dry.'

There was a click and he was gone. They looked at each other.

'Well that's that,' Susie said, putting her phone away.

'Good call,' Travis told her, and she gave a slight smile.

'Can't have the boss thinking I'm a chicken shit, can I?'

Travis went to the mini bar and checked the supplies. 'Not much here,' he said. 'I don't know about you, but dinner was a long time ago.'

'I hear you, let's eat.'

**14**

———

Cabin fever finally overtook Brad and he caught a cab to the airport.

The driver couldn't believe his luck with the size of the fare from Pukekohe to Onewhero then all the way to Mangere. Brad, on the other hand, nearly had a coronary.

He sucked it up and took the next hit when he checked in, deciding to wait for the red eye flight and save himself almost half a fare. The landing at Wellington airport was typically bumpy and he again wondered why the hell he'd ever transferred down here where it always seemed windy and wet-say what you like about Auckland, but the weather didn't always suck balls.

He got out of the Arrivals Hall quickly with just a carry-on bag, made his way to the taxi rank outside and gave directions to a house around the corner from his own in Johnsonville. It was nearly one a.m. when the cabbie dropped him off and Brad peeled notes off his rapidly depleting roll of cash. He waited until the cabbie disappeared from sight before hiking down to the corner and having a recce of his own street.

It was quiet and still, which made it that much easier to spot the car on surveillance just a couple of houses from his. It was a small hybrid hatchback, not the sort of car usually used by cops, and he guessed it was media instead. Some headline-hungry reporter who had ID'd him and tracked him down. Brad made a mental note to up his game in the personal security stakes.

He hugged the shadows and made his way towards the car, approaching from behind before darting to the back of the car and hunkering down. He felt faintly ridiculous-he was almost as big as the car itself.

He could hear soft snoring and the windows were fogged up. Whoever it was, was clearly desperate for the story but didn't have the stamina to see it through. Still, they were a factor to be dealt with.

Brad carefully unscrewed the cap from the tyre valve and inserted a small piece of gravel before screwing the cap back on just enough to open the valve and let the air begin to leak out. The cap helped muffle the hissing sound. He moved round to the driver's side and did the same to the other back wheel, before crab walking back to the exhaust pipe. Not having any bananas at hand, he made do with a rolled up copy of the local rag that he'd purloined from a neighbour's letterbox. He jammed it in as far as it would go, and eased his way back into the shadows.

Knowing which neighbours had security lights and animals made it easy for Brad to dodge through properties and scale fences before dropping into the back yard of the house he rented with two others.

His flatmates had the upstairs rooms, which he was happy with since he was subject to callouts and it wasn't fair to disturb them at un-Godly hours when the pager went off. Reece was a personal trainer and was usually at his girlfriend's place-his WRX wasn't on the driveway, which was a good sign. Alexa was a different story, and he sometimes wondered how they were attracted to each other given their immense differences. She was an accounts clerk for a hardware chain, lived on movies and takeaways and rarely went out. Peeking through the window to the internal garage, he could see her pink Getz parked up, fluffy dice hanging from the rear view mirror.

The back door opened silently and Brad padded through the ground floor in the dark to his room. He shut the door behind him and turned on the bedside light. Nothing appeared to be disturbed, aside from a pile of freshly folded washing on his dresser-one of Alexa's habits. He grinned to himself when he saw she'd even folded his underwear.

He dragged a black kit bag from under his bed and began piling stuff into it-clothes, laptop, gym gear, a couple of books, Kindle, iPod, and a folder of personal documents. He grabbed the emergency fund of cash from under the bedside table and stuffed it in his pocket. He put the bag by the door and opened the wardrobe door again. Pushing the clothes to the side, he unlocked his gun cabinet.

Inside were some of his guns, the others being stored at the station in the squad room. Ever since arriving back in Wellington-he couldn't bring himself to refer to it as Welly, that was just *way* too pretentious-he'd had a niggling itch at the back of his mind. He felt unsafe and exposed. The feeling was only heightened by the surveillance on his house.

No better way to relieve that than by going armed for bear. He lifted his Lithgow L1A1 SLR from the safe and hefted it in his hands. It was an Army-surplus 7.62mm battle rifle with a 20-round magazine. Brad had four loaded mags in the top part of the safe, which he unlocked with another key. He put the rifle in a soft carry case with the magazines and put it with his bag.

The next item he removed was a Mossberg 500 pump action 12-gauge, complete with a sling and a bandolier of shells. He had not had his pistol license long, and the only pistol he owned was the original hand cannon wielded by Dirty Harry, "the most powerful handgun in the world." Seeing Clint Eastwood blowing away bad guys with it as a kid, Brad had always had his heart set on one. It was a blued Smith and Wesson Model 29 revolver with a six inch barrel and chambered in .44 Magnum.

Brad had won competitions with it at his pistol club and got a thrill from its raw power every time he used it.

He was about to grab the holster for it when the door squeaked behind him and Alexa appeared.

She squealed when she saw the massive pistol in his hand and put her hand to her mouth. 'Holy shitballs, what the bejesus is that frickin' thing?'

Brad quickly slid it into the tan leather Galco holster on the duty belt and put the weapon down on his bag. Alexa was half his size and dressed in short cotton pyjamas that did nothing to hide her pert breasts. Her sandy hair was tied in side pig tails and she wore black rimmed glasses.

He felt foolish standing there surrounded by weapons with a half-naked girl before him.

'Sorry, I didn't mean to disturb you.' He gestured weakly to his bag. 'Just came to get a few things.'

'I was awake anyway, 'she said. 'Reading. I got the latest Michael Connelly today.'

He knew she was an avid fan of crime fiction, because she often quizzed him about Police matters. He suspected she was secretly writing a book of her own, given some of the questions she'd asked.

'I heard, obviously,' she told him. The small hand she put on his thick arm was warm and her eyes were concerned. 'Are you okay? I mean, you know...it sounded pretty bad. I saw your picture.'

Brad shrugged, unsure what to say. Deep and meaningful's had never been his strongpoint. He realised he hadn't actually spoken to a friend for more than a couple of minutes since the job went down.

'I'm okay,' he said quietly, unable to meet her eyes. 'It is what it is.' He paused, then blurted, 'It just sucks.' He shook his head ruefully. 'Sorry, that sounded pathetic. What a twat.'

She made a sympathetic sound but said nothing. Brad felt his cheeks getting hot and he suddenly wanted to get out of there.

'Your colleagues have been around, a few of them. I think they were from your squad.' She wrinkled her nose when she smiled. 'They were fit looking guys, anyway. Just not as...big, as you.'

Brad nodded. That fit. They would have found it strange that he'd suddenly disappeared.

'Has anyone else been around?' he asked. 'Any reporters?' He hesitated for a moment. 'Or anyone else who might have been a bit nosey, or out of place?'

'Yeah, a couple of reporters came around. I just refused to open the door, told them to go away or I'd call the cops. They went away.'

'Cool, thanks. Sorry about the hassle.' He grinned half-heartedly. 'What a shit flatmate aye? Only been here a few months.'

She squeezed his arm. 'It's okay. As long as *you're* okay.'

He nodded and patted her hand with his big mitt.

'So I guess you're moving out then?' she said, looking up at him. She was close enough for him to feel the warmth of her body against his skin. She had a fresh-shower smell in her hair.

'For a while, anyway.' He didn't have an answer because he didn't know.

'Well, goodbye then, I suppose.' Alexa smiled coyly now and Brad felt a flutter in his guts.

*A flutter? What am I, sixteen?*

'I guess so.'

She leaned up on tip-toe and put her arms around his neck, pulling him into a hug. He hugged her back, feeling her breasts crushing against his broad chest. She pressed against him and tilted her head. Brad felt her lips on his cheek then her hands moving, turning his head and drawing his mouth to hers. She kissed him softly at first then harder, with more intensity, and he kissed her back.

Her tongue was warm and inquisitive and he responded, lifting her off her feet and cupping a hand under her butt to hold her up.

Alexa moaned in his ear, a more guttural, animalistic sound than he'd ever imagined the studious accounts clerk to be capable of, and she manoeuvred him towards the bed.

Brad decided there was no point in protesting. Some things just had to be done.

TITO FELT a bead of sweat trickling down his back as he waited by the door to the clubroom.

The door opened and Kruger's huge frame filled it. He glowered at the Mexican gangster and waved him in. The door shut behind him and Tito became acutely aware that he was only the third person in the room. Kruger towered behind him and Jonah Jones sat at a bar leaner.

Tito crossed to the President, staying silent and waiting. His body still ached from his last beating and he figured keeping his trap shut was wise.

Jonah eyed him coldly, and Tito felt his scalp prickling as beads of nervous sweat broke free and began to soak into his hair. One began an agonizingly slow trickle down his temple, tickling like a fly walking on his skin. He fought the urge to wipe it away.

'You know me and Kruger been at the cop shop all day,' Jonah began. 'Got fucken grilled by some fucken D's who thought they knew it all. They got nothin' concrete, but they know enough to look pretty hard at us. Got our lawyers down there and told them two things.' He cocked a half smile at Kruger over Tito's shoulder. 'Told 'em Little Ray broke away from us and was de-patched. It hurt like a motherfucker to disown a brother Bandit, but Little Ray would've understood. Told them any shit he was into was his own shit, nothin' to do with the club.'

Tito nodded eagerly and nearly spoke, but caught the President's look and held his tongue.

'Second thing we told'm was they could suck my big fat cock if they wanted anything else. We walked outta there a few hours later after they finished fucking us around, they ain't got shit on us. Oh,' he grinned properly now, 'aside from the big man there, who accidentally walked into one o' them and knocked him on his faggot arse.'

Kruger gave a low chuckle behind Tito.

'They weren't too happy with that but the lawyer was right there and said it was an accident, so they had to let us go.' Jonah's expression went serious again. 'The point of this conversation, Tito, is that for now we're in the clear. I got no doubt the pigs'll carry on tryin' to get to us, and it'll be a long game, but for now I reckon we're okay. Still got a thorn in our side though...a debt we gotta clear.'

Tito was trembling with anticipation, his eyes locked on Jonah's weathered face.

'That one pigshit killed three of our brothers. Even our buddy Johnny Reb'-as they had nicknamed Mitchell during his short stay with them-'couldn't drop the cunt. He's either one lucky mother-fucker, or very fucken good.'

He paused now, drumming his fingers on the table top in front of him.

'We know who he is. We know where he lives.' He sat up more erect, looking his minion straight in the eye. Tito didn't need to know, but Jonah had a direct line into a freelance journalist with a nasty meth habit. 'He needs to be taken down for what he done. This is your opportunity to prove yourself again, Tito. You fucked up the other day in here, and you lost a lot of respect from the brotherhood for it.'

Tito nodded apologetically, still silent.

'So the job is yours. It's a hit and you're pullin' the trigger.'

Tito nodded again, breaking into a grin. He was so excited he coulda pissed his pants.

**15**

———

Ingoe woke them at seven am.

Travis rolled off the couch when Susie parked herself at his feet with her cell phone in her hand. He'd crashed there under a blanket while she took the bedroom.

He rubbed his face and yawned before sitting again, glancing at Susie. Her long thick hair was tousled and she was wearing a white T shirt with a gaudy *Welcome to Bangkok* logo on the front. Below that she wore just light blue satin knickers, and her long legs were smooth and shapely. He could see her nipples protruding through the thin cotton T-shirt.

If she noticed him noticing, she didn't seem to care. He wondered momentarily what it would be like to make love to her. Travis shook his head at himself and tried to focus on the phone, from which Ingoe was talking on speaker. It wasn't easy to focus.

'So not much news on the death of Paul Watkins, unfortunately,' Ingoe was saying. 'Early days for the investigation into that, but the best we know so far from Major Dang is that a man was seen standing near him while he was waiting to cross the road. Nothing more.'

'Thai or foreigner?' Susie asked.

'Thai apparently. No ID on him or even anything to say he was involved. Easy enough to give someone a shove and not be seen, though.'

Travis and Susie glanced at each other, a silent agreement passing between them; too coincidental to be an accident.

'Now, the cops here have made some advances in their investigation, but only as far as dragging in some of the Southern Bandits bikies. They don't have enough evidence to charge anyone though- the gang leaders are saying that Little Ray was out of the gang and playing his own gig.'

'Pfff,' Susie snorted.

'Agreed,' Ingoe replied, 'but they have nothing else.'

'Any updates on The Pastor?' Susie asked.

'Not much, but we do have some intel on his crew now.' They heard a rustle of paper in the background as Ingoe checked his notes. 'He has two guys with him most of the time. One is a local Thai bloke called Prasong, nothing else known. Apparently he's some kind of criminal that Stephenson has taken aboard, even lives with him.'

'What, like together?' Travis asked.

Susie cocked an inquisitive eyebrow at him, amused.

'I don't care if he's gay, but it could be relevant,' he said defensively.

'That's not clear,' Ingoe said. 'Apparently he's a real bad bastard though. Used to be a cage fighter in the underground scene in Bangkok.'

Travis let out a low whistle. He knew a bit about that scene, none of it good.

'His other guy is a Rhodesian-not Zimbabwean-named Terence Yates. Fifty eight years old, ex-mercenary.'

Susie made a scoffing noise, which Ingoe obviously heard.

'He's no has-been,' he warned. 'He was a Selous Scout back in the day then spent another couple of decades or so in different war zones. Pretty much every agency in the world has had a look at him. This guy has seen it and done it. If he could read and write properly, he could write the book. Don't underestimate him because he's an old fart.'

Susie's brow was furrowed as she absorbed the info.

'Selous Scouts were a Special Forces unit,' Travis told her. 'Similar to the SAS. Real hard arses.'

'I'll flick you through the address details and whatever else we have for him.'

'We'll have a recce,' said Travis, 'once Brad gets here we'll regroup and suss out a more pro-active approach.'

'How're the local authorities dealing with last night's events?' Susie asked. 'We haven't seen any media yet.'

'Gangland stuff. The usual gang on gang shooting. Haven't got anything back from the prisoner they got yet.'

'Is Major Dang on that?' Travis asked.

'So he says.'

Travis grunted dubiously.

'I know what you're thinking, Jack,' Ingoe said. 'Let's hold on that for now. Last update for you is a possible player to be aware of. Ex-SEAL named Johnny Mitchell.'

Travis pricked up his ears. The US Navy's Sea, Air, Land specialists were right up there in the pecking order of Tier One outfits.

'Thirty five year old US citizen, served nine years in the Navy including four with the SEAL teams. We know he did tours in Iraq and the 'Stan, plus whatever else we don't know about. He's been on the circuit since then and has popped up in various zones, including Somalia.'

'Pretty standard tourist spot,' Susie remarked.

'What's his deal then?' Travis asked. 'SEALs don't tend to go rogue.'

'Good question. Apparently his marriage fell apart and he was short on cash. He sold some operational details to a journalist and got caught out. Got DD'd and out on his arse. Interestingly, Philip Stephenson has just returned from Somalia. Had two days in the Mog, travelling with his two buddies.'

'DD'd?' Susie asked.

'Dishonourable discharge. Kicked out.'

She nodded.

'When was this Mitchell guy last there?' Travis asked. 'And have they travelled together?'

'Don't know either. The Yanks aren't talking to us about Mitchell.'

'Any reason?'

'Not so much. They might do in time, but right now we've got nothing.'

'Helpful.'

Susie shook her head in frustration. Travis couldn't help but notice her breasts moving when she did so.

'So you reckon Mitchell may be linked to Stephenson, is that the theory?' Travis asked.

'It's a pretty good theory. Mitchell was here until yesterday, when he flew to Thailand. He was in NZ at the time of the robbery.'

'Interesting. You're thinking he was involved?' Even as he said it, Travis knew. 'The guy Brad shot it out with. He was the guy.'

'And he probably trained those gangsters,' Susie put in.

Travis nodded. 'Exactly.'

'The Southern Bandits had a big funeral for Little Ray, apparently bikies from all over turned up. Interestingly, two known members of the gang were absent and haven't been seen for a few days.'

'So Brad was right when he said two guys,' Susie said.

Travis nodded. Inwardly he was impressed, but he kept it to himself for now.

'That's all for now, team.' Ingoe yawned. 'I'm hitting the pit, and I'll be in touch as soon as I know anything else. I'll get Brad in the air first thing.'

'If he's coming over,' Travis said quickly, 'I'll get him to bring some things with him.'

'On him, or in the diplomatic pouch?' Ingoe enquired.

Travis twitched his head. 'Diplomatic pouch might be best.'

'Send me a list,' Ingoe told him.

They rang off and Susie tossed her phone onto the coffee table, folding her legs under her on the couch.

'Interesting,' she said, stifling a yawn and running a hand through her hair.

'Uh-huh.' Travis stood and headed to the kitchenette. He flicked the kettle on and came back.

Susie looked at him in his briefs. His torso was toned and muscular, marked here and there with scars. He saw her looking and quickly grabbed up his cargo pants.

'Good idea,' she grinned, 'put some pants on, would you?'

He gave her incredulous. 'Really?'

Susie unfolded her legs and stood. She sauntered towards the bathroom. He watched her go and he knew she knew. She was undeniably attractive.

'I'm going to take a shower,' she tossed over her shoulder before she shut the door.

'Lucky you,' he muttered, pulling on his pants. 'I need a cold one.'

**16**

———

Alexa allowed him to make a sideways shuffle from the flat, leaving her to lock up behind him. There had been no tears, just a long lingering kiss before she shut the car door and hit the button for the garage door.

The rumble of a 5.0 litre 308 cubic inch V8 filled the garage as Brad fired up his car. The navy blue 1973 Holden Statesman De Ville was his pride and joy.

He backed out of the garage, gave Alexa a final wave and rumbled up the street. He slowed as he past the sleeping journo, and gave him a blast on the horn. The man woke with a start and looked around. When he saw Brad grinning at him from a metre away he fumbled for the key, firing up the hybrid. Brad gunned it and peeled rubber as he roared away.

As he got to the corner he saw the hybrid U-turning behind him. The little car got around then ground to a halt. Brad gave a friendly toot on the horn and left him behind.

KISS blasted from the stereo as Brad hit the motorway and pointed the nose north. He sang along as he drove, more of a low growl than the high notes Paul Stanley could hit on *Crazy, Crazy Nights*, but he didn't care.

He left Johnsonville at 2am and filled up at a gas station, stocking up on a large black coffee, a pie and a couple of supposedly-healthy-but-laden-with-hidden-sugar muesli bars. With few other cars on the road he made good time, keeping a careful eye out for traffic cops as he sat in the fast lane with the stereo rocking and caffeine in his veins.

He passed through locked down towns and hit the Desert Road, surrounded by ruggedly beautiful bleak landscape hidden by the inky blackness. The Army camp was still as he rolled past and pulled into a service station. He stretched his legs, used the toilet out the back and bought more supplies-another large black coffee and a bag of peanut M&Ms. The station attendant behind the Night Pay window was wide awake and chatty, asking Brad how far he had to go and warning him of cops on the road ahead.

'Saw two carloads of 'em heading north just an hour ago,' he confided, tapping his nose conspiratorially. 'Unmarked cars, too.' He jabbed a dirty finger towards the Statesman on the forecourt. 'You might be able to outrun 'em in that beast, though. What's that, a 253?'

'308,' Brad replied, tucking his wallet back into his pocket. 'Thanks for the heads up, mate.'

He was glad for the warmth of the Holden after the chill outside.

*Why is Waiouru always colder than a witch's tit?* Brad wondered as he nosed back out to the road. A logging truck thundered past and he gunned it onto the highway, taking a hit from the coffee. Something about the station attendant's warning rang alarm bells with him, and the more he thought about it, the more it didn't make sense.

Two carloads of traffic cops in unmarked cars. Not just cops, but traffic cops. That meant they were probably in hi-viz vests and in uniform. Traffic cops didn't travel in carloads-pairs, yes, but not carloads. And where would two carloads of traffic cops be going in the early hours of the morning?

He berated himself for not asking more questions. Maybe he was just being paranoid; but maybe not.

Brad had long learned to trust his instincts, and right now his gut was telling him there was something wrong. He pulled the Statesman to the shoulder of the road, put the coffee down and popped the boot.

A minute later he was ready. The SLR was loaded with a full mag and one up the spout, resting nose-down in the passenger's foot well. The Smith and Wesson was holstered on his hip. The Mossberg was fully loaded and lying on the backseat. He got back into the car and changed his mind. He unholstered the Smith and put it on the passenger's seat. Not a soul had gone by while he had been stopped, and he felt completely alone out here in the barren wilderness.

As he eased off the shoulder again, Brad was satisfied with his preparations. And the further he drove, the more certain he became that it was necessary.

He was in the windy dips north of Waiouru, carefully manoeuvring around the hairpins, when he noticed a set of headlights behind him. No, not headlights, just sidelights, and a good hundred metres back. He hadn't seen any vehicles off the road, so either they had been well hidden or had flown up behind from miles back.

His alarm bells rang louder. He shook a handful of M&Ms out and crammed them into his mouth. He turned down the stereo-Whitesnake were blasting out *Here I Go Again*-and crunched the peanut candy, washing them down with the dregs of his coffee.

He came up out of the dips onto the flat and saw a checkpoint straight ahead. Cones in the middle of the road, an unmarked Holden Commodore sedan on each side of the road, both displaying red and blue flashing lights on their dashboards. He could make out a driver in each vehicle.

A uniformed cop stood in the road facing him, a torch with a red cone on it in his hand. More figures in hi-viz vests stood at the side the road.

Four things immediately struck Brad as being all wrong about the checkpoint; bad place for a checkpoint; too many cops; unmarked cars; and the flashing lights were on the dash, not affixed to the top of the windscreen or hidden behind the grill.

He slowed as he got closer, quickly counting up the figures. Eight all up, all in hi-viz vests. Five of them stood back behind the Commodore on the left, partially obscuring them from his view.

The cop in the road waved the torch at him, signalling him to come forward. Brad kept the Statesman rolling slowly forward, reaching across to the passenger seat and sliding the Smith into his lap. As he did, he noticed another thing; the hi-viz vest the cop wore had no Police decals on it.

He was twenty metres away from the cop now, and his alarm bells were deafening. He wound the window down and stuck his head out.

'What's the problem, officer?' he called out.

'Just move it forward, buddy.' The cop waved impatiently with the torch.

'What's your QID?' Brad hollered, referring to the unique six digit personal identifying number each cop had.

'My what?' The cop's face screwed up and he turned side-on, exposing a tat on his neck.

Every cop knew what a QID was, and they knew their own by heart.

Brad braked hard and slapped it into reverse, rocketing backwards quickly and hitting the high beams to blind the men in front of him.

The cop in the road shouted something and his mates poured onto the road. Shots rang out and a few even hit the body of the Statesman. The corner approached fast and as he reached it, the car coming up behind appeared from the blind spot. The rear of the Statesman crunched into the front left wing of the car, a red Ford Falcon wagon.

Brad gassed it and rammed the Falcon sideways across the road, causing it to slide backwards into the low ditch at the side of the road beneath a high bank. He whacked the gear stick into Drive again and motored forward but saw a line of men across the road only about forty metres ahead. They had ditched the hi-viz vests and were aiming weapons at him. Muzzles flashed and bullets impacted the car.

More firing sounded behind him and the rear windscreen shattered. He shoved the door open and hurled himself out, the Smith in his hand and M&Ms flying everywhere. He hit the tarmac and rolled, the Statesman continuing to roll forward and take fire.

He could see two guys coming from the Falcon, lit up by their one remaining headlight. One had a sub-machine gun in his grip and the other wielded a long of some sort.

The SMG opened up and ripped a long burst into the back of the Statesman, blowing the taillights and popping the boot open.

Brad let out a growl in his throat and took a double handed grip, sighting down the long barrel as he lay flat on the roadway. The two men were only about fifteen metres away now, and he saw the second guy see him. He shouted out a warning to the sub-gunner and started to bring his rifle around.

Brad was faster.

The Smith boomed, flame belched from the barrel and a huge .44 Magnum hollow point took the sub-gunner in the chest and blew him off his feet. He fell backwards and emptied his gun at the stars. The second man faltered and hesitated, standing still long enough to sign his own death warrant. Brad triggered a second shot that took him in the guts and dropped him to his knees. The third Magnum round literally tore his head from his shoulders, just like Clint had said it would.

Rounds started coming his way now and he pushed up, scrabbling back to the side of the road and the relative concealment offered by the scrub there. The night was lit up by muzzle flashes and rounds were flying all around. Brad scrambled further back, keeping low and moving to his right. Whoever these jokers were-and he had a fair idea-they weren't disciplined shooters and had no apparent game plan.

That was good, but in their favour was vastly superior numbers and automatic weapons. Unless something dramatic changed, Brad knew he would be overrun sooner rather than later.

With that in mind, he changed tack and moved back to his left, scrambling quickly through the scrub towards the top of the dip. It was treacherous underfoot and he was mindful that the gully would appear at any moment, potentially spelling his end if he wasn't careful. He got to a position as close to the two dead men as he could get, took a breath and broke from cover.

The gangsters were busy shouting at each other and loosing off wild shots into the darkness where he had been moments before, and he made it to the dead sub-gunner.

The SMG was an old Sterling 9mm with a side-mounted magazine, and the gangster had a spare mag tucked into his waistband. Brad found the mag release and dumped the empty, clipping the new one into place and chambering a round before someone spotted him.

Rounds started coming down and he sprinted forward, jamming the Smith into the holster and firing the Sterling from the hip, pumping short bursts at the figures ahead of him. He got behind the Statesman, which had rolled off the road and ended up half in a ditch, the motor still running.

Ricochets sparked off the body of the Statesman as he scrabbled round to the left, yanking the rear door open and grabbing the Mossberg. He slung it across his back and reached through to the front passenger's seat for the SLR. He knew the big battle rifle would up his chances of survival significantly. A long burst of automatic fire punched through the windscreen and seat in front of him and he felt pieces of glass and dashboard plastic tearing at him.

He ducked back and unleashed the Sterling with one hand, spraying the magazine empty through the blown-out windscreen where he could see the outline of a man rushing forward. The guy flopped sideways and Brad dropped the SMG, ducking back inside and grabbing for the stock of the SLR.

More rounds filled the interior of the Statesman, ripping the seats to shreds and exploding glass all around him.

Brad threw himself back into the ditch, hearing bullets snapping past him as he took cover. He scrambled back through the ditch and into the scrub beyond, unslinging the Mossberg and flicking the safety off. He got it into the shoulder as he hustled through the low scrub.

He heard a tyre explode behind him and more shouting. Coming up in a crouch, he scanned the road-the gangsters had helpfully left the headlights of their cars on, providing a decent back light. Five of the gangsters were right up by the Statesman now, raking fire into and around the car. Two others stood back near the two cars, and the other two were in the middle of the road, half way between the two groups.

As Brad watched his car get shot to shit, he felt the anger rising.

'Fuckers,' he muttered. He sighted on the closest of the gangsters, who had a sawn off shotgun in his hands. He squeezed the trigger and the Mossberg bucked. The man dropped instantly and the guy nearest him turned and stared with his mouth open. Brad pumped the slide and sent a blast of 00 buckshot at him. He saw him fall and moved left. Five metres later he stopped again and snapped two quick shots at the three guys still near the car before moving again.

Bullets whizzed overhead into the wild blue yonder. Brad took another position at the knee and sighted on the two guys in the middle of the road, who were now closest to him. One had an M3 "grease gun" in one hand and a cell phone in the other. The second had a pistol of some sort drawn, hanging at his side. They were watching their men at the car still cutting loose at the undergrowth.

The guy with the phone, who Brad assumed to be the leader, looked worried. Neither seemed to have any idea of his presence.

He tucked the stock into his cheek and fired a round, gut shooting the leader and sending the phone and M3 flying. The second man turned and ripped off a shot that went wide. Brad took him in the shoulder with a shot, knocking him down. The man writhed on the ground, clutching his shattered shoulder. He'd dropped his gun and Brad left him-wounded men caused the enemy more problems than dead ones.

The three guys near the Statesman started up the road towards him, firing wildly.

'Go go go!' one was shouting, firing a Mini 14 from the hip like he was Arnie.

Brad took a few seconds to reload the shotgun from the sleeve on the buttstock. The three were getting closer, the guy with the Ruger still shouting encouragement to his mates.

Brad picked on him next and triggered a shot just as the guy stumbled and nearly went down. The wedge of heavy buckshot skimmed just over his head and produced a shriek of terror. The guy pinned the trigger back and shot out his magazine into the ground, rounds pinging off at all angles. One ricochet took out the leg of one of the men in front of him and he went down, screaming.

One of his buddies stopped to help him up and together they ran at a fast hobble.

Brad let the group go past and scoop up the man who had been shot in the shoulder. He screamed as they lifted him. Brad heard the leader calling out weakly after them.

'Hey, ese...c'mon, ese...don' leave me man...'

The two guys from the cars came forward to meet them and one of the guys continued past, grabbing the leader under the arms and dragging him backwards like a rag doll until the guy with the Mini 14 came back to help.

Brad watched them go. They reached the cars and piled in, one of them pausing long enough to unleash a burst of fire back down towards the ambush site. Brad frowned and came up to his full height.

The man unleashed another long burst while his buddies got the cars ready.

Brad sighted on the guy, now forty metres away, and pumped off two shots. One took him in the legs and knocked him back into the car he stood beside. The second tore through his right elbow, almost severing the arm.

The man was screaming like a banshee as someone pulled him into the car and they peeled away, one of the cars throwing a U-turn to get round and chase the other vehicle.

Brad stayed standing and kept the Mossberg at the shoulder, rock steady. He sighted on the rear of the back car and began to squeeze off shots, steadily pumping rounds into the back of the car. He saw the taillights explode in red clouds and the rear windscreen shatter.

It was strictly beyond the effective range of a shotgun but he wanted to discourage them from returning. He sent the last round as the cars disappeared into the distance.

Brad lowered the Mossberg and automatically slipped his last couple of shells into the tubular magazine.

The silence of the desert was broken only by the strains of Knightshade coming from the stereo in the destroyed Statesman. He surveyed the scene below him, partially illuminated by the moon. Three gangsters lay dead on the road near it, weapons discarded nearby. Further back was the crashed Falcon wagon with two guys lying dead on the road. All of them wore some parts of Police uniform.

Brad made his way down onto the road. In front of him he could make out the shapes of a revolver and the M3, both lying near pools of blood. He'd have bet the house it was the same M3 used in the bullion robbery, and the same one sold by Malcolm Cook.

He spotted the cell phone dropped by the leader and checked it. The line was still open and he held it to his ear. Even over the partial deafness from the shooting he could hear someone breathing at the other end. He dug out his own phone and held it beside the recovered phone.

'So I guess you're the big cheese,' Brad said.

There was silence for a moment then a rough-edged voice sounded in his ear.

'Who is this?'

'I'm the guy you fucken pussies can't kill.'

The man gave a sharp intake of breath.

'That's right, mother fucker. Your Mexican mate's got his guts hangin' out and the rest of them ran away. The ones that could, anyway.'

'You made a bad mistake, arsehole,' the man breathed. 'You don't wanna fuck with us.'

'Wrong, cock sucker,' Brad growled. '*You* don't wanna fuck with *me*.'

'We'll meet again,' the man replied. 'This ain't over, pigshit.'

'Huh.' Brad snorted. 'I haven't seen you yet. Feel free to get your balls outta your panties and give it a crack.'

'Watch your back you cunt-you won't see me coming.'

'Huh.' Brad snorted again. 'Don't worry mate, you'll see me face to face when I slit your fucken throat.'

With that he disconnected the call and pocketed the recovered phone. He hit Stop on his own phone and ended the recording, then pocketed that phone too.

He checked both ways; still no traffic. He ran to the Statesman and grabbed his torch, then ducked back into the scrub and scouted round to recover as many of his spent shotgun shells and ejected wadding that he could find. He pocketed them and ran back to where he'd discarded the Sterling sub-machine gun. He used his T shirt to quickly wipe it free of prints, then did the same with the spent magazine he'd dropped.

He heard the rumble of a gear change in the distance and spotted a truck approaching a couple of klicks or so away from the south. It had to get through the hair pins to reach him, so he still had some time.

He took another half minute with his phone, snapping photos of the scene and the dead men, then ran back to the Statesman.

Broken glass jabbed him as he got behind the wheel and clicked the stereo off. The engine was still running and he shifted it into reverse with difficulty-something was grinding in the gearbox.

The car protested when he revved it to get it back on the road and rammed it into Drive again. Steam was blowing from the radiator and as he got moving it seemed like every warning light on the dash was lit up. With the headlights having been blown out he drove by moonlight, nursing the destroyed car north as quickly as he dared before he reached a rough turn off into the scrub. In his rear view mirror he could see the headlights of the truck arriving at the scene and slowing to a stop. Approaching in the distance was another truck, heading south.

In minutes the balloon would be going up and he needed to make himself scarce.

The Statesman limped along the rough path until it came to the dead end of a turn-around area where hunters and hikers parked up.

The Statesman ground to a halt, shuddered and died. Brad glanced to his left, where the SLR rested against the passenger's seat.

The stock was smashed by bullets and it looked like the receiver had taken a hit as well.

His classic car and his classic battle rifle, both fucked. What had started out so promisingly had really turned into a shit night.

Brad plucked his phone out. Time to make a call.

JED INGOE WAS USED to being woken at unusual hours for unusual matters, but the call from Brad Travis at 5am was a new one.

Ingoe had rolled out of bed, trying not to disturb his sleeping wife, and quickly attached his prosthetic leg. He made his way in the darkness to his study downstairs, hit the desk light and got to work. Within twenty minutes he had a team of operators from the Group racing south in a chopper from Papakura to pick Brad up from an RV in the wilderness. They would extract him back to Auckland and a couple of operators would remain with the Statesman, which would be recovered by a covered truck being organised from Waiouru. Ingoe then woke the Director and updated him.

The Director thanked him for the call and said he would take care of it.

Ingoe ended the call and put the phone down. The cops would be on it by now, unaware it was a national security matter-he could leave it to the Director to get a handle on it now.

He ran a hand through his short grey hair and reflected on Brad's sit-rep. Five dead gang members, probably three more badly wounded, two wrecked cars, automatic weapons, and shell casings and blood everywhere.

Ingoe wondered just how the fuck they were going to keep a lid on this one.

Paul Watkins' apartment was on the seventh floor, a small box in a tower of boxes.

The building manager had already had Watkins' uncle and a couple of embassy staff there wanting access, so was not surprised when Travis and Susie turned up.

'You no come last time,' he said, hesitating with a key in his hand.

'No,' Travis agreed. 'This is Paul's sister, we've just flown in.'

Susie gave a realistic enough mournful look and suppressed a sob into a tissue.

'We'd just like the opportunity to get some family heirlooms and things before the funeral,' Travis told him. 'Come on man, help us out here aye?'

The manager wasn't entirely convinced but he gave up the key anyway. They left him in the ground floor office and took a rickety lift to the seventh floor. The car was barely big enough for four people.

'Jesus,' Susie commented as the lift gave a deep groan and shudder. 'I'm guessing there are no safety standards here.'

The doors creaked open and they quickly alighted, both glad to be rid of the certain death trap. Watkins' apartment was to the left and across from the lift lobby, and they were inside in seconds, shutting the door behind them.

The apartment was a four room affair, with a separate bedroom and bathroom, a tiny kitchen and a living area.

'He clearly doesn't entertain much,' Susie observed, looking around. 'I'll take the bedroom, you do in here?'

Travis nodded and they set to work. The search took less than half an hour. They didn't expect to find anything untoward, since there was no reason to suspect Watkins himself of anything, but it always paid to be cautious.

They found that Watkins lived a minimalist lifestyle with one set of everything and everything fastidiously clean and in the right place

'Hardly the crazy backpacker on his OE, is he?' Travis called out from the living area. 'All I've found is copies of Lonely Planet books and some aerogrammes from his Nana.'

'I've got his laptop,' Susie replied. 'No password, fortunately. Apparently he's a bit of a gamer and likes European porn.' She came out of the bedroom and set the laptop by the door to take with them. 'Oh, and a little stash of weed wrapped up in a sock.'

'That's a bit more backpacker-like,' Travis grinned.

'Not really a backpacker though, was he? If he was, he wouldn't be tapped as a courier.'

Travis replaced the cushions on the two-seater sofa, and shrugged. 'I've got nothing,' he said. 'I wonder what the embassy staff and his uncle took.'

'I didn't see anything obviously missing,' Susie noted. 'I'll check with the embassy after this.' She shrugged. 'There may not have been anything to take.'

'Let's go.'

They stepped out into the hall and Travis locked the door behind them. As he turned to speak, he saw a flicker of movement down the hall near the entrance to the stairs.

'Down!' he shouted instinctively, grabbing Susie's arm and hunching down. A shot rang out, whistling over their heads.

Travis ripped the Sig from the hip holster and snapped a double tap in return, unable to see the enemy due to the light in his eyes from the large window at that end of the hall.

He scuttled across the hall, keeping low and his pistol raised. A head popped out from the stairs and he fired again, knowing he'd missed but wanting to at least keep the attacker at bay.

Susie was tucked in behind him, her pistol drawn and her back against his as she covered the other end of the hall.

A door opened and a head popped out. It was a middle aged woman who disappeared as soon as she saw the white woman's gun aimed at her.

'Hit the button!' Travis hissed. 'It's the only way down.'

He saw a hand appear at floor level with a pistol in it, and three shots sounded, blowing holes in the skirting board near his feet. He sent a shot back and the hand disappeared from view again. He briefly considered a frontal assault down the hall, but knew that he would be horribly exposed. The better call was a tactical withdrawal, and he was horribly mindful of how many walls a .357 SIG round could travel through.

Two more shots sounded and he felt the rush of wind as the bullets passed overhead, smashing a large pot at the end of the hall.

The lift arrived with a thunderous groan and the doors dinged open. The unseen shooter fired again as Susie dived into the lift and Travis scrambled after her. He paused in the doorway and saw the shooter start to come into view.

The shooter was a wiry Thai but Travis couldn't make out any other features. The shooter's pistol belched flame again as he started to duck back but Travis obstinately held his ground, sighting down the stubby barrel. He triggered a single shot and ducked back into the lift, where Susie was desperately jabbing the Door Close button.

Travis automatically swapped his spare mag into the Sig and slid the partially-spent mag into his pocket. He looked at Susie, who was still clutching her own Sig and the laptop.

'What the fuck was that about?' he wondered aloud.

PRASONG IGNORED the pain in his left arm and instead hit the talk button on his walkie talkie.

'Go,' he said, and shoved the radio back in his pants pocket. He switched the magazine on his Glock 17 for a full one, and checked his arm. The enemy had creased it with his last round, leaving an ugly gouge that was leaking blood, but he knew he wouldn't die; he'd had worse and survived.

He started to descend the stairs.

IN THE BASEMENT of the building, Terry Yates stepped back from the elevator control box and took cover in an alcove.

His training with the Selous Scouts had included demolitions, and Terry was something of an expert with explosives. He activated the circuit and heard the detonation in the control panel from the small explosive charge he'd placed there.

Smoke puffed out and he quickly recovered what remained of his gear, before heading for the exit.

Above him he imagined he could hear the elevator plunging down the shaft towards the ground seven floors below.

IN THE TINY box high up the shaft the two Kiwis heard a far-off crack echo towards them and felt the elevator lurch beneath their feet.

'Fuck!'

Travis reached for Susie and the elevator dropped like a stone, throwing them both off-balance. Susie screamed and he heard an animal-like snarl erupt from his own mouth as he hit the wall and bounced off.

Something in the back of his head prodded him in that first second and he instinctively threw himself across the small space into the opposite wall and back again. Some long ago lesson told him that elevators could be thrown off balance and jammed, if the safety brakes didn't activate.

From what he'd seen of this elevator so far, he wasn't counting on any safety features working.

A terrible metallic screeching and tearing sound could be heard from outside the elevator and Travis threw himself across the space again, staggering with his footing as the tiny car plunged away-he felt almost weightless with the ground dropping from underneath him.

He slammed the wall with his shoulder and felt the elevator sway. Susie quickly cottoned on and joined him, holstering her gun and dropping the laptop as she crashed into the wall beside him then pushed off again.

Together they hit the opposite wall and the elevator gave a definite sideways lurch, groaning and screeching in protest.

'Again!'

They threw themselves across the small space and slammed into the opposite wall, feeling a sickening lurch as the car was thrown at the wrong angle and jammed against the wall, tilting at a slope that made them both grab for the handrail.

'Jesus Christ!' Susie panted, her eyes wide with fear.

Travis sucked in a breath and looked to the ceiling, already working on an escape plan.

He reached up.

STANDING at the basement exit with his walkie talkie in his hand, Terry frowned. The elevator should have hit the ground by now, killing both the agents on board. He dug a cheap cell phone from his jeans pocket and checked for a signal. It was strong.

Terry thanked his lucky stars he'd taken a back-up precaution, and dialled a number from memory.

He hit Send.

JUST AS TRAVIS' fingertips brushed the ceiling a trio of small explosions sounded simultaneously beneath the car and the floor blew apart.

Travis dropped like a stone through the large ragged hole that appeared in the centre of the floor as smoke and dust gusted into the elevator. Watkins' laptop sailed past him into the darkness below.

His heart leaped into his mouth and he grabbed desperately for a hand hold, anything to save himself from falling to his death.

Susie saw a blur of movement as he dropped and instinctively snatched at him, seizing his left arm near the elbow with her right, halting his progress but jerking her forwards towards the gaping hole. Her feet were precariously balanced ion the very edge against the wall and she was holding onto the handrail with her left hand. Her grip slid and she saw him drop until she caught his wrist and felt his fingers close around her own wrist, painfully tight.

She shrieked and gripped harder, his eyes bugging as he stared up at her, dangling in space below the elevator, completely helpless.

Travis scrabbled with his feet for a purchase but they kept slipping. He kept his eyes locked on Susie, whose face was screwed up with the effort of holding him. He grabbed for the edge of the hole in the floor with his right hand, managing to get a grip with his fingertips. He saw Susie's feet slipping towards the hole as she strained under his weight. Her skin was slick with sweat and her fingernails dug into his wrist.

'Hold on,' he panted, edging his right hand around for a greater purchase. He found a small patch of floor hard against the wall that was still intact and didn't move when he pulled on it.

He managed to get his elbow onto it and heaved, trying to haul himself up. He felt Susie being dragged down as he did so and he tried to release her wrist but she held on in a death grip.

'Let go,' he rasped, and saw the horrified look on her face. 'Do it!'

She refused, not realising what he meant.

'I'm not letting go!' she hissed through clenched teeth, hauling at his arm.

He felt himself swing like a pendulum below the elevator, which was still groaning and creaking loudly. His left boot hit the wall and he felt a hint of purchase beneath his toe. He pushed off, jerked free of Susie's grip and lunged upwards with his left arm outstretched.

His fingertips snagged the handrail and he clung on for dear life. Levering with his right elbow and with Susie pulling at his left, he managed to work his way back into the car, getting a knee then a boot onto the tiny floor space where his elbow had been moments before.

Leaning back against the wall with sweat streaming down their faces, they stared at each other, breathing hard.

'Hold on?' Susie panted. 'Really?'

'All I could think of.' He looked to the service hatch in the ceiling again. 'Gotta go up. This thing'll probably fall.'

He carefully climbed up onto the handrail and braced a hand against the ceiling while he pushed it at the hatch. It was stuck fast and he slammed it with the heel of his hand, finding where it was secured. He'd done plenty of training in elevator shafts over the years on counter-terrorism duties and knew that, far from what was portrayed in movies, service hatches were usually fastened from the top. At least this one felt like it wasn't top-quality hardened steel.

'Gunna have to shoot it open,' he told Susie, drawing his Sig.

'Won't it ricochet?' she balked.

'Yep, and that might kill one of us. But if we don't get outta here this thing will drop and we'll both be dead anyway.' He shrugged philosophically. 'Better to die tryin'.'

'Cheerful bastard.' Susie carefully moved to the corner away from his angle of fire.

'Here we go.' He turned his face away and fired a shot into the edge of the hatch. The sound was deafening in the enclosed space. The round ricocheted off the ceiling and wall and down into the blackness. They each checked themselves but were unharmed. Travis slammed the hatch again and it moved further, so he gave it another round.

He holstered the Sig and hit the hatch again, finally popping it open with the third impact.

'Climb up,' he told Susie.

What?' she shouted, deafened by the gunshots.

He jabbed his finger at her feet then the handrail and she nodded. He caught her hand and helped her up. Her face was white and he could tell she was way outside her comfort zone. He wasn't exactly ecstatic himself.

She got up on the rail and looked dubiously at the small hatch in the ceiling.

'Built for Thais,' she commented.

'You'll be alright, fatty,' Travis said, giving her a grin. 'Get your hands in and pull yourself up; I'll push you up.'

Susie got both hands onto the edges of the hatch, took a deep breath and pulled upwards as she pushed off from the handrail. The elevator shuddered with the movement and shifted slightly with a metallic screech. Her legs kicked wildly and Travis copped one in the chest as he grabbed for her. He seized her right foot and heaved, but she kicked free. He planted a hand on her butt instead and shoved hard.

Her legs and then feet disappeared from sight and he could hear her above him. The elevator lurched alarmingly and he heard something metallic snap.

'Hurry up!' Susie urged him, and he edged closer to the hatch before getting his hands up onto the rim.

The elevator made a loud cracking sound and shifted again, dropping an inch or so. Travis pushed off and heaved up, scrabbling for purchase. He got his hands flat and levered up, scraping his side on the edge of the hatch as he wriggled through the small gap. Susie got her hands under his arms and hauled at him, and in seconds he was sitting beside her on the filthy dirty roof of the ancient elevator car.

Dim light came from lights at intervals up the shaft above them. None of the doors appeared to be open up there.

'Follow me,' Travis rasped, his throat dry with the exertion and dust.

He found the rungs on the wall that were used by service technicians, and started to climb. Susie followed him and they climbed to the floor above. Travis got a foot onto the lip of the doorway and reached across, working his fingers into the gap between the doors. He could hear movement on the other side and prayed it wasn't the bad guys. If they opened the door, he and Susie would be trapped like rats in a barrel.

He pounded his fist on the metal of the doors.

'Help! Open the door! Help!'

He continued to haul at the door, feeling them budge open slightly. He hauled again, straining every fibre in his body and praying to gods he hadn't recognised for a lifetime.

The doors gradually started to open and a crack of light appeared. He could hear voices speaking excitedly in Thai on the other side.

'Feel free to help,' he grumbled.

Suddenly the end of a metal bar appeared in the gap and he could feel someone levering the doors from the lobby. He continued to pull and together he and the unseen person worked the doors open far enough for a head to poke through and peer at them.

'Okay, mister?' an older Thai man enquired.

'Yeah, brilliant,' Travis replied, pulling the door open properly. He pulled himself up and stepped into the doorway, quickly scanning for enemy as he got free of the shaft. The sign by the lift said they were on the third floor.

Susie appeared beside him, grabbing his shoulder for support as her feet found terra firma. Her face was smudged with dust and grease and her clothes were filthy. He guessed he didn't look any better.

The older man with the pry bar looked them up and down and shook his head. 'Crazy tourists,' he said.

Susie peered back into the shaft and saw the elevator car still jammed there. She looked back at Travis.

'Pessimist,' she said. 'It hasn't moved.'

He was about to reply when there was a wrenching tear of metal followed by a groan and a creak, then the elevator fell down the shaft.

They jumped back as the crash echoed up the shaft and a cloud of dust blasted up and billowed out into the hall.

Travis clapped the older man on the shoulder. 'Thanks mate.'

He grabbed Susie's hand and they hit the stairs. The building manager was in the lobby shouting into a cell phone and waving his hands excitedly when they got to the ground floor, and Travis tossed him the key to Watkins' apartment.

He jerked a thumb at the elevator doors as they headed for the exit.

'You might want to get that serviced,' he said. 'It seems to be playing up.'

**18**

———

Brad had spent nearly three hours being debriefed by the Director and Ingoe. They fed him and had him physically checked out by a Service doctor, who found no injuries aside from some minor scratches and bruising from shrapnel, plus some decent bruising to his right shoulder from diving out of the car.

'Your car's a write off,' Ingoe told him at the conclusion of the debrief. 'It's stashed at Waiouru, but you won't be driving it again.'

'Great,' Brad grunted. 'This op is costing me a goddamn fortune. Better go car shopping.'

'No time for that,' the Director said, 'you're off to Thailand.'

Brad eyed him carefully as the older man topped up his cup from a tea pot.

'What, Uncle Jack got himself in the crap?'

The Director poured his tea. Ingoe's face was impassive.

'They could do with a hand over there. Sounds like they're storing up a hornets' nest.' The Ops Officer checked his watch. 'You're wheels up in about four hours.'

'Luggage?'

'Trixie will sort you out.'

'Vehicle?'

Ingoe tossed him a set of keys. 'Jack's truck's downstairs. Leave it in the long term park'

Brad nodded.

Ingoe glanced at the Director. 'I've gotta go, sir. I have somebody arriving about now.'

The Director dismissed him with a nod. Once the door had closed, the Director fixed his gaze on Brad. 'So,' he said. 'You've killed between six and ten men in the last few days.'

Brad stayed silent.

'You okay with that?' The Director's shrewd eyes gave nothing away.

Brad considered his response carefully. He had the feeling it carried weight with the Director. 'It's been a busy week,' he finally rasped.

The Director said nothing. Brad waited. He'd had enough debriefs by shrinks to know they wanted you to fill the silence. He didn't.

The Director finally nodded slowly and took a sip of his tea. 'Good luck in Thailand,' he said.

Brad took that as his cue and left. The Director's PA, Trixie, handed him a bulky envelope on the way out to the lift. On the way down to the basement he checked the contents-plane ticket, new passport for Bryan Taylor bearing his photo, a new platinum card in the same name with a post-it note attached showing the PIN, a new smart phone and five grand's worth of baht.

He was already sterile, so filled his pockets with the gear and headed across the basement garage to Travis' double-cab Colorado. As he headed for the exit he saw a young techo parking a late model fire engine red Monaro in a service bay. Ingoe was standing by the lifts with another man.

The second man made eye contact with him, and Brad felt a jolt of recognition. Captain Craig Archer of the Group, who he had met on a training exercise some time ago when he was still on the Auckland team.

Brad gave him a nod of recognition and rolled on past. He presumed Archer was now part of the Division.

He smiled to himself and rolled out to Queen St, heading for the motorway. He gave himself three hours to do what he needed to do and get to the airport.

His first stop was the Sylvia Park shopping centre. He needed to get himself kitted out with sufficient clothes and gear for the trip, given it was now unwise to return to his flat. Twenty minutes at an outdoors store gave him most of what he wanted. Another ten minutes at a menswear store completed his shopping, and he was back on the road, heading south.

Reaching Jack's home, Brad let himself in and checked the details on the text Ingoe had sent him. He found Travis' safe keys, and went out to the garage. The external back wall was two metres from the interior wall, and he found the door handle that was concealed alongside a shelving unit. Unlocking it, Brad discovered the shelving unit itself swung out completely and was actually the door.

He found a light switch and stepped inside the long narrow cavern. The wall to his left bore rifles and shotguns on individual horizontal racks. The last metre or so of the wall carried pistols on individual mounts. A two-tier shelving unit at the bottom carried storage bins with holsters, magazine pouches, and slings. He saw a bin of different scopes, and a bunch of various cases.

The wall to his right had racks of different camping gear, including boots, packs, clothing and sleeping gear.

'Fuck me, Jack,' Brad breathed. 'Preparing for Armageddon?'

He moved to the far wall and unlocked a large safe there. It was stacked with boxes of ammunition in different calibres and weights.

Brad let out a whistle. He felt like a kid in a candy store.

He checked his list and got to it.

THE SERVICE on the Thai Airways flight was to the usual high standard, and Brad demolished every piece of food put in front of him.

The flight attendants in the Business Class section were all of indecipherable age and beautiful and could have been sisters. Brad's seat companions, however, were standard Kiwi tourists and unintentionally did their best to ruin his flight.

He got the window and offered to swap with the wife for the aisle seat, to give himself more leg room. The guy politely declined on behalf of his dolly-bird wife, who was too busy flicking through the latest Cosmopolitan to reply. Brad could see the headline of the article from where he sat-something about how getting your bloke to open up about his feelings would lead to more explosive orgasms. He groaned inwardly.

'She gets up a lot for tinkles,' the guy explained, and his wife elbowed him sharply. 'Well you do.'

'It's not my fault I have to,' she snapped, 'and he doesn't need to know anyway. Just shut up.'

The guy gave Brad an exasperated "Whaddaya do" look and popped his ear buds in. He had the build of a prop and a buzz cut, and some kind of a tribal tat curling down his arm from under the sleeve.

Brad could hear some kind of hip-hop blasting from the guy's iPod and curled his lip with disgust. He glanced down at the pocket on the seat back in front of the guy. The hardback book tucked in there was the latest from a former British SAS guy who had a string of books ghost-written under his name and had appeared on TV. The guy had paid full price for it from an airport bookshop.

Brad's lip curled further and he shook his head in disgust as he turned back to the entertainment guide, looking for a movie.

The guy caught his look and nudged him as he took his buds out again. 'Something the matter, fella?' He looked down at the hardback. 'You don't like my book?'

Brad shrugged, non-committal because he didn't care enough to argue the point with the guy. 'If you wanna read it mate, fill your boots.'

Brad turned away again and the guy snorted dismissively, not wanting to let it go. He gave his wife a mocking grin and jerked his thumb in Brad's direction.

'Like he's ever had the balls to put his arse on the line for his country, aye?'

The wife gave a simpering smile that nearly cracked her thick foundation. Brad kept his mouth shut. The guy turned back and gave him a look of derision.

'Until you've served, fella, you don't get an opinion.' He glanced down pointedly at his tat. 'Know what I mean?'

'Big difference between service tats that mean something, *fella*, and tough stamps that don't mean shit,' Brad rasped, starting to lose his patience.

The guy opened his mouth to retort but caught himself. Brad was leaning slightly towards him now, in his body space, his eyes fixed intently on the guy's face. His arm was planted firmly on the armrest between them, the bicep straining against the sleeve of the T-shirt.

It became suddenly apparent to the guy that not only was his fellow passenger huge but he was also one very scary dude. He turned back to his wife and patted her hand reassuringly.

'Not worth worrying about, babes,' he said weakly.

Brad could see the disdain in her eyes as she looked at her husband. He shook his head again and sat back. The couple immediately started whispering heatedly to each other, the gist of which seemed to be her berating him for being a fucking pussy and him pleading with her.

Brad put his earphones on and found a movie, a decent Liam Neeson thriller. He liked Liam Neeson; he had a very particular set of skills.

As he watched Neeson smash and bash his way through bad guys, Brad thought about the couple beside him, and the passengers all around him, and reflected on himself. They were nothing like them; he was nothing like them. He felt like an island in an ocean of dreariness. They were like mice on a wheel, stuck in an endless cycle of mundane daily life, paying bills, doing chores and just fighting to stay awake.

If he was honest with himself Brad had to admit that, the trauma of colleagues being killed and wounded aside, the action of the last few days had been a rush. STG guys trained hard for such situations, and he was proud that he had survived two intense firefights against superior numbers and had acquitted himself well.

Most guys went a whole career without ever having a single contact or pulling the trigger. He knew only a handful of guys who'd killed in the line of duty, and rarely was it more than one bad guy who went down. He knew that he was therefore unique, for the Wellington bullion robbery alone, let alone the second incident on the highway.

He looked around at his fellow passengers again. No, he decided, he was definitely not one of them.

He settled back in his seat and closed his eyes, getting rest while he could.

## 19

Another change of hotels had seemed an obvious safety measure, and Travis and Susie had made every effort to throw off any watchers.

They took a tour bus around the city and ditched the tour partway through, criss-crossing the city on a succession of cabs and tuk-tuks before they were satisfied they were clear. They changed their outfits twice with purchases from cheap stores and vendors, ditching their old clothes as they went. Finally they hit a mall and topped up their bags with more clothes, plus some emergency food supplies in case they ended up on the run-after the events of the last couple of days, anything seemed possible.

They finally booked into another large hotel where they could melt into the background, taking a suite on the eleventh floor and getting their bags taken up by a porter. Shutting the door behind him, Travis leaned against the frame and rubbed his face. He had to admit, it had been a hell of a day.

He looked across at Susie, who was calling down for room service. He smirked as he listened to her order, which consisted of coffee and a double order of pasta.

'Sick of Thai food already?' he asked, securing the door and drawing his weapon.

'I'm starving,' she said with a grin that was too strained not to be forced. 'And yeah, maybe I need a taste of home.' She sniffed suspiciously at herself. 'And a shower.'

Travis unclipped the holster from his belt and checked the spare magazine, now reloaded. He didn't have a cleaning kit, so simply field stripped the gun instead and unloaded both magazines to check the ammo. Susie watched him refill both magazines while he sat at the table.

The food arrived and they wolfed it down, eating in silence, each lost in their own thoughts.

Susie piled the dishes back onto the tray and put it on the bench. She wiped her hands on the thighs of her pants and headed for the bathroom.

'You want first shower?' she called out.

'You saying I stink?'

She poked her head out the door and grinned cheekily. 'Sure am. Sort yourself out, would you?'

She was only gone a few minutes when he heard the bathroom door open and the sound of running water.

'Can you have a look at this, Jack? I think it needs some attention.'

He pushed up from the couch and turned to see her standing in the bathroom doorway. The fluffy hotel towel barely reached from her breasts to her thighs. She was looking at him innocently, running a hand through her tousled, wavy hair.

He tried to ignore his thoughts and squeezed past her into the bathroom. She didn't move aside.

Travis looked at the shower, which was flowing freely. He checked the temperature, which was fine. Shaking the water from his hand, he started to turn.

'So what's...wow.' His jaw dropped when he turned round.

Susie was leaning against the vanity with one foot up on the edge of the bath, her knee bent and the long leg that came with it almost fully exposed.

'There's nothing wrong with the shower,' Travis heard himself say from a long way off.

'I know,' she replied softly, 'I didn't mean the shower.' She dipped her head and glanced away then quickly back at him again. Her breasts pouted under the towel as she took a deep breath. 'I meant me.'

'Wow,' he said again, forcing himself to take a step back. 'I don't know if this is such a good idea...' He caught her look. 'I mean it's a great idea, but maybe not great timing...'

Susie's chin jutted defiantly. 'In case you don't recall, Jack, we almost died today. I don't know about you super-ninja-commando guys, but spooks like me don't have I-almost-died-today days very often, so you'll have to forgive me if I kinda take it to heart.'

'It has been a few months,' he conceded, and she frowned at him.

'Are you making fun of me, Jack?'

Travis looked at her in her fluffy white towel, her skin smooth and tanned, her wavy dark hair framing her beautiful face and falling to her shoulders, her full lips moist and inviting.

He shook his head fervently. 'No ma'am, I am not making fun of you, believe me.'

'I'm attracted to you, Jack. I don't have much luck with men and relationships, and at the rate we're going I may not see another sunset, so why waste time?'

She gave him that cheeky grin. 'Sometimes you've gotta give it the Nike approach.'

Travis shook his head in amazement and turned to go, a jumble of thoughts running through his head. He took a step towards the door then hesitated.

'Fuck it,' he muttered, and turned back.

'Just do it,' she corrected.

'Whatever.'

She stepped into his arms and their lips locked, tongues searching urgently and hands groping at each other with desperation. In seconds his shirt was off and his jeans were hitting the floor.

Any thoughts of showers were discarded as quickly as their inhibitions.

TERRY YATES DIDN'T GET worried too often, but he was seriously concerned right now.

Standing on Stephenson's deck and watching the younger Kiwi pacing relentlessly, Terry couldn't help but start looking past the here and now. He'd just broken the news to his boss that two of the boys they used in the Mog had been killed. Shot in the back and dumped in a ditch, apparently by the other two boys. The weapons were gone again and Ashkir was having a Warp Factor Ten shit-fit. Added to that the failed hit on the Kiwi spooks in the apartment block, which should have been a sure-fire hit, had gone badly with Chambers. He had already had a piece of Stephenson about that, giving him the message that failures like that had a significant bearing on his suitability for future jobs.

However you looked at it, the picture was not a pretty one.

Watching Stephenson now, pale faced and sweating, chewing his nails and staring at the ground as if hoping for a divine intervention, Terry wasn't counting on him for an answer to the problem.

He glanced to his right, where Prasong stood impassively. The Thai's face gave nothing away. Unlike his boss, he could've been a world class poker player.

'Fuck!' Stephenson said for the hundredth time.

'Whatever we do, Phil,' Terry said, 'it better be bloody quick, huh?' His eyes flicked to Prasong for support. 'That bastard Ashkir is sure to keep his word, you know?'

'I fucking know that!' Stephenson exploded, glaring at him. 'I fucking know that, Terry!' He shook his head and chewed his thumb nail as he started pacing again. 'Fuck...'

Prasong glanced between the two men, his eyes flat. His English wasn't good enough to follow each word, but he got the gist of the conversation. He didn't like that Somalian man Ashkir; he was a very bad man.

He glanced back to Stephenson. He could tell the boss was on the verge of cracking. Prasong said nothing. He completely trusted his boss and would wait for him to tell him the next step. Terry, on the other hand, he wasn't so sure about. His mate looked like he was ready to run for the hills.

Prasong sighed inwardly at the thought. If that happened, he had no doubt that Stephenson would instruct him to kill the Rhodesian mercenary. That wasn't an ideal situation, but that didn't matter. Stephenson was the boss, and Prasong would do what he asked.

Keeping his hands in his pockets, Prasong ran his thumb over the Bali-Song knife there. It was scalpel-sharp and well used.

He eyed Terry's whiskery throat.

PARKED in a battered van just a hundred yards from Stephenson's villa, Johnny Mitchell listened intently to the directional microphone in his lap.

It was trained on the villa and was strong enough to pick up the conversation even through the walls. He cracked the tiniest of smiles as he listened.

There was no doubt that things were going to rat-shit for these guys, and that worked well for Chambers and, by association, him.

Although Stephenson had a finger in many pies with his wheeling and dealing, Chambers was a man of great influence in these parts. Stephenson could parade around like a peacock all he liked, thinking he was a fixer and throwing about his stupid nickname like some kind of hallmark, but Chambers was the real deal. It amused Mitchell to imagine how shocked Stephenson would be to find out that behind most of the deals he thought he had arranged, lurked the shadow of Chambers. If Stephenson, The Pastor, fancied himself as some kind of artist then the camp Englishman was an ever present but rarely seen Svengali.

He even had tame cops on the payroll, which was why it was so easy for him to find out about the two New Zealand agents arriving in Bangkok.

It hadn't been so easy to get some decent heavies, however, and Chambers had been severely pissed when the hit on them had failed. Obviously they weren't normal spooks; maybe whatever the Down Under version of the CIA's Activity was. Whoever they were, they were a problem that needed to be dealt with. Stephenson had jumped at the chance to get some payback at his former employers, but clearly his boys weren't up to the task.

Mitchell considered the two thugs for a moment. He had the utmost respect for fellow former operators, but he was confident he could deal with the old Rhodesian dude okay. The silent Thai dude was a different story. Something about that little freak gave Mitchell the shits. He knew plenty of ruthless killers-hell, he counted himself as one-but little Prasong was something else altogether. If he had the chance he'd put a bullet in the back of his head and be done with it.

Mitchell fired up the van and listened to its crappy engine rattle. It was time to get moving.

Chambers would want a sit-rep sharpish.

SUSIE LAY on her side and traced a lazy finger down Travis' chest, tickling the hair there and making a slow track to his midriff.

The air-con was cool in the bedroom and the sheets were rumpled. Her finger reached the pink-white scars on his hard stomach, partially concealed by hair. They were like hard ridges and valleys to her touch. She noticed he had suddenly tensed under her attention, and she looked up at him, realising he was awake.

His hand came down from behind his head and gently but firmly moved her hand back up to his chest. He patted her hand and held it there.

'Sorry,' Susie said softly, 'I didn't mean to...sorry.'

'It's okay.' His eyes were dark and unfathomable.

Susie opened her mouth to speak again, but paused and bit her lip. No matter how curious she was, he obviously didn't want to talk about how the scars came to be, so she decided to leave it. For now, at least. She changed tack instead.

'So, good idea or bad idea?' She propped herself up on her elbow and half lay on him.

'What, this?' He waggled a finger between their naked bodies.

'No, landing on the moon. Of course this.'

He shrugged non-committedly. 'Seemed like a good idea at the time...'

She raised an inquisitive eyebrow. 'And now?'

'Well.' He grinned. 'If you're going to go out, you may as well go out with a bang.'

She laughed and he shifted his leg, rolling her on top of him.

'You sure?' Susie asked as she felt his arousal. She shifted her hips and moved against him. 'You're kind of old, I'm not sure how strong your heart is...'

He cupped her breasts with both hands and gently teased the nipples. A low moan sounded in her throat. She arched her back and eased her hips down.

'Let's just see what happens,' Travis told her with a grin. 'I'm prepared to put my life on the line.'

'Gee,' Susie breathed, rocking slowly, her hands firmly on his chest. 'What a guy...'

**20**

_____

Jonah Jones had a contact in the cops, a call-taker in the Comms centre who had family connections to the Southern Bandits.

His contact had been a great help over the years, and as far as he knew, had never fallen under suspicion. She had access to the national intelligence system and had used it to give him many tips and bits of intel. The intel had both helped him avoid capture and to gain leverage over people of use to him.

Accordingly, when his cell phone rang at 3 a.m. and her name appeared, he took the call. The conversation was brief.

Jonah hung up the call and flopped his head back onto the pillow. His contact was on night shift at Comms and had got wind of a planned operation by the Special Tactics Group in conjunction with the Wellington CIB who were investigating the bullion robbery.

At 5 a.m., the Southern Bandits pad was to be hit and Jonah and Kruger would be arrested. They would be appearing in court charged with the robbery and the murders of three cops.

Jonah rolled out of bed and punched up another number on his phone. There was a delay then the connection was made. He felt a surge of relief when the Englishman answered.

'We need out,' he said shortly. 'Immediately.'

'How many?'

Jonah didn't even blink. 'Just two,' he said.

There was a pause as the Englishman took that in. 'No problem. Same place, you'll see us when we get there.' There was another pause. 'You will owe me, of course.'

'Of course.' Jonah had known that was coming, but it was unavoidable. 'Thanks.'

'Travel safe.' The Englishman gave a chuckle and hung up.

Jonah stood in the darkness of his room and pulled on his jeans. He headed down the hall to Kruger's room and softly tapped. Two of the other rooms were occupied by club members, but he had no intention of disturbing them.

The door cracked open and the gigantic Sergeant-at-Arms stood there in his undies, his tats standing out in the hallway light against the whiteness of his skin.

He said nothing, still sleep dazed. His girlfriend snored in the bed behind him.

Jonah put a finger to his lips to indicate silence. Kruger gave a short nod.

'The cops're coming,' Jonah hissed. 'Hitting us in two hours. They're coming for you and me.'

Kruger scowled.

'We've got a flight. Gotta go now.' Jonah watched the big man's face for any sign of doubt. There wasn't any.

Kruger glanced at his girlfriend and stepped back into his room. Jonah waited. A moment later the man was back carrying four things- his patch, jeans, his favourite boots, and his Auto Mag.

Jonah grinned and led the way.

Ten minutes later the young prospect on sentry duty heard his President's voice come through the intercom beside him. The speaker box was mounted to the wall and the barrel of an M1 carbine leaned against it.

'Open the gate, Deano.'

He peered down into the yard from the guard post on the roof. He saw Kruger staring up at him, pointing at the high wrought iron gates at the front of the property.

Deano wondered what he was doing, but didn't question it. You didn't question Kruger or Jonah. He hit the buzzer and the gates started to swing open. He heard the rumble of motorbike engines and a moment later saw the two hogs rolling out onto the street, both riders fully patched up and carrying duffle bags slung over their shoulders.

They roared away up the street and Deano closed the gates behind them.

Silence fell on the street again.

THE HANGAR at Koh Samui airport was leased by a private charter company named Millbank Airways, an oblique reference to Richard Chambers' long distant past as a surveillance officer for Britain's MI5, the Security Service, which was based at Millbank in London.

A one-plane outfit with only two pilots, it carried out legitimate charter business interspersed with very non-legitimate smuggling operations. Simon Kenny, the captain of the shabby but reliable old DC-3, had been a top pilot for Qantas before being sacked for repeated drunken episodes. Chambers was certain that he flew drunk half the time. His co-pilot was a Liverpudlian named Hammond, who barely spoke and who nobody could understand when he did.

They had done the bullion run from New Zealand to Australia and on to Bangkok, then to the Middle East from there.

Since that run, they had been carrying out legit business delivering cargo around the region and keeping up an air of normality.

Johnny Mitchell pulled up in a beaten up old van while Kenny and Hammond were sitting in front of the hangar in their normal pose, newspapers open and coffee mugs at hand. Both wore scruffy shirts that were originally white and tan cargo shorts. Kenny's gut hung well over the front of his pants. The plane was in the hangar behind them. They looked up as the van arrived in a cloud of fumes and Mitchell jumped out.

He grinned as he strolled over to them, his hands in his pockets.

'To what do we owe this pleasure, cobber?' Kenny asked, not bothering to get up. It was too hot and besides, he couldn't be fucked.

'Clear your diaries, gents,' Mitchell told them. 'Mr Chambers would like you to pick up some cargo in En-Zed. Priority load.'

'Oh yeah.' Kenny grunted and put his broadsheet down. 'What is it?'

'Does it matter?'

'Not really. When does he want it by?'

'Priority.' Mitchell's grin stayed in place. 'Like, now.'

Kenny pushed himself up with a groan and glanced at his Scouser co-pilot. 'Come on you whinging Pommy prick, time to earn your keep.'

**21**

———

Disembarking at Koh Samui Airport took longer than Travis would have liked.

He bit his tongue but his face gave the game away. Susie smiled to herself as they shuffled their way down the aisle amongst the throng of tourist passengers.

A fat man pulled his carry-on bag down from the overhead locker and inadvertently thumped Travis in the chest with it. He didn't seem to notice until Travis glared at him. The man gave him an innocent look.

'Don't mind me,' Travis grumbled.

'Whatever, pal,' the fat man said, waddling ahead of him.

'Easy, tiger,' Susie said softly, seeing Travis' shoulders bunch with tension. 'Be a tourist, okay?'

He nodded reluctantly and shuffled on.

Coming through into what amounted to an Arrivals Hall, they spotted Major Dang and his team waiting outside for them by a pair of Land Cruisers. All of them wore dark shades and earpieces.

'Cool,' Travis grunted. 'Low profile.'

Susie laboured behind him, wrestling with the trolley carrying their bags. 'Mmm, nice. They look like the Secret Service.'

Travis shot them a smile and headed over.

Susie struggled with the trolley, which was determined to crab walk sideways. 'Thanks, but I'm okay.'

'Good.' Travis slipped on his own shades. 'Equal opportunities, y'know.'

As he got to the welcoming party, Travis noticed that Dang was accompanied by the same guys he'd originally clashed with in Bangkok. He hoped that all was forgiven, otherwise this could be an uncomfortable time.

Dang gave him a tight smile and stepped forward to shake hands briefly. Sergeant Mookjai glowered at Travis from behind his shades and made an aside to the two colleagues standing near him. Both of them grinned and Travis got the feeling they weren't just being happy-go-lucky.

'Thanks for the welcome,' Travis said to Dang. 'Is it not a bit overt though?'

'Overt?' Major Dang frowned at him.

'You know...obvious?' He indicated the shades and earpieces. 'You look like a bunch of cops.'

Mookjai sneered and interrupted. 'We *are* a bunch of cops.'

Travis gave him a cold look and turned to the Major, expecting some level of understanding. He didn't get it.

'*We* run this town,' Dang told him, 'not the criminals, and certainly not *you*. You are guests in our country; you do not come here and tell us how to do our job.'

Susie had joined them by now and stood listening.

'Do I make myself clear?' The Major's voice was trembling with barely controlled anger.

'Crystal,' Travis replied evenly.

'Good. You have caused us enough problems. You would be best to stay out of our way, I think.' He glanced at his men. 'It would be best all round.'

Travis held his hands up in surrender. 'Hey, sweet as mate.' He glanced at Susie and gave her a grin. 'It's been a pretty eventful trip so far, and I for one am happy to sit by the pool and kick back for a bit.'

Susie opened her mouth to object but saw his look and shrugged instead. 'Sure, whatever.' She gave Dang a bright smile. 'You guys are the professionals; we'll leave you to do your thing.'

Dang nodded, unsmiling. He clearly wasn't buying their charade. 'That is good. We will tell you when you are needed.' He finally smiled but it was a thin, unpleasant smile. 'Don't expect a call in a hurry.'

Mookjai chuckled and the other two men smirked.

With that they were ushered into one of the Land Cruisers, and one of the sidekicks took the wheel. Dang joined him in the front and they pulled away from the kerb.

Travis noticed that their luggage was put in the other wagon, with Mookjai and the second man.

'Any reason our bags are travelling separately, Major?' he asked.

Dang met his eyes in the rear view mirror attached to his sun visor. 'No reason,' he said.

Travis turned to Susie, beside him in the back seat. 'Obviously Sergeant Mookjai wants to try your knickers on.'

Dang scowled but Travis heard a titter from the driver. Dang scowled at the man and he shut up.

The rest of the drive was in silence.

The resort they had booked was south of the airport in the Lamai area, looking out to the Gulf of Siam.

The Special Branch cops dropped them at the Reception and while Susie checked them in, their bags were unloaded and Dang took Travis aside.

'I have your guns and passports,' he said, eyeballing Travis coolly. 'You will not be needing either of those items here. When it is time for you to leave, you will get your passports back. Besides, it is illegal for you have firearms here.'

Travis opened his mouth to object but thought better of it. This was how it was going to be, and he knew that to push the issue would just cause them more problems. Dang had made it pretty clear they weren't wanted; whether that was because of their earlier run-in, the subsequent gun battle, or something else, he didn't know. Their uncertainty over the Major's trustworthiness had led to them not reporting the attempt on their lives at Watkins' apartment block to the local authorities. Ingoe was aware and had agreed it was better to roll with it and see what shook out.

Travis simply nodded and put out his hand. Dang waited before shaking it reluctantly.

'I will be in touch,' the Major said briefly.

'Well, you know where we'll be.' Travis gave him a grin. 'A few cocktails by the pool won't hurt.'

Major Dang did not smile. 'Do not take me for a fool, Sergeant-Major Travis.' He gave a slow nod and now his lips twitched in a thin smile. 'Yes, I know who you are.'

Travis shrugged. He wasn't surprised.

'Koh Samui is a beautiful island with many wonderful sights to see and things to do. I suggest you make the most of being a tourist for a short time.' He held Travis' gaze evenly. 'Like any tourist destination, it is not always safe here. In my experience, Sergeant-Major Travis, it is usually the foolhardy and curious who get themselves in trouble.' His thin smile now took on a cruel veneer. 'Sometimes they even get hurt.'

Travis took a slow breath in through his nose, feeling the anger pushing up inside.

'Do I make myself clear...*Mr* Travis?'

Travis gave a curt nod. Dang turned to go, but Travis caught his elbow. The Major turned back and they were eye to eye.

'I get your point, Major Dang,' Travis rasped quietly. 'But don't ever threaten me or my partner again.' His eyes narrowed. 'That would be a mistake.'

He saw Dang's eyes flick over his shoulder at the same time as he felt a gun barrel dig into his kidney. Sergeant Mookjai's voice sounded in his ear.

'Take your hand off Major Dang,' the man said coldly, 'or I will kill you right here.'

Travis removed his hand and straightened up. The gun barrel dug harder into his back and Mookjai breathed in his ear. His breath smelled of fish. The man gave a low chuckle.

There was a blur of motion and a second later Travis was face to face with Mookjai. The Sergeant's gun hand was bent back on itself and his Colt Commander was facing towards his own gut. Both men were trembling with the strain of their silent battle. Mookjai's face bore a grimace of pain.

'Say the word, shit head,' Travis growled. 'And I'll drop you with your own gun.'

'That's enough.' Major Dang's tone was sharp. 'Stand down. Both of you.'

Travis slowly released his opponent but twisted the Colt from his grasp and retained it.

Mookjai stepped back and gave him a murderous look. 'That was a mistake.'

Travis dropped the magazine and racked the slide, popping out the chambered round. 'Then you should have thought first,' he said calmly. He palmed the gun and mag to Major Dang, who tucked them under his shirt unobtrusively.

Travis cocked his finger and thumb like a pistol and pointed it at Sergeant Mookjai. 'Catch ya 'round, hotshot.'

He turned his back and walked over to where Susie waited by the bags. She gave him quizzical.

'A pissing contest at the Reception desk? Really?'

He gave her grumpy. 'He started it.'

She shook her head sadly. 'They don't play nicely, do they?'

Travis gave her a slight smirk. 'I think I might be off Major Dang's Christmas card list.'

Susie sighed. 'Everywhere you go,' she said, grabbing her bag.

The villa they had was near one of the six pools and had a small private garden. A path led down to the stunning white sand beach. The resort had outdoor areas for dining and drinking, and some guests were already doing both. Their porter opened up the villa and placed their bags for them, took his tip and left, all with a gracious smile and a happy air.

'People are all so relaxed and happy here,' Susie remarked, admiring the view from the seaside window.

'Huh.' Travis grunted as he rummaged through his bag. 'I can't believe I'm getting paid to come to a place like this.'

Susie turned to speak and he held a finger to his lips. She waited while he finished with his bag and moved on to hers.

When the search was complete, he showed her several tiny electronic items on the bedspread. He had found two listening devices and four GPS tracking units. They were the latest kit but with limited range, indicating that whoever Dang had monitoring them was close by, and they had been expertly concealed in their luggage. The tracking devices had been slipped into the lining of Susie's hand bag and their footwear, and the bugs were hidden in the outer lining of each of their suitcases.

He silently pointed them out to Susie. She raised an eyebrow in surprise.

'Bastards,' Travis said aloud, 'they *have* taken our passports and guns.'

'Is that what your, ahh, conversation was about?' Susie enquired, clicking on.

'Yeah, Dang told me they had done that and he'll give them back when we leave. He also warned us off doing anything aside from touristy stuff, basically said if we poke around we'll end up getting hurt.'

'The cheeky prick!' Susie sounded outraged. 'Wait till that gets reported back; he'll be on traffic patrol before the week is out.'

'Probably with that lady-boy Mookjai swinging on his pole.' Travis couldn't help himself. Susie shook her head reproachfully, as if he was a naughty schoolboy, but he caught the whisper of a smile in her eyes.

'Well,' she said. 'We're a bit screwed then, aren't we?'

'I don't know about you,' Travis said, 'but I could do with a swim.'

## 22

Brad was extremely grateful for the efficiency of the embassy staff at Bangkok when he landed.

After making his way through Customs he was met on the other side by a driver holding up a sign with B. Taylor printed on it. He was a compact Asian, possibly Singaporean, with spiked hair and a hatchet face.

Brad made himself known to him and together they carried Brad's bags outside to an air conditioned BMW. The driver spoke with a Kiwi accent and introduced himself as Joe.

'I'll take you to your hotel,' he said, peeling away from the kerb to a blast of horns. Brad grabbed the armrest for support and reached for his seatbelt. 'Someone else has delivered the diplomatic pouch for you.' He gave Brad a knowing look.

Brad said nothing. Fortunately for him, considering the amount of gear he'd brought over, the diplomatic pouch he'd sent to Jack was anything but a pouch.

THE SERVICE in the poolside restaurant was excellent and the food was outstanding.

Naked flames flickered from stands beside the pool, glinting orange and red on the rippling surface of the water. Travis and Susie watched the other diners and beyond them, the sun setting on the ocean.

Travis finished his lobster and sat back, wiping his mouth with a satisfied smile. 'That was fantastic.'

Susie took a sip of Riesling, condensation trickling down the sides of the glass. She still had half of her own lobster to go. She saw Travis eyeing it hungrily.

'Hands off,' she warned.

He gave her his best innocent look. 'I'm just concerned about the high calories in that,' he told her. 'I'm thinking of your health. If I can reduce that risk for you, I think it's the right thing to do.'

She squinted at him. 'Are you calling me fat?'

'Whoa!' He raised his hands defensively. 'Hell no. I ain't no stupid.'

'Good,' Susie forked another piece of perfectly cooked, soft tail flesh into her mouth. She smiled at him as she chewed. 'Because I have been feeling a bit...out of shape lately.'

'Are you serious?'

Travis had a vivid image in his head from earlier that day. After unpacking the diplomatic so-called-pouch, which he was pleased to see contained all the gear he had requested, they had swum in the pool and she had insisted he go ahead of her, leaving her to get changed alone in the villa. He had taken it as a hint that the sex in Bangkok had been a mistake and she was deliberately removing the intimacy of being naked in front of him. He'd been disappointed, and had brooded over it until she appeared at the poolside.

The black and white zebra striped bikini had barely held things in place and she had turned heads when she dropped her towel. Tossing her hair and pulling it back into a bun, she had stared at him from behind oversized dark glasses, saying nothing. That was okay by Travis though; he wasn't sure he could have spoken anyway.

She had seemed to enjoy his reaction but after the swim, had again insisted on privacy while she dressed. It had been bugging Travis all afternoon. She was a seriously beautiful woman and he felt a strong attraction to her.

Susie snapped him out of his flashback.

'I can think of one thing that's good for working off the calories.' Her hazel eyes twinkled mischievously in the light.

'What? Showering alone?' He knew he sounded petulant as soon as he said it.

'Not quite what I was thinking.' She gave a slight shrug. 'But if you prefer that...'

'Hmmm...' Travis tried to recover from his childish response. 'Another swim then? Or a set of press-ups?'

'If by press-ups,' Susie said, finishing her lobster and picking up her wine glass again, 'you mean going back to our room and doing naked press-ups on top of me, then yes, press-ups.'

Travis cocked an eyebrow and tried to hide a grin. 'I don't know about you, but I'm okay without dessert. Let's go.'

He started to get up and she playfully sipped her wine.

'I kinda fancy a coconut mousse parfait, myself.'

He leaned over her chair and put his mouth close to her ear. Her hair tickled his face as he whispered.

'I'll make it worth your while.'

'Is that a promise?' She bent her head to look at him, their noses brushing gently, their faces so close together that his eyes seemed huge.

Travis nodded slowly. 'Oh yeah. It's gunna be a long, slow agony.' His lips twitched. 'And you'll love every second of it.'

Susie gave an involuntary shiver. 'Big talk, soldier. I hope you can deliver.'

AN HOUR LATER, Susie had to admit it was worth skipping dessert.

They had made love with a passion she had not known before, taking their time and exploring each other with a desire that made her tingle all over. They ended in a sweaty tangle on the floor near the bed, their pulses thumping and a sleepy, satisfied glow descending on them.

She rolled on top of Travis, propping her chin with a fist on his chest. She could feel his heart banging in his ribcage but already dropping to a normal rate faster than her own. His eyes were half closed, a happy smile on his face.

'Like the cat that got the cream,' she smiled, reaching up to run a finger down his cheek.

'I hope you're not expecting too much from me right now,' he replied. 'I'm shattered.'

'Oh.' Susie shifted her hips against him. 'Are you sure?'

'Well...'

'You don't seem so sure...' She continued moving, then suddenly felt his torso tense up beneath her. She looked down, still moving her hips, and saw him staring sideways at something beneath the bed.

'Stop.' His voice was quiet but forceful. 'Susie, stop now.'

She froze, unsure what was wrong but recognising the urgency in his voice. 'What is it?'

He slowly put his hands up to her arms and started to lift her. 'Get up very slowly,' he said quietly, his eyes still locked on the floor under the bed. 'Keep away from the bed and stand on a chair.'

She started to raise herself up but couldn't resist a peek under the bed. She saw something moving slowly in the near-complete darkness. It moved into a tiny sliver of light from the window shutter, slithering towards them across the wooden floor. It was a snake, silver with black shapes, and as her eyes grew accustomed to the gloom she could see it was over a metre long.

Susie's heart leaped into her mouth and she felt her hands begin to tremble. She was terrified of snakes. She pushed herself up and in two steps was standing on a chair, feeling ridiculous. She self-consciously covered her crotch and crossed her other arm across her breasts.

She watched as Travis slowly got to his feet and moved away from the bed, moving decisively but without panic, not wanting to alarm the snake. He hit the lights and looked round for a weapon. He quickly moved to the bathroom and grabbed the small rubbish bin there, then took a broom from the wardrobe.

'It's coming out,' Susie told him, watching the reptile slither out into the open. Its tongue flickered and it seemed to be coming towards her. Her mouth felt like it was full of cotton wool.

Travis seemed to be taking his time getting ready to deal with it, while she stood naked on a chair waiting to get bitten. The snake was longer than she originally thought, more like a metre and a half. Its tiny eyes and flickering tongue gave it a demonic appearance and she dreaded to think what it could do to her.

'Any time today would be good,' she croaked.

'Stay calm,' Travis said quietly, 'it's okay. We don't want to spook it. I just want to help it into a nice quiet place for a sleep.'

Susie frowned as she saw him scoop up a couple of items off the small kitchen bench. Her can of hair spray, a book of resort matches, and the sharp vegetable knife they had used earlier to slice fruit.

She glanced down again, seeing the snake move closer, its head weaving as it looked around. She was certain it could smell her fear. Surely any second now it would strike. She desperately needed to pee.

Susie saw Travis put the rubbish bin down. 'What are you doing?' she squeaked. 'Can't you catch it?'

'Bin's too small,' he said soothingly. 'And there's no lid. I need to either kill it or keep it enclosed securely.'

'So you're going to kill it then?'

The snake slithered closer. By Christ it was an evil looking bastard.

'That's the plan.' Travis moved softly towards the reptile from the side, keeping low and ready to move. When he was a metre or so away the snake stopped and turned towards him, assessing the newcomer for a threat.

'I take it you've done this before then?' Susie asked.

Travis gave a brief shake of his head. 'Never.'

'What?' Susie's voice rose to a shriek.

'It's alright,' he said. 'I've seen it on You Tube.' He gave her a grin he probably though was reassuring. It wasn't.

Susie watched as Travis leaned the wooden handled broom against the wall and stuck the knife between his teeth. He looked like a naked pirate, and in any other circumstances she would have laughed.

He struck a match and held it up, letting the flame take hold. The snake stared at it and moved closer, seemingly interested. It slid closer, now less than a metre away. The match was half burned.

Susie watched, fascinated and horrified at the same time. Travis was like some kind of snake charmer and she fervently hoped he knew what he was doing. She saw his right hand move up and suddenly a column of flame burst forth from the can of hair spray. It took the snake full in the face and she saw Travis step forward, enveloping the head and upper body of the snake in the fireball.

Susie thought she heard a shriek of some sort, but wasn't sure if it was her or the snake. She covered her mouth in horror.

In the next second Travis had discarded the can and the match and slammed the head of the broom down across the snake's neck, pinning it to the floor with all his strength. He snatched the knife from his teeth and stabbed downwards, missing with his first strike. The snake writhed in agony, flicking its tail wildly and trying to break free, but to no avail.

Travis' second strike drove the vegetable knife through the top of the snake's skull and he twisted savagely, wrenching the knife around to do ultimate damage. The blade pierced the floorboard and stayed there, keeping the snake in place as it continued to twitch in its death throes.

Travis straightened up, breathing heavily, staring down at his beaten foe.

Susie took her hand away from her mouth and started to get down, but Travis held up a hand.

'Wait there,' he ordered. 'I'll clear the room first.'

She stood on the chair, shivering despite the heat, while he first checked his bag then under the bed. He armed himself with his K-Bar knife and the big stainless revolver-he'd told her it was called a Python, and the irony was not lost on her. He then methodically checked every nook and cranny of the villa. Finally he announced it was clear and went back to the snake. He scooped it into the rubbish bin and tied the bag off, then helped Susie down from the chair. Her legs were wobbly beneath her.

'What the bloody hell was that doing in here?' she said, her eyes still wide with fear.

Travis' eyes were dark and focussed. 'Good question.'

It took them only a minute to get dressed and tuck Travis' weapons away again, and two minutes for a porter to arrive at the villa. Faced with a dead snake and two indignant guests, he summoned the duty manager. Travis explained how they had found the snake and managed to kill it, and made a point in front of Susie of playing it down. The manager opened the bag and examined the snake.

'I know it was probably over the top,' Travis said, 'but even though it's probably only a harmless grass snake, I wanted to play safe. Now, we'll be needing a new room...'

'Oh no sir,' the duty manager said, shaking his head vigorously and pointing at the dead snake in the bin. 'That is not grass snake. That is viper.'

Susie's hand shot to her mouth again. 'A viper?'

'Yes ma'am.'

'Is it poisonous then?'

'Oh yes ma'am, very bad snake. Very much poison.' He nodded vigorously again. 'It bite you, it will kill you. Dead,' he added, as if concerned she didn't understand.

'It's okay,' she replied, feeling a shudder deep within her, 'I got it the first time thanks.'

Travis took her elbow and steered her inside.

'You didn't really think it was a grass snake, did you?' Susie said.

Travis gave a slight shrug. 'Na. But there was no point alarming you even more. You don't like snakes?'

Susie pulled a face and shook her head. 'They're horrible. I'm with Indy on that one.'

Travis frowned quizzically. 'Indy?'

'Indiana Jones.' She adopted a man's voice. '"I hate snakes"? No idea?'

Travis grinned and grabbed his bag. 'I obviously need to get out more.'

He glanced at the blood stain on the floor while he packed, and had a flash of revulsion as he relived the incident. Death by snake bite would be a horrendous way to go, and he knew they were lucky to have escaped this time. Maybe next time they wouldn't see it coming. If they had been in bed instead of on the floor the viper would have naturally been attracted to their body heat, and once that happened a bite was almost inevitable.

One thing was clear above all else; this was no accident. Somebody had put that viper in their room, and their intention was clear. But who? Major Dang? The Pastor? Somebody they hadn't yet identified?

Right now it was too much to try and figure out. The priority was to get settled in another room and keep safe until morning, when they could begin to try and unravel the web they had found themselves in.

## 23

Johnny Mitchell had been pounding the streets of Bangkok at
11pm when the phone in his fanny pack started chirping. He
eased to a stop and grabbed it out, breathing hard. His T-shirt
was soaked in sweat and his heart was up around 145 bpm.
He had about another half hour to go and disliked being interrupted.
Chambers' name appeared on the screen.

'Yeah boss.'

'Johnny, I've made a mistake.' Chambers' voice sounded strained.
'I need your help.'

'Okay, I'm just...'

'Now. Come to my place.'

Mitchell let out his breath and silently cursed, but kept his tone
civil. 'Will do.'

Heading back towards his apartment, Mitchell had a feeling of
foreboding. He instinctively knew what was coming. Richard Chambers had very unusual tastes in sexual partners, and it turned
Mitchell's gut to think about it. He knew there had been an incident a
while back, just before Mitchell linked in with Chambers, involving a
transvestite prostitute. The problem had been made to go away that
time but Chambers hadn't learned his lesson, and Mitchell had been

needed to fix a couple of problems since then. His gut told him this one was going to be worse.

Mitchell had always thought that even though the Englishman was a weird dude he paid well, and his eccentricities were tolerable. He was starting to wonder if that assessment still held.

Forty minutes later when Mitchell got to Chambers' luxurious penthouse suite, his faith in his instincts was justified. Chambers met him at the door, his face pink with excitement. He wore a short silk robe that kept flapping open at the front. It was obvious he had nothing on underneath.

Chambers let him in and shut the door behind him. He took Mitchell through to the stark white kitchen where he sloshed gin from a bottle into a tumbler on the bench, spilling some over the side. He took a decent slug and sucked his teeth.

Mitchell waited.

Chambers put the tumbler down with a clunk. 'In there,' he said vaguely, waving towards his bedroom.

Mitchell walked to the open door and surveyed the scene. A semi-naked Thai lady boy lay sprawled on the king size bed, his face turned sideways and staring towards the door in a grotesque mask of death. His tongue was partially poking out and his face had a bluish tinge under his makeup.

He wore a red suspender belt and a white feather boa. By the tightness of the boa around his neck, Mitchell judged that to the instrument of death.

Mitchell returned to the kitchen, where Chambers was half way through his gin.

'What d'you think?' Chambers asked, already slurring his words.

'Well he's dead,' Mitchell said flatly.

'I know that,' Chambers spat, 'I fucking killed the little prick, didn't I? I know that.' He wiped the back of his hand across his mouth. 'For fuck's sake, I can't believe it...what a fucking mess.'

Mitchell took a deep breath and let it out slowly, watching his boss. The more he looked the more he saw a pathetic but psychotically dangerous old man. In the back of his mind, it clicked with Mitchell that this was the end of the road.

'Nothing we can't fix,' he said carefully.

Chambers met his gaze and studied his face, seeming to assess him for several moments. 'Good,' he said finally, 'you're a good man, Johnny.' He managed a weak smile. 'This is the last time, I swear.'

'You said that last time,' Mitchell blurted without thinking.

A flash of anger crossed Chambers' face and his eyes became two small black beads that bored into Mitchell's head. Gone was any trace of a sexually dysfunctional old man.

'You don't speak to me like that, Johnny,' he hissed through clenched teeth. His knuckles were white on the tumbler. 'You don't ever speak to me like that again.'

Mitchell held his tongue and felt a flutter of disquiet in his chest. 'Sorry boss,' he said as soothingly as he could manage. 'That wasn't fair.'

Chambers still eyeballed him, and Mitchell could feel the rage generating off him. He waited.

Finally Chambers took another slurp of his gin and let out a heavy sigh. The tip of his pink tongue flickered across his thin lips.

'It's okay,' he said, 'let's just get this mess cleaned up. And after that, I think I might need to move, lay low for a while.'

Mitchell glanced at him again, and the older man gave a firm nod. 'To the island.'

THE DC3 WAS MET on the tarmac by a pair of white Land Cruisers with several Thai men standing around it.

Jonah Jones eyed them as he descended the stairs, his gut telling him they were cops. Not cops like what he was used to though.

Major Dang met the two bikers at the foot of the stairs. He wore mirrored shades and a blank face.

Jonah put out his hand, figuring he should be friendly. The Major ignored it and simply studied him silently for a long moment before speaking.

'Come,' he said simply, turning on his heel.

The two men followed him to the first Land Cruiser. One of the men there opened the rear door. Another stepped forward with his hands out to take their bags.

Jonah shook his head and made to get in the back, keeping his bag with him. The man insisted, reaching for the bag. Kruger made a growling noise in his throat and reached out a paw.

There was a blur of movement and the man whipped a pistol from beneath his shirt, pointing it at Jonah's head. A hammer clicked behind him and Kruger felt the pressure of a gun barrel against his ear as Sergeant Mookjai stepped in from the side, his Colt up and ready to go.

The bikie enforcer was so much bigger than the sergeant that if Mookjai had fired he would have taken the top of Kruger's head off.

'Our turf,' he said firmly, 'our rules.'

Jonah eased back from the Land Cruiser, holding his bag out at arms' length. Kruger reluctantly dropped his own bag.

'Your weapons, too,' Mookjai said.

'We're unarmed,' Jonah said.

Mookjai snorted. 'Don't play me for a fool.' He jabbed Kruger's ear with the Colt. 'Take out your pistol with two fingers and hold it out.'

Kruger lifted his shirt and carefully withdrew the Auto Mag, passing it to one of the other cops. Jonah was similarly relieved of his Glock, and Major Dang stepped forward.

'Let us start again,' he said calmly. 'We know who and what you are, gentlemen. Do not think you can come to our country and call the shots, as they say.' His expressionless gaze shifted between them. 'If you think we are fools, or can be bullied, then you must think again. If you don't play the game by our rules, we will kill you.' A mirthless smile cracked his lips. 'If you do as we say, then we will get along...swimmingly. Do we understand each other?'

Jonah nodded. Kruger just stared at the older man like he wanted to rip his head off and take a dump in the cavity.

'Good.' Dang nodded again. 'Then let us go.'

Kenny and Hammond watched the display with amusement from the aircraft door. Kenny shot a wave to the departing vehicles and turned to his co-pilot.

'Righto, that's that mate,' he grinned. 'No flights booked. Let's get fucked up.'

Hammond grinned and said something unintelligible.

Kenny grinned. 'Sweet as mate, sounds good.' He began to descend the stairs.

Hammond shook his head and followed. He'd just told Kenny that he had a sore gut and didn't feel like a drink.

Didn't that Aussie fucker even speak English?

## 24

Brad arrived on Koh Samui later the same morning and with his bags in tow he made his way out into the sunshine to hail a cab. He noticed a Thai couple in their thirties hanging around with just shoulder bags, looking very much like cops pretending to be locals. They saw him see them and they both immediately looked away.

He ignored them and grabbed the first cab that appeared, opening the door to speak to the driver.

A Thai man in a smart suit appeared at Brad's side with a broad smile and an extended hand.

'If you would like to come with me sir, your shuttle is over here,' the man said, gesturing towards a white Land Cruiser nearby.

Brad looked at him. 'And who are you?'

'I am your driver, sir.' The man smiled wider. 'It has been arranged for you.'

'By who?' As far as Brad knew, nobody but Jack and Susie knew he was coming.

'It has been arranged,' the man repeated, gesturing again towards the Land Cruiser.

'Not by me it hasn't,' Brad told him bluntly.

'Please sir, if you would like to come with me…'

'No,' Brad said, 'I wouldn't.' He turned back to the cab driver, and heard a short burst of Thai from the smiling man behind him.

The cab drivers' face fell and he put the car in gear, moving off quickly. Brad turned to the smiling man with a scowl.

'Who the hell are you?' he rasped.

'I am your driver, sir. Please…' The smile never faltered, and the man gestured again towards the Land Cruiser.

'What's my name?' Brad asked him.

The man paused before returning to his refrain. 'Please sir, if you would…'

'No,' Brad snapped, 'I wouldn't.'

He grabbed up his bags and started to walk away.

'You won't find another cab, sir,' the smiling man said behind him.

Brad stopped and turned to look at him. 'What?'

'There are no cabs available for you, sir.'

Brad tossed his head towards the taxi rank, where drivers waited for a fare.

'Then what are these, an optical fucken illusion?'

The man still smiled. 'They are not available for you, sir. Please, if you would…'

Recognising a brick wall when he saw it, Brad relented. He followed the man to the Land Cruiser and as he put his bags in the back, a second Land Cruiser slid to a stop beside them.

Another Thai man alighted and took the bags from him, carrying them to the second vehicle.

'What the fuck is this about?' Brad growled at the smiling man.

'Nothing to be concerned about, sir. Please take a seat and enjoy the ride to your resort.'

Brad figured he may as well roll with it and see what happened. The second Land Cruiser tucked in behind them for the journey, and Brad could see a second man in the vehicle with the guy who'd taken his bags.

The driver played some kind of techno pop on the radio

throughout the drive, which did nothing to lighten Brad's mood. Finally they arrived at the resort and he was let out at Reception.

One of the men from the second vehicle dumped his bags on the step and the smiling man accompanied Brad to them.

'Obviously my bags have been searched,' Brad said, 'even though I'm travelling on a diplomatic passport. Is this how you treat all your guests?'

The smile disappeared. 'Consider yourself lucky you are allowed here. Check in with your colleagues and heed my advice; stay out of trouble.' The man smiled coldly. 'And watch out for the snakes in this area. They can be murder.'

Brad scowled. He reached down and scooped up his bags. Turning his back on the driver, he tossed an aside over his shoulder.

'Thanks for the ride, Major.'

Major Dang watched him go, scowling to himself. He glanced over to Mookjai, waiting by the second Land Cruiser. The sergeant gave a nod to confirm he had completed his task.

Dang nodded back. 'Let's go.'

BRAD FOUND Travis and Susie by the pool, relaxing on loungers with drinks close at hand. Susie had a glossy magazine open beside her and was people watching. Travis appeared to be asleep with a paperback open on his lap.

Brad ran an approving eye over Susie's figure, clad in a red bikini.

'Good flight?' Travis asked, sitting up and sliding his dark glasses down his nose.

'Fine. Got a welcoming committee from your mate, gave me a free ride.'

'Two Land Cruisers? Took your bags separately?'

Brad gave a tilt of the chin.

'May as well go unpack and settle in. De-bug while you're there,' Susie advised.

Brad flicked his chin again and moved away.

'Man of few words,' Susie observed wryly and picked up her magazine.

'Uh-huh.' Travis nodded.

Susie glanced at him sideways. 'Obviously runs in the family...'

**25**

---

Kablan and his three men had settled into a hotel in Nathon, taking two rooms to share. They travelled on Nigerian passports and encountered no problems on the way.

They were met at the hotel by a diminutive Thai man aged somewhere in his sixties. Kablan had never met him before but the man had had dealings with Ashkir and arrangements had been made.

The man carried a small rucksack with him, and was searched by one of Kablan's men before being allowed into Kablan's room.

The door was closed and two of the men stood guard while Kablan and his second, Gobey, spoke to the man. They sat on the floor facing each other.

The man handed over the rucksack, and Gobey checked it. Inside were four Chinese Type 54 pistols, variants of the Russian Tokarev TT-33. Gobey checked them and gave Kablan a nod.

'They'll do,' he said.

'What about rifles?' Kablan said. 'I don't see any rifles in there, old man.'

The old man didn't flinch. He withdrew a set of car keys from his pocket and passed them over.

'Downstairs,' he said, 'in car.'

Kablan tossed the keys to Gobey and jerked his thumb towards the door.

The room remained silent until Gobey returned a couple of minutes later. Kablan looked up questioningly as he entered.

'Chinese AKs,' the wiry Somali said.

'Bullets?'

'Enough.'

Kablan turned back to the old Thai man. 'You can go,' he said dismissively.

The old man pushed up with surprising ease for a man of his age. He said nothing as he moved to the door.

One of the guards let him out and closed the door behind him again.

Kablan tossed a pistol to each man, keeping what looked like the best one for himself. He slid a magazine into place and racked the slide. He glanced at Gobey, who was loading his own weapon.

'It is time to visit Mr Stephenson,' he said.

THE SUSPENSION of the grey Mazda sedan the old man had supplied creaked under the weight of the four men as Gobey pulled up outside Stephenson's villa.

The four Somalians alighted and approached the house.

They were met on the front path by Prasong.

Kablan noticed that the expressionless Thai had both hands behind his back. He glanced towards the house, and spotted the older white man there, his hands out of sight below the solid railing of the deck. His face was watchful, flicking from Kablan and Gobey on the path to the other two who had fanned out behind them.

Kablan stopped in front of Prasong and the two men stared at each other.

'Tell him we're here,' he said.

There was a pregnant pause for a long moment. Nobody spoke. Fingers curled around weapons, waiting for the go.

Stephenson appeared beside the older white man.

'What d'you want?' he called out.

'Our boss wants to make sure you keep your deal,' Kablan said, his good eye never leaving Prasong's face.

'The deadline hasn't expired yet,' Stephenson replied. 'There's no need for you to be here.'

'My boss would disagree, Mr Stephenson.' Kablan turned his head and fixed his eye on Stephenson. 'You know the terms of his agreement.'

'Yes I know the terms,' Stephenson snapped, the tension clear in his voice. 'The deadline has not arrived yet, so you can just go.'

'We will go peacefully,' Kablan agreed, giving a slow nod. 'This time. Do I make myself clear?'

Stephenson said nothing. His face was pinched and pale.

'Do I make myself clear?' Kablan repeated.

Terry hefted the AK in his hands so that they could see it. 'Just fuck off you dirty kaffir,' he snarled, 'before I blow your shit away.'

Kablan stared at him, recognising the accent. He didn't like white Africans. 'You,' he said, 'you will be first.' He kissed two fingers and pointed them at Terry like a pistol, blowing him a kiss. 'Till we meet again.'

The four Somalians backed off to their car and departed.

A hundred metres down the road, Johnny Mitchell watched from his battered van with growing interest. He took out his cell phone and rang Chambers.

**26**

———

Susie watched Brad constantly throughout lunch. Every time he looked at her she smiled. Finally he put his fork down and pushed his plate back.

'Am I a monkey in a zoo?' he grumbled.

She smiled again and gave a short laugh. 'Sorry, I'm just amazed at how much you can eat.'

'Gotta feed the beast.'

Travis emptied his water glass and refilled it. Without prompting he topped up Susie's too, a move that didn't go unnoticed by his nephew.

'So what's the plan?' Brad asked. They had filled him in on the snake incident which, considering Dang's comment to Brad, they were now attributing to him and his team. He had also found tracking and listening devices in his own luggage, similar to those found by Travis and Susie.

'I think our first step should be to find the listening post,' Travis said. 'It's gotta be handy.'

'Judging by the type of gear they used it's gotta be within a couple of hundred metres,' Susie said. 'A guest at the resort, maybe. Or at least based in a room here.'

'Probably one of Dang's guys,' Brad said. He gave a wry shake of his head. 'I'd love to wring that prick's neck.'

'All in good time,' Travis said. He looked to Susie. 'Given the Service's relationship with him, do you foresee any issues with us going up against him?'

Susie waggled her hand from side to side. 'Could be/maybe. The Director doesn't tend to look too favourably on us taking out our contacts.'

'Even if he's corrupt and obstructive?' Brad queried. 'What kinda bullshit policy is that?'

'It's not a policy as such,' she replied, 'more just a matter of good manners.'

Brad grunted and reached for a banana.

'If we had the right kit we could track it straight away,' Travis said. 'But we don't, so it's down to the old Mark One.'

Susie frowned quizzically.

He tapped his eye. 'Mark One eyeball. I think we split the resort into sectors and go hunting.'

His companions both nodded agreement.

'Speaking of kit,' he said, looking to Brad. 'No issue with getting what we need?'

Brad grinned. 'None at all. Your mate Jedi has an Aladdin's Cave down there. He queried a couple of items but gave them up anyway.'

'Good.' Travis slid his dark glasses back on. 'Right, first things first; I'll take the villas and cabins, Susie you take the garden rooms, Brad you do the suites-the main building over there.' He checked his watch. 'No rush, take your time. Better go grab our shorts,' referring to pistols rather than clothing, 'and meet back in the pool when we're done.'

'Meet back in the pool,' Brad echoed with a grin, pushing up. 'It's a tough life.'

He loped away towards the villa and Travis started to get up. Susie stopped him with a hand on his arm. He sat back down.

'You never told me. Your sister.'

He looked sharply at her. She waited. His brow furrowed.

'You don't have to tell me,' she said softly, 'if you don't want to.'

'It's okay.' Travis sat back and rubbed a hand down his thigh as he gathered his thoughts. 'She was older than me...good fun, a real hard case. Easily led though. Got a bit wayward at high school and ended up pregnant.'

Susie nodded silently.

'Things went pretty much bad to worse after that. She got into drugs and all the shit that goes with that. The young fella was taken off her, she went downhill and ended up dead pretty soon after.'

Travis' face clouded over and Susie waited some more. He took a moment to regroup before continuing.

'The young fella was taken in by our folks, I went off and joined the Army and that was pretty much me off the scene for the next twenty odd years.'

'So your parents raised him?'

'At first, then he got shipped off to an aunty and uncle.'

'The father?' Susie prompted.

'Waste of space, never showed any interest. I don't think he was even named on the birth certificate.'

Susie pulled a face. 'How did she die, if you don't mind me asking?'

'Overdose,' Travis said shortly.

'And what's Brad's beef with you then?'

Travis started to shrug then gave an almost imperceptible shake of his head. 'I wasn't there. For either of them.'

'You were a bit young, to be fair,' Susie said.

'I understand where he's coming from. I could've done more.'

Susie opened her mouth to speak but saw the look on his face and closed it again.

'This is my chance to make it right,' Travis said softly. 'I know what he's going through now, and I won't let him down again.'

MAJOR DANG SCOWLED as he listened to Mookjai's sit-rep, not interrupting but feeling his rage build.

At the same rate as his rage built his member deflated, and the topless young "massage therapist" who had been working on him tried her best to get things going while he sat with the cell phone clamped to his ear.

Dang slapped her hand away irritably and rolled sideways off the mattress on the floor. He struggled into his pants and shoes, snapped 'Wait there' and disconnected. He pulled his shirt on and angrily threw back the curtain which separated their "cubicle" from the rest of the room-four similar cubicles were curtained off, two of them in use.

The middle aged madam standing by the till gave him a sharp look as he stalked towards her. He thrust a couple of notes at her and went for the door. The driver waiting for him at the kerb jumped with surprise and scrambled to open the car door. Dang ignored him and got in, slamming the door behind him.

The driver knew better than to speak-obviously this hadn't been a normal "happy ending" massage.

Dang's mood had not improved when they arrived at the resort where the New Zealanders were staying.

He made his way to the room in the main building where their listening post was, and was met at the door by Sergeant Mookjai. Looking into the room past him, Dang saw the duty monitor, a young constable. The man was sitting on a chair at the table, which was covered in pieces of broken electronic equipment. He was nursing his right wrist and had wads of bloodied toilet paper protruding from both nostrils. He looked both forlorn and scared.

'He says a very big white man came,' Mookjai informed his superior. 'Hit him with the door and nearly broke his arm, then broke all the equipment. It is smashed.' Mookjai's face was tight with anger. 'It is them, for sure.'

'No doubt,' Dang agreed.

'I will go now,' Mookjai told him, giving a curt wave to a couple of his men. 'We will bring them in for questioning and things will happen.' He looked knowingly at Dang.

'No,' Dang said, 'I think we will be smart about this.'

'But sir...'

'No.' Dang's tone was firm now. 'I understand your sentiments, Sergeant, however we have to remember these are not the usual stupid tourists who we can play with. These are Government people, and we will risk an international incident if they were to...become injured.' His dark eyes glittered. 'No, I think we can do better than that.'

**27**

---

The island lay seven miles off the east coast of Koh Samui.

It was a square mile of rock covered with dense jungle, and had previously been home to an addiction-rehabilitation centre run by Buddhist monks in the seventies and eighties.

The monks were long gone but the centre remained, Spartan concrete buildings with no insulation and few windows.

Johnny Mitchell loathed the place-you could almost feel the dying spirits of the junkies who'd spent time there-but it had proved very useful over the years. A number of people had met their demise here.

The tide carried them into the sheltered bay on the southern side of the island, Mitchell cutting the engine of the small fishing boat as they neared the wooden dock. He looped a rope over the mooring hook on the dock and tied them off, the waves slapping at the sides of the boat. The smell of the sea air was heavy. Mitchell felt alive when he was at sea. He leaped nimbly out and helped Chambers up before grabbing the bags. Chambers led the way from the dock up the narrow goat track towards the centre of the island, his flashlight beam bobbing and swinging as he stumbled over the rough ground.

Mitchell followed several metres behind, as sure footed as a mountain goat despite the terrain underfoot. They reached the clearing near the middle of the island which contained the buildings and Mitchell quickly moved forward, scanning the area with a night vision monocular before physically clearing each building. Once he was satisfied, Chambers joined him and they moved into the main building.

It had originally been the administration and teaching block of the facility, housing a kitchen, a couple of offices, a chapel and an auditorium of sorts. Mitchell had spent time here over the last year between jobs doing what he jokingly called renovations including a master suite, a bunkroom and some special additions.

While Chambers settled himself into the master suite Mitchell went out the back and fired up the diesel generator to get the lights going. He came back inside to find Chambers waiting for him in the auditorium, his hands clasped together as if he were praying and an almost apologetic look on his pink face.

'I really am sorry for the inconvenience, Johnny,' Chambers said. 'I know this is not your favourite place, but it really does serve a need, doesn't it?'

'It does,' Mitchell acknowledged. He watched Chambers carefully. The man had always been somewhat unstable, but tonight was something different. He seemed more fucked up than normal, and Mitchell wasn't sure if it was because of the accidental death-well, as accidental as it could be when you were choking someone with a scarf while fucking them in the ass-or something more. He hoped it wasn't anything more than that. The Englishman walked close to the edge on a good day as it was.

'Tomorrow is a new day, is it not?' Chambers' eyes sparkled now and he smiled like a child, full of innocent excitement.

Mitchell said nothing. He had the impression he didn't need to; this was a one-sided conversation and he was merely a spectator.

'I find that I'm rather disappointed in my friend Philip,' Chambers continued. 'He and his minions have really let me down this time, and I fear they have reached the end of their usefulness, don't you?'

Mitchell remained silent. Chambers' gaze went right through him and he felt a chill run down his spine.

'It's so sad when a relationship breaks down Johnny, but if the trust is gone, what is left?' Chambers spread his hands now like a preacher at the pulpit spreading the Good Word, only Mitchell knew what was coming and there was nothing holy about it.

'You want me to get them out here,' he said flatly, and Chambers' face lit up like a cherub.

'Oh Johnny, you really can read my mind,' he cooed. 'That's just the ticket indeed. And while we're at it, we'll deal with that bloody fool Dang too. He's annoying me as well.' Chambers smiled coldly. 'He and his cohorts are bringing the New Zealanders out here, so I think we will deal with all of them at once.'

'Boss, do you think...'

Chambers cut him off with an icy glare. 'Yes, I do think actually Johnny. I think those useless bloody bastards need to be taught a bloody lesson, all of them. Open up the pit and let them fight it out. Whoever survives, walks away.'

Mitchell nodded slowly, being carefully to keep an eye on Chambers without eyeballing him. An intense feeling of evil was creeping over him and the hairs on his neck were standing up.

'No worries Boss,' he said coolly, 'I'm all over it.'

'Splendid.' Chambers clapped his hands together and smiled brightly. 'I knew you'd be just the man for the job, Johnny. Now if you'll excuse me, I'm going to turn in. It's been an eventful day.'

With that he was gone with a swish of his robes, back towards the master suite.

Mitchell watched him go, finally letting out his breath. Whatever else happened, he decided, he was doing nothing without a gun strapped to him.

## 28

The tapping at the door was soft at first, just enough to stir Travis into cracking an eye open. He listened, the feel of Susie's warm nakedness comforting against his skin. The tapping escalated to a firm knocking and he sat up, snatching his jeans off the floor.

'What is it?' Susie said sleepily, sitting up and rubbing at her face.

'Don't know.' Travis pulled his jeans up and tugged a singlet over his head, grabbed his Colt Python then padded towards the door, checking out the window as he reached for the handle.

In the ambient light he saw Major Dang, Sergeant Mookjai and two others standing outside. His levels of alertness shot straight up and he backed away from the window, waving at Susie to get her attention.

'Get dressed,' he hissed urgently,' trouble!'

No sooner had the words left his mouth than the door crashed open and slammed against the wall. The four men burst in, all carrying weapons. Travis brought the pistol up and snapped a fast double tap into their mass, seeing the closest man clutch at his chest and begin to fall. He stepped left and fired another double tap, before Mookjai got his own weapon on line and fired.

Twin darts stabbed into Travis' torso and bolts of electricity slammed into his nervous system. Mookjai kept the pressure on and Travis danced a macabre dance, losing his gun and unable to fight the power that surged through him, locking up his muscles and completely incapacitating his body.

He hit the deck and Mookjai gave him another burst for good measure, causing Travis' limbs to flail about helplessly. The man beside Mookjai dropped on Travis' back and wrenched his arms behind his back, cuffing them securely before frisking him.

Susie wasn't sure if she'd screamed or not. She had dived for the newly acquired Glock 26 when the door smashed open, but ended up lying half out of the bed with the sheets tangled round her legs while Major Dang shone a bright torch in her face and smiled evilly down at her, his foot on her gun. His own pistol was aimed between her eyes, ready to spread her brains across the bed.

She froze, suddenly aware of her nakedness.

'Sit up and don't be silly,' he said quietly. 'I will be happy to kill you if you do not.'

Travis was just starting to get his senses back when a rag was jammed in his mouth and a hood was yanked over his head. He was dragged to his feet and hustled towards the door, the men holding him being sure to bounce him off the doorframe as they went through, causing an explosion of pain in his head.

Behind him, Susie was allowed to dress under the watchful eye of Dang and the first man through the door, who now had two fresh holes in the front panel of his body armour. Once she had three-quarter pants and a T shirt on Susie was also cuffed and secured with a rag and a hood.

The other man took her arm and walked her quickly out of the room. Dang scooped up Travis' Python and tucked it into his belt with a smirk.

Travis felt sand under his feet and heard surf as he was hustled roughly away from the resort. He splashed into water and felt the wooden side of a boat against his legs. He was partially lifted before being dumped into a boat, landing unceremoniously on the floor and receiving a kick in the ribs from whoever was on board. He rolled to the side and tried to get to his knees, before a gun butt crashed into his skull and knocked him flat again. He lay there, disoriented and wondering what the hell was going on.

He heard more people arrive and a few seconds later a soft body landed half on top of him. He recognised Susie's scent. They both wriggled to untangle themselves and ended up lying more or less side by side.

More people climbed aboard the boat then they heard a louder splashing and heavy grunting as others arrived.

There was the sound of straining and the boat rocked before a heavy impact beside Travis. From the size of the object and the muffled growling coming from it, he was pretty sure the new arrival was Brad.

An outboard motor started up and the boat moved off, bumping across small waves and gradually picking up speed. Travis was aware of the sound of a second engine nearby, keeping pace with them.

He got as comfortable as he could and breathed through his nose, getting himself together and gathering his wits. He pressed against Susie, willing her to stay calm. Things were looking dire and he couldn't help but wonder if they were about to meet a watery death. Kidnapped and taken out to sea, nobody would ever know what happened to them. He forced the thought from his head and concentrated on what he knew and what he could do.

Mookjai focussed on the dock as the boat pilot brought them in close, cutting the engine and letting the current take them in.

The other boat docked first, the three men on board with Major Dang alighting quickly and mooring their craft before beginning to unload their supplies. The Major stood back and watched.

Mookjai glanced down at the three prisoners in the bottom of the boat, all three lying still and silent. The big one stirred and made muffled sounds, probably curses given their previous interaction- when they had captured him in his villa they had tasered him twice before getting him fully under control. Before the first dose though he'd got his hands on one of the lads and battered him around the head before throwing him against the wall.

That cop, Decha, sat over the big man, watching him carefully. When he stirred this time, Mookjai watched Decha stamp his foot down hard on the man's head, producing a grunt and more muffled curses. The other two lads chuckled and Mookjai hoped for Decha's sake that the big man didn't get loose. He turned his own attention to Travis, the older man, who lay in the middle. From Mookjai's experience it wasn't the young hot heads that posed the most danger, it was the older, wiser men. They had experience and cunning on their side, and this one was certainly battle hardened. Mookjai would dearly love to plug him and drop the body overboard, but orders were orders.

The woman had remained silent for most of the journey. He wasn't sure whether she was too terrified to move, or had simply retreated inside to re-gather herself. He didn't care either way-nobody walked away from the island.

They moored and began to unload. Susie was pulled to her feet first and manhandled onto the dock, waiting with one of the men while they went back for Travis.

The boat rocked as they jerked him roughly up. Mookjai jabbed his gun barrel into Travis' ribs and pulled him close.

'Please be stupid,' the cop hissed. 'Gimme excuse.'

Travis remained silent, but Mookjai could feel the vibes coming off him. The Kiwi let them haul him awkwardly up onto a wooden dock, where Mookjai held him near Susie.

Three of the men went back for the big man-Big Bad Brad, Mookjai thought-and wrestled him up onto the dock. As soon as his feet were stable the big man lashed out with his head, crashing his skull into the face of the man on his left arm. As that man cried out a big foot drove backwards into the man behind Brad, standing right at the edge of the dock. The man squealed and flew backwards, over the boat, hitting the water with a loud splash.

Decha jabbed his stun gun into Brad's gut and gave him a long burst, making him jerk and thrash uncontrollably before collapsing to the ground like a felled tree.

Mookjai stayed back with his two prisoners, keeping an eye on Travis. He half expected-hoped-the Kiwi would react, but there was nothing. Either the man had complete faith that his nephew would be okay, or he was one cold bastard.

The cop hauled himself out of the water and received a burst from Major Dang, who was clearly not impressed. The other man was wiping blood from his face and shooting daggers at Brad's hooded face.

'If you ladies are quite ready, let's go,' Mookjai snapped. He shoved Travis forward, keeping the Commander ready just in case.

**29**

———————

They made their way to the goat track, where they were met by the American, Mitchell. He had an Uzi submachine gun forward slung and a pair of night vision goggles pushed up on his head. He gave no greeting, just led them silently up the path to the buildings, veering off from the centre to a side building. As they entered it, Mookjai realised the building had been gutted and turned into an arena of some sort. The walls and roof were intact, but all that remained of the floor was an outer ring, circling a pit that filled the centre of the building.

The pit was probably four metres deep and twice that in circumference. He could see a door inset in a wall below, and a matching door to the side up at ground level.

Mitchell led them to the door and unlocked it with a large key. The stairs behind it were concrete. Lighted torches flickered at regular intervals down the wall, giving the whole place an almost prehistoric feel. It was cold and draughty.

At the base of the stairs was a room which had five cells off it, like some sort of medieval dungeon.

Mitchell opened the door of the first one. Brad was led in first, followed by Travis. Both were forced to their knees, looking away from the door. Susie was last in, and when she was pushed to her knees Mookjai stepped forward with a set of handcuff keys. He freed her hands and removed the hood and gag. She shook her head and licked her parched lips, looking round in the dim light.

Mookjai handed her the key and backed out of the cell. The door clanged shut.

'Unlock them,' he said, indicating the two men with his pistol.

Susie unlocked the cuffs from the two men and made to pass the cuffs back through the bars.

Travis stopped her, eyeing Mookjai with undisguised disdain.

'When you feel like fighting like a man,' he rasped, 'come and see me.'

Mookjai stiffened and Mitchell stepped calmly forward, lifting the stubby snout of his Uzi. It was pointed at Susie's gut. At this range it would shred her in a second.

'Pass the cuffs back, pal,' he said coolly, 'or I'll punch her ticket. *Comprende?*'

Travis turned his gaze to him, taking the three sets of cuffs to the bars and holding them out by a finger. He ran his eye up and down Mitchell, coming to rest on his face.

'Call yourself an operator?' he said coldly. 'You look like a fucken mercenary to me. A man without honour is no man at all.'

Mitchell flushed and his jaw set. 'I always thought you Kiwis were overrated, boy.'

'Ha.' Travis gave a short, barking laugh. 'Where I come from, DD spells coward. Guess you just weren't up to it...*boy.*'

He gave a derisive snort and dropped the cuffs on the floor, before turning his back contemptuously. The unspoken message was clear.

Behind him, Mitchell slowly bent and picked up the cuffs, tossing them away to the side. 'Your time is here,' he said.

Mookjai led the way back up the stairs and the door at the top banged shut.

The only light in the dungeon was the flickering torches from the stairs, casting moving shadows in the musty darkness.

The dirt floor felt damp and cold. The concrete block walls were blackened with mould. The whole place had the rank stench of death about it.

'I wonder how many people have died down here,' Brad mused aloud.

Travis shot him a look. 'Yeah, let's be positive about it. Nice one.'

Brad shrugged. 'Just making conversation. So, when did you two hook up?'

'Fuck me,' Travis muttered as Susie flushed. 'You're a bloody great conversationalist aren't you?'

'Well there's not much else going on down here is there?' Brad shook the bars with both hands. They were solidly bedded in.

He looked around. There were no windows and no obvious means of escape.

'We could try digging our way out under the bars,' Susie suggested.

Travis had been running his fingertips all over the wall behind them. 'Nothing there,' he said, straightening up and dusting his hands off. He took an inventory of them all. Aside from what they were wearing, they had nothing to hand.

He wore faded blue jeans and a grey singlet. Susie's ¾ length pants were khaki green and the T shirt over her pink sports bra was white. Brad wore DPM camo pants and a black T shirt. They were all bare foot.

They were locked in the dungeon of an island prison, surrounded by armed criminals. He couldn't think of a time he'd been in a more dismal position.

'No worries,' he said with a grin, 'we've got them on the ropes.'

## 30

When Major Dang, Sergeant Mookjai and their men entered the auditorium of the main building, they found Chambers sitting at a long conference table.

He beamed at them across the table. He was clad in a long white robe like some kind of Roman emperor.

Also at the table, but sitting apart from him, were Philip Stephenson and his two henchmen, Prasong and Terry. All three looked distinctly uneasy, although Stephenson tried to force a smile.

Dang glanced down to his right and saw a small pile of weapons on the floor. He looked at Mitchell and noticed the Uzi barrel held steady at his navel.

'Weapons on the floor, gents,' the American said softly. 'Nice and easy.'

Dang gave a nod and complied, his men following suit. They took seats across the table from the Englishman, Mitchell standing guard at the door.

'Welcome, gentlemen,' Chambers beamed, looking round at each of them in turn. 'Welcome to my island paradise. I thought it prudent for us to get together one last time.'

He placed his hands flat on the table and adopted a contrite look.

'Due to unforeseen circumstances, it is time for me to move on, at least for a time. However, before I do, there are arrangements to be made. These arrangements affect each and every one of you.' He smiled thinly. 'Business, as they say, is business.' He made a steeple of his fingers and leaned forward, elbows on the table. 'The line of work we are all in is a precarious one at best. It is a constantly changing beast. Dynamic, you could say. It is exciting and dangerous and thrilling.' His eyes gleamed as he spoke. 'With that comes inherent risk and the need to be adaptable. That suits me-I am a chameleon. I have changed form many times over the years, and it is my adaptability that makes me strong.' He pounded a fist against his chest. 'Some might say invincible. *Indestructible*.'

Chambers cast his gaze around them all again, the fervour within radiating from his face. The room was deathly silent.

'Alongside me I need men who are also adaptable and resilient. I need men with forward thinking. Yesterday is gone, tomorrow is the future. My operation is sleek and deadly accurate. There is no room for idleness and dead wood. No room for time wasters and dreamers. No room for yesterday.'

Sitting at the end of the line furthest from the action, Terry listened to the man talk. There was no doubting the man was bat-shit crazy, and the more Terry listened the more he realised that every man in the room was pretty much fucked. He glanced casually across at the Thai cops sitting opposite them. The boss, that Major Dang, was completely impassive as he listened. His sergeant looked permanently pissed off, like he wanted to smash the first person to look at him sideways. The rest of them looked like they didn't know what the fuck this crazy bastard was talking about. Fair do's, Terry figured, they probably only spoke enough English to shake down tourists.

Looking to his left, Terry could see Stephenson was churning everything over in his head. He knew the boss was seriously concerned. Prasong, as always, gave nothing away.

'All of you have been with me on this journey and have proven your worth previously.'

Terry saw Dang's chest puff out and a self-satisfied smirk settle on his face. Cocky bastard.

'But recently all of you,' Chambers jabbed the table top with a finger for emphasis, 'all of you, have let me down.'

Terry saw Dang's smile fade and grinned inwardly.

'This is your chance to re-engage with me. Prove your commitment again.' He looked at each in turn. 'I take it that each of you has followed their instructions?'

There were slow nods, and Mitchell stepped forward.

Stephenson removed a small but hefty black velvet bag from an inside pocket and passed it the American. Dang did likewise with a larger bag which clanked as he handed it over. Mitchell checked both bags quickly before giving Chambers a nod. Terry knew that the bag Stephenson had just handed over contained two million US worth of uncut diamonds. He presumed Dang's bag contained something of similar value, presumably gold coins by the sound of it. He'd heard a whisper the Thai cop had got his hands on some Nazi gold a while back.

'Very good,' Chambers purred. 'This is a good start. The ability to follow instructions is important. So far you are all even. So far.' He steepled his fingers again. 'The second part of this evening will be a true test of survival. I need men that I know will live and die for the cause. And kill for it.' He smiled coldly. 'As you know, the intelligence service of New Zealand has rather naively sent some agents after us. Well, I presume, after our friend here, The Pastor. After some quite feeble attempts by all of you to shake them from our trail, they have finally ended up here and are currently under lock and key.'

Dang got that cocky smirk back again. Terry wanted to rip it from his face. Obviously the crooked cop thought he had the upper hand now.

'The second part of this evening will sort the men from the boys, and whoever proves themselves to be a boy, will not be continuing this journey.' He smiled again, the psycho cherub coming back. 'And to the victor the spoils!'

Stephenson opened his mouth, cutting off Chambers' diatribe mid-flow.

'So what it boils down to is you want to up sticks and fuck off to Somalia to run your operation from there, and we've all pissed you off enough that we have to fight it out to see who gets to be your bum-boy?'

Chambers' eyes were like shards of ice. 'Don't ever interrupt me, you arrogant little bitch. And if you speak to me with that insolent tongue again, I will cut it out and feed it to you.'

Stephenson visibly paled and his Adam's apple bobbed up and down.

Chambers stared at him balefully for a long time before speaking again. 'In essence, yes. That is what I am proposing.'

'With respect, you do know that the Somali's want my head?' Stephenson pressed anxiously.

Terry cringed, waiting for his boss to take a bullet from the American.

'I am aware of that, and it makes it more interesting don't you think?' Chambers replied, his icy glare changing in a second to a cherubic smile. 'Of course I am aware.' His smile got wider, his eyes glinting with amusement. 'I arranged it!'

Stephenson's jaw dropped open and Terry saw Mitchell push the door open behind him. In walked two grizzled looking bikers, both big men in black jeans with Southern Vikings patches on over T shirts.

Terry eyed them curiously. Jonah Jones and his buddy Kruger. At Mitchell's word they added their weapons to the growing pile on the floor. Terry noted that Kruger's was a huge AutoMag .44. Obviously got a small cock, he mused.

Once they were seated on Chambers' other side, Mitchell opened the door again and disappeared. He was back a few seconds later, holding the door open to let four men walk in. Each of them had an AK front slung.

Terry heard Stephenson give an involuntary gasp as he laid eyes on Kablan, the half-blind sidekick to Ashkir. Kablan leered at him across the room.

'We meet again, Mr Stephenson,' he grinned. 'Mr Ashkir will be most pleased, I dare say.'

'Weapons,' Mitchell said calmly, 'on the ground.'

Kablan glanced at him and gave a sneer. 'I surrender my weapon for no man. Especially,' he stepped into Mitchell's personal space, 'an American pig dog.'

Mitchell's expression did not change. 'All your weapons on the ground,' he said quietly, gently raising the barrel of the Uzi. 'Now.'

Kablan didn't flinch. His thick lips curled back to reveal yellowed teeth.

Terry felt the atmosphere tighten. It was like the air was getting sucked out of the room. All eyes were on the two men. Even Chambers seemed lost for words.

But no, as Terry looked down the table at him, Chambers was not lost for words at all; he was grinning with anticipation. He was loving every second of it, the psycho bastard.

Mitchell took a slow breath in through his nose, started to exhale, and squeezed the trigger.

The Uzi chattered and six rounds blasted through Kablan's gut, one of the rounds knocking the man behind him into a spin. As the leader started to fall his two remaining men grabbed for their weapons. Gobey got both hands on his AK and started to turn before Mitchell put a burst through his rib cage then another into the man beside him. Both men fell and Mitchell blasted the next burst into the first man he'd wounded, now struggling to hold himself up against the wall. He slid down it, leaving a large bloody smear. Terry noticed that his left eye was dangling from the socket onto his cheek.

Ricochets pinged off surfaces all around the room.

Mitchell moved from man to man, putting a short burst into the head of each of them. He stood over the four bodies and automatically changed magazines, racking a fresh round into the chamber.

Gun smoke hung in the still air, mixed with the pungent metallic odour of blood.

Terry stayed perfectly still. He was both shocked and impressed. This guy was a fucking killing machine. No sympathy for those dirty black bastards though, they could go to hell. He flicked his eyes to Chambers.

The pink-cheeked Englishman was glowing, his eyes bright. If Terry was a betting man, he'd bet the sick fuck had just shot his bolt. Everybody else looked stunned.

'Well,' Chambers said finally, 'I guess that evens up the odds somewhat, doesn't it?'

He looked around the assembled faces again, grinning widely.

Kruger shifted slightly in his chair. 'Mean,' he grunted.

'That, gentlemen,' Chambers said, 'is what happens when people cross me.' His expression turned serious again. 'I recommend you do not make the same mistake.'

'So what exactly is it you want from us then, Richard?' Dang asked. 'If you looking for people with influence,' he gestured towards his team, 'this is us here.'

Chambers smiled at him like a kindly uncle.

'We will see,' he said, 'we will see.'

'THAT WAS A LOT OF SHOOTING,' Travis noted, standing at the cell bars and trying to see up the stairs.

'What the fuck are these clowns doing?' Brad growled.

The door opened at the head of the stairs and footsteps descended.

'Whatever it is,' Travis remarked, 'it's happening now.'

Johnny Mitchell appeared with five Thai cops trailing behind him. Brad stepped up to the bars, recognising Decha as the one who had tasered him. A scowl settled on his face.

Decha scowled back, holding Brad's gaze as the five men were led to the adjoining cell.

'Wait here,' Mitchell said, locking the door behind them.

He went back upstairs, leaving the two groups to glare at each other through the bars.

'I get my hands on you, you little fuck,' Brad snarled, 'I'll break your scrawny neck.'

Decha snarled a reply, the words in Thai but his meaning clear.

'I have a very bad feeling about this,' Susie whispered to Travis, holding his arm.

'I have to admit,' he said drily, 'things aren't really looking up.'

Travis watched Mitchell carefully as the American moved to the door across from them and unlocked it with a large old fashioned key. The door opened and beyond it he saw what looked like a dirt pit.

Mitchell turned and gave a cocky smirk as he headed back to the stairs.

Travis turned to his two companions.

'Brace yourselves,' he said, 'this is gunna be game on.'

**31**

Mitchell made his way back towards the main building, his mind buzzing. The bush sounds were loud around him, the night pitch black. He didn't need the NVGs on his head though, having followed this track many times.

Just twenty yards from the main building, he spotted a flicker of movement at the corner of the building. He paused, the Uzi coming up in his grip. He watched as a man slipped round the corner of the building and headed towards him, glancing over his shoulder but unaware of the threat ahead of him.

'Hey buddy,' Mitchell said, flicking his torch on, 'goin' somewhere?'

Terry froze in the torch beam, his hands up to shield his eyes. 'You scared me half to death, man. I'm just...ahh...'

Mitchell nodded, even though the other man couldn't see it. 'Getting the hell outta Dodge?'

'Na man, I was just...ahh...' Terry shook his head in exasperation and put his hands up. 'Okay man, you got me. I was getting the hell outta here. This is some crazy shit going down, you know?'

He tried to squint past the light and Mitchell cut it, taking a careful step sideways in case the old timer tried to rush where he'd last seen him.

'Anyone else coming with you?'

'Na man, I just said I was goin' for a piss and ran. I don't know what those dumb shits are doing man, but I ain't stickin' around.' He stared at Mitchell's faint outline in the darkness. 'That guy, your boss? Man, he is off his goddamn rocker. He's talking all this shit about competing to add value to his operation,' he gave a snort of disgust, 'but what a crock of shit, man. If anybody gets off this island alive, I'll eat my bloody hat mate.'

Mitchell half smiled to himself. The man wasn't wrong. Chambers had four mil now to assist his escape and resettlement plans, and the rest was just for his own entertainment.

'Go on,' the American said softly. 'Get going. I won't stop you.'

'Come with me man,' Terry urged him. 'I know your background, we could be a good team. Leave this shit behind.'

'Thanks buddy,' Mitchell replied, 'but this is me. This is what I do now.'

He paused for a second, common sense tugging at him. He shook it off. More than anything right now, he wanted to wipe that smug look off Jack Travis' face. He was a fucken Navy SEAL, goddamnit. Nobody dissed the Navy SEALs.

'Take the boat with the white seats. I got a bag stashed in it with some things you'll need. Kind of an insurance policy for me, but I guess I won't be cashing it tonight. He jerked his head towards the dock. 'Get going before they come looking.'

Terry didn't hesitate, just hurried off into the darkness without a backwards glance. Dawn was not far off and he needed to make tracks fast.

Mitchell headed towards the main building.

CHAMBERS WAS NOT IMPRESSED that Terry had escaped, but in the bigger scheme of his plans for the night it was really inconsequential.

He couldn't shake the nagging doubt that Mitchell had lied to him, but it didn't matter right now. The grizzled old mercenary was just one man; there were plenty more still there and blood would be spilt. Looking at Stephenson and his side kick, Prasong, Chambers was confident they had known nothing of their comrade's escape plan. If anything, Stephenson seemed more anxious than before. That was good.

First on the agenda was Major Dang and Sergeant Mookjai, up against Jonah Jones and Kruger. When Chambers broke the news to them both pairs of men stiffened and quizzical looks were exchanged.

'I thought we were fighting those other arseholes,' Jonah said, jerking a thumb over his shoulder.

'All in good time, my friend, all in good time,' Chambers replied. 'Maybe.' He smiled and indicated the two Thai cops. 'You need to get through these two men first.'

Kruger grunted. It seemed about the extent of his vocabulary tonight.

Jonah frowned then shrugged. 'No problem.'

Dang licked his lips cautiously as he eyed the two large bikies. Although Mookjai was fit and strong, he was painfully aware of his own physical abilities.

'It would seem to be a good idea for us maybe not to fight among ourselves,' he suggested, in what he hoped was a wise tone. He held Chambers' gaze across the table. 'We are on the same side, are we not?'

'No.' Chambers' right hand moved and he produced a Browning High Power from underneath his robes. He pointed it at Dang's face. 'I think you're missing the point, Major Dang.'

The shot was loud and sharp and Dang's brains splattered across the wall behind him. Mookjai reacted instantly, grabbing at a pistol concealed beneath his clothing. Mitchell took one step forward as he fluidly drew his Beretta, and pumped a round through the sergeant's right ear. The body collapsed against his dead commander.

Chambers closed his eyes and delicately sniffed the blue-grey smoke curling from the barrel of his Browning. He inhaled it and let out a satisfied sigh, before tucking the pistol away again. Mitchell holstered his Beretta and stepped back, impassive.

'Does anybody else have anything they would like to contribute?' Chambers looked each of the four remaining men in the eye. 'No, I thought not.' He pushed up from his chair. 'Let us move over to the arena.'

Mitchell waited until the four men had stepped outside into the darkness before stopping Chambers and taking him aside.

'The other five cops, boss?' he asked. 'You want them in the ring too?'

Chambers checked his watch and pursed his lips for a moment. 'No, I think not. They are superfluous to requirements now.'

'So?' Mitchell raised his eyebrows questioningly.

Chambers gave an almost imperceptible shrug. 'Kill them,' he said.

TRAVIS, Brad and Susie had a plan formulated when Mitchell reappeared at the stairs. He walked to their cell door and inserted a key in the lock, then stepped back and aimed the Uzi at them through the bars.

'The girl comes out,' he said, 'any tricks and I'll just start shooting.'

'If you're going to do that anyway,' Travis replied, 'what have we got to lose?'

Mitchell shifted the Uzi barrel and fired a short burst into the cell next door. One of the Thai cops took all the rounds in the gut and collapsed to the floor, rapidly leaking blood.

'You want more blood on your hands?' Mitchell asked.

'You gutless fucken shithead,' Travis snarled, 'put it down and come in here!'

The remaining four Thais were in shock, huddled over their fallen colleague.

Susie stepped forward and reached for the key.

'No,' Travis said.

'He's going to just keep killing people,' Susie said firmly. 'I don't want other peoples' deaths on my conscience.'

'He'll kill you,' Travis told her as she pushed the cell door open.

Mitchell saw a shift in Brad's posture as he readied himself, and the American moved the Uzi towards Susie.

'I wouldn't,' he said softly.

Susie stepped out and closed the door behind her, locking it. Travis could see her eyes were wet and her chin was trembling, but she put on a brave face.

'It'll be okay,' she said shakily to him. 'They just want me as a bargaining chip.' A tear broke free and rolled down the side of her nose. 'You do what you do best.'

Travis felt helpless with impotent rage as he watched Mitchell escort her upstairs. Five minutes later the American was back, tossing handcuffs to the four remaining Thais and getting them to cuff themselves together, back to back. He then escorted them up the stairs and silence fell again.

Travis and Brad looked at each other in the semi-darkness.

'This is it, boy,' Travis said. 'This is balls to the wall.'

Brad nodded.

They both heard a far off popping of shots, at least twenty in all. They looked at each other again, both men wearing grim expressions. An understanding passed between them.

Nothing needed to be said.

**32**

———

Chambers sat on his throne and clapped his hands with delight.

'Bring in the Christians!' he chortled, his face the excited pink of a child.

The door opened and Brad stepped through, scanning around him. Kruger glared at him from across the pit. He was bare-chested and wore black jeans with his motorcycle boots.

Brad was surprised at how huge he was, and immediately assessed him for strengths and weaknesses. Probably a 'roid user, undoubtedly a drug user, unquestionably a killer. But also carrying weight round his gut and probably out of condition.

Brad met his gaze and held it, jaw jutting and game face on. He rolled his shoulders and shook his arms out.

Kruger eyed him across the gap, and cracked his knuckles. Brad took deep breaths in through his nose, oxygenating his blood and getting ready. Any second now, he would be fighting for his life.

Above them, Chambers clapped his hands again, the slap of skin on skin cracking loudly in the arena.

'Let the games,' he hollered, 'begin!'

With that, Kruger began to move forward, arms wide and a snarl on his face. Brad shifted, keeping his feet wide for balance and his hands loose, reading his opponent's body language and planning his moves. Kruger was a monster, no doubt about that, and if Brad let him get his hands on him he'd be in trouble.

The circle they were creating was getting gradually smaller, and Kruger made a sudden rush at him, arms wide and roaring like a bull.

Brad stepped left, brushed the right hand aside and slammed a jab into the big man's side ribs. He'd hit other guys with that shot before and put them down. Kruger grunted and swung a back hand that glanced off Brad's skull and sent him off-balance.

The big bikie turned and brought his fists up in a boxing stance. They were like Christmas hams and each knuckle bore a death's head tattoo. Brad continued to circle him, assessing and manoeuvring.

Kruger came in another rush, more refined this time and without the roaring. He edged close enough to start throwing big meaty jabs, which Brad could easily dodge, then tried a surprise front kick to the knee.

Brad saw it coming a mile off and stayed low, weaved and blocked the big boot with both hands, keeping it down. He seized the boot and yanked it round, twisting the foot and turning the leg with it. Kruger had no option but to turn and save his ankle from being broken.

He took air and came down hard on his front, his right leg still locked behind him. He went to push up, but they both knew he was in serious trouble now.

Brad kept the leg locked straight and high and drove his foot down between Kruger's legs, slamming into his genitals. The man let out a *whoof* of air and started to fold. Brad braced the boot between both hands and snapped it round viciously, hearing a dull crack muffled by the heavy boot. Kruger let out a shriek of pain. Brad twisted harder, hearing the bones crunch, and flipped the monster bikie onto his back.

Kruger reached up for his wounded ankle and shrieked again when Brad threw the leg down and stepped back. Kruger rolled onto his other knee and swung wildly at him. Brad easily avoided the swings and circled him, knowing he had the upper hand now and taking a moment to size up his options. Kruger struggled to turn with him but couldn't keep up, whipping round from side to side with his wounded leg stuck out in front of him.

Brad moved in quickly, landing a resounding double slap to Kruger's ears and following it through with a driving knee to the right side of his head as he went off balance. Kruger was thrown to the left and caught himself on one hand, his head ringing as he saw Brad appear in front of him.

The stiff fingers of Brad's left hand jabbed into his eyes and as Kruger reeled back in agony he never saw the strike that killed him. With his full power behind it, and no thought of mercy, Brad drove his big right straight into Kruger's throat. The blow crushed his larynx and cut off the air.

Kruger clutched at his throat, blood already trickling from his left eye, and collapsed backwards. He gasped and flopped and Brad turned his back on him, breathing hard. In seconds the Sergeant-at-Arms, the enforcer, was dead.

A long slow clap sounded from above. Brad glanced up to see Chambers on his throne, a smile of admiration on his face.

'Bravo, young man, bravo.'

Brad sucked in air and shook his arms out.

The door opened and Prasong and Mitchell appeared. They grabbed Kruger's arms and dragged his lifeless form out of the pit.

'That is not the end, of course,' Chambers called out.

Brad spat. 'Bring it on,' he growled.

Before the door closed, Jonah Jones stepped through. He wore his Southern Bandits patch vest over a bare chest, and like Kruger, still had his jeans and motorcycle boots on. His fists were already clenched and the pupils of his eyes were pinpoint tight and locked on Brad.

'I told you we would meet again,' he bellowed, strutting up and down his side of the pit.

'I'm glad you stepped out from behind your mummy's panties,' Brad growled.

Chambers leered down from above, loving the atmosphere. 'On with the show!' he called, clapping his hands.

The two men began to circle each other like gladiators, both ready and poised. It was obvious to Brad that while Kruger was huge and brutal, Jonah was the real danger man of the two. Smaller and lighter, definitely, even giving a couple of inches and a few kilos to Brad, but more mobile and conditioned than the Sergeant-at-Arms.

Brad let Jonah kick things off, which he did with a double jab and a side kick, all of which Brad managed to block, but it gave him an insight into his opponent's abilities. He was fast enough and had some power in his strikes, and clearly some knowledge of fighting moves.

They thrust and parried for a minute, each assessing the other, before Jonah went for a sneaky jab to the face which he intended to follow up with a full haymaker.

Brad weaved and let the jab sail past his head and instead of stepping out, he moved in. He sensed the haymaker coming and blocked it with his left forearm, the impact jarring him up to the shoulder. He ignored it and seized hold of Jonah's hair instead, yanking the head forward and slamming his forehead into the gang leader's face. The nose split under the blow and blood sprayed out. Jonah staggered back, one hand at his face, the other flailing wildly.

Brad slapped the hand away and landed a solid left hook to Jonah's jaw, spinning him away into the wall of the pit.

He danced back, sucking in air and reassessing.

Jonah took a few moments to get himself together before shaking tendrils of blood from his hands and stepping up again. Whatever he was on was doing a good job of masking his pain.

He wiped his hands on the back of his jeans and came forward, blood flowing freely down his mouth and chin.

Brad let him come then stepped in with a snap kick to the thigh and a right jab. Jonah took the kick and didn't blink, and blocked the jab away. He came in fast, landing a decent double jab to Brad's jaw and opening a cut above his left eye with a good cross.

Brad wiped the blood away and got space.

'I meant to tell you something,' Jonah grinned, circling around again, 'when I mowed your little buddies down...they pissed their pants and squealed like pigs.'

He laughed a nasty cackle, obviously trying to goad Brad into doing something reckless.

Brad let him have his fun; it just made him more determined to win this thing.

'I thought your Sergeant-at-Arms was supposed to be some kinda mean son of a bitch,' he replied. 'Kruger was a fucken pussy, just like the rest of your boys.'

Jonah's expression darkened. 'I'm gunna make you pay for killing him. He was my brother.'

'Does that make it incest then?' Brad sneered, and Jonah frowned, confused. 'You know, when he was bouncing on your cock.'

Jonah's face went dark and he rushed in fast and hard, swinging and jabbing in a blur.

Brad took a couple of hits but blocked or dodged most of them, until he felt a slice across his left bicep. He glanced down and saw a clean cut had opened up, and it was as he danced back that he saw the box cutter knife in Jonah's right hand.

'How d'you like that?' Jonah snarled with a grin, blood still dripping from his chin. 'I'm gunna stick you like a pig, bitch.'

'Bring it on then, sweetheart,' Brad rasped. 'Let's boogie.'

He feinted a couple of strikes and let Jonah grab his right wrist, seeing the knife come up for a slice, before he clamped a paw on Jonah's right wrist and locked the hand still in mid-air. He squeezed hard enough to make Jonah's hand go white and pink, twisted his own wrist free, and turned Jonah's right wrist back on itself.

The box cutter fell free as Brad twisted the wrist until he heard a snap, smacked a back hand into the gang leader's face to keep him occupied, and wrenched the arm in and around, getting it up behind Jonah's back.

Jonah let out a scream and scrabbled at him with his free hand, trying to get a hold. Brad forced him to his knees and slammed a knee into his back, arching him backwards.

He let the man go and moved around him again. Jonah forced himself unsteadily to his feet, his right hand hanging limply at his side. His face was bloodied and he was in obvious pain, but he wasn't giving up.

Brad quickly checked the cut to his bicep-it was deeper than he'd first thought, and needed stitching. He wiped blood from his eye and readied himself.

Jonah scooped up the box cutter in his left hand and stayed low, weaving like he knew something about knife fighting. Brad moved, keeping space and assessing the options.

Suddenly Jonah charged in, slashing with the knife and forcing Brad back. He bent and threw a handful of dirt in Brad's face, temporarily blinding him. Brad felt his back hit the pit wall and knew he was on the ropes.

He dodged left and felt Jonah impact his right side, then another cut to his right hip. He hissed and kept his eyes closed, reacting instinctively.

His left came through in a thunderous hook to Jonah's head and he seized the collar of the patch vest and yanked his opponent forward, slamming a knee up into his gut.

He stepped away from the wall, dragging Jonah like a doll, and landed another knee to the gut. He felt Jonah sag and quickly wiped his eyes, blinking rapidly to get some vision back.

Jonah's left came up with the box cutter again, going for Brad's face. Brad blocked the strike and gripped the wrist, twisted hard and drove his fist into Jonah's eye, opening up a gash on the eyebrow. With his opponent temporarily dazed, he ripped the knife from Jonah's hand and seized him by the hair again.

Drawing Jonah's head back, he exposed the throat. He stared into Jonah's eyes from inches away. He saw the fear there, and the realisation. They both knew what was going to happen.

'I told you,' Brad whispered, and drew the knife straight across Jonah's throat.

The carotid artery was severed immediately and a jet of dark arterial blood shot across the pit.

Brad pushed the dying man away from him and let him fall to his knees, Jonah's eyes wide with terror and a dark stain showing at the crotch of his jeans. Blood flowed down his bare chest and his artery continued to pump out jets as his heart raced.

It took several seconds before the body slumped over sideways. Brad watched it fall and looked down at the knife in his bloodied hand.

The door opened again and Mitchell appeared this time, coolly aiming his Beretta at him.

'Toss the knife,' he said.

Brad tossed it to him and the former SEAL kicked it back behind the door. Prasong came through now and dragged Jonah's body away. A large blood stain remained on the dirt where he'd lain.

'Well done,' Chambers called down, 'I thoroughly enjoyed that one. Very gladiatorial, well done indeed.'

'You know you're fucken mental, don't you?' Brad rasped.

The Englishman smiled back, placating. 'Oh believe me, Mr Travis, I am very self-aware. Now, you may have a rest and gather yourself.' He gestured to Mitchell. 'Bring in the next one.'

Mitchell turned to go, and Chambers spoke again.

'Oh, Johnny. Make this one a double, would you?'

Mitchell nodded and guided Brad out of the pit, back to the cell.

Travis gave his nephew an enquiring look. 'You alright?'

Brad nodded briefly. 'Kruger and Jonah,' he said. 'Both dead.' He glanced back at Mitchell, waiting impatiently at the door. 'Apparently you're getting a double.'

'Hurry up,' Mitchell said.

'Fuck off, dickhead.' Brad had just killed two men with his bare hands; he was beyond caring what the ex-SEAL thought.

Mitchell's eyes narrowed dangerously. 'I can't wait for my turn with you, buddy.' He gestured with his gun barrel to Travis. 'Come on, old timer.'

Travis scowled at him then turned to Brad. 'Really? I thought I was having a young day.'

'Don't get sensitive,' Mitchell told him with a sneer, 'your day's about to get worse anyway.'

'Why, do I have to have sex with your Mum?'

Mitchell's nostrils flared but he held his tongue. He waved Travis out and escorted him to the pit, shutting the door behind him.

## 33

Travis took in the pit in a glance, noting the blood stains. He wondered who his two opponents were going to be; presumably Prasong and Terry. Brad's efforts had obviously whittled the list of candidates down somewhat.

He looked up and saw Chambers gazing down from his throne.

'Enjoying the show up there?' he asked sarcastically.

'Oh yes, I'm having a lovely time,' Chambers purred, making a steeple of his fingers before him. 'I'm particularly looking forward to this round. I have the feeling it will be quite...scintillating.' His smile got wider and he clapped his hands loudly. 'Let the games begin!'

The door opened and two men entered. First was Prasong, clad only in gym shorts, his body completely devoid of any fat. He was all hard muscle and sinew. Travis' eyebrows shot up when he recognised the second man.

Philip Stephenson smirked as he strolled into the pit. He was also clad only in shorts and was leanly athletic with a hard torso.

'What, surprised?' He rolled his neck, loosening up. 'Didn't know I was a fighter?'

The two men began to circle him. Travis felt over dressed in his jeans and singlet.

'Easy mistake. I never was, until I met my friend here.' Stephenson tossed his head towards the silent Thai. 'I lost a bet, the cost of which was a round with this guy.' He shrugged. 'Needless to say, he wiped the floor with me. I took him on as his manager and he taught me. Of course I'm nowhere near his league, but I'm no slouch either.'

'We'll see,' Travis replied evenly.

The Pastor nodded and smiled. 'We will.' He put his hands together in mock prayer. 'Let us pray.'

He bowed his head and closed his eyes for a brief moment.

'What the fuck?' Travis said, rolling his eyes at the theatrics. 'Stop jerkin' off and get on with it.'

Stephenson's eyes snapped open and he turned his gaze on Travis. He had taken on a new demeanour and Travis could feel the purpose and murderous intent emanating off him.

'Prayer time,' Stephenson whispered.

Prasong and Stephenson approached him in tandem, keeping wide enough for Travis to have to use his peripheral vision to keep an eye on both.

Prasong made the first move, a blur of strikes and kicks as he worked his way in closer. Travis ducked, blocking and parrying but getting a couple of decent hits to the torso before his back hit the wall. Stephenson moved in then too, snapping a front kick to Travis' right hip and a side kick to the gut, both good solid hits. Travis sucked it up and blocked a burst of punches from Prasong, each blow like being hit with a hammer.

Stephenson took his turn, a flurry of strikes coming at Travis as Prasong edged back. Travis took a good hit to the jaw but blocked the rest, and slipped sideways past an over-zealous jab, slapping the punch away and landing a hook to the side ribs. He followed it with a jab to the kidneys as he worked past Stephenson and drove a knee into the former spy's left thigh, causing it to buckle.

Realising his boss was in trouble, Prasong moved in but Travis gripped Stephenson's shoulder and shielded behind him.

Stephenson slammed his elbow backwards into Travis' ribs,

breaking his hold, and whirled with his other elbow, going for a head strike. Travis ducked under it, hooked him in the ribs again and drove the heel of his hand straight up under his arm into his jaw.

Stephenson's jaw slammed shut and his head snapped back. Travis delivered a brutal short side kick to Stephenson's right knee. The knee folded inwards and he started to drop, gasping with pain.

Prasong came over the top with a hammer blow to the side of Travis' head, knocking him away from Stephenson. Prasong moved past, closing in with a double side kick to Travis' back which sent him staggering across the floor.

Stephenson hobbled to the wall on his damaged leg while Prasong continued the attack.

Travis turned to confront him and copped another kick in the chest, slamming him back against the wall. He covered in time to block a burst of punches and pushed Prasong away, but took another couple of good hits to the face. One opened a cut on his left cheekbone, which felt like it was cracked.

Prasong stepped back to quickly check his boss, just for a split second, and Travis moved fast.

His front kick to Prasong's gut knocked the man backwards and he moved in with a double cross to the jaw. Prasong recovered quickly, landing blows to Travis' head and forcing him back again. Travis rolled with it and got the Thai's right hand, locking it securely in his grip and pulling him forward. Prasong twisted to get free, Travis' hand slipped with the sweat on their skin and Prasong landed a nasty shot to his neck.

Travis took it, seized the hand again and turned, locking it under his arm and getting his back against Prasong as he swung on the arm to hyper-extend it.

Prasong knew what he was doing and fought to get free, slamming his elbow repeatedly into Travis' back. Travis gritted his teeth against the pain and hung on.

With a surprise twist, Prasong turned and got his left hand up into Travis' crotch from behind, gripping onto his testicles and crushing. White hot bolts of agony shot through Travis and he let go, staggering away. Stephenson moved in from his right, hobbling fast but getting to Travis before his opponent could defend himself.

Stephenson drove his fist into Travis' ribs first then his kidneys as he turned away, following with an elbow slamming into his back.

Travis dropped to his hands, feeling his singlet rip open as Stephenson hung on. He caught himself and took a kick to the side of the head from Prasong. He drove his foot back, connecting hard with The Pastor's left knee cap, blasting straight through and folding it completely inwards. Stephenson screamed and went down on his face.

Prasong flew in with kicks to the side, sending Travis into a rolling collision with Stephenson. The Pastor was still screaming as Travis rolled over him and pushed himself up fast enough to downward block another kick. He caught Prasong's foot and heaved, flipping the Thai up and back.

As Prasong went with it into a perfect back flip, Travis returned to where Stephenson lay writhing. He delivered a solid kick to Stephenson's jaw that drove his head into the dirt, knocking him out cold. Travis' balls throbbed with the effort. He yanked the ripped singlet off and tossed it aside.

Prasong gave a flying roundhouse kick that would have taken Travis' head off had it connected, but Travis got his hands up in time and caught the foot high in mid-flight, twisted and pulled to defeat the fighter's recovery attempt. Prasong was falling when Travis slammed a heel into his crotch and braced himself with his hands up, keeping Prasong's right foot high.

Prasong landed on his hands and ignored the pain in his groin, pushed up and kicked back with his left foot, catching Travis on the shoulder but failing to break his grip. Travis kicked him again to the gut, landing three strikes then twisting the foot again and flipping Prasong a complete 360. The little Thai broke free and vaulted to his feet, half spun, and smashed him in the face with a back kick so fast Travis never even saw it until it landed. He crashed back into the wall, tasting blood from his nose and his eyes filling with involuntary tears.

Prasong saw him on the ropes and came in for the kill. His

hammer-like fists slammed into Travis' chest with a tap-tap of jabs, then he stepped back and threw himself into a spinning roundhouse kick to the head.

It was the sort of shot that could snap a neck or put a target out cold, if it connected.

Travis sensed it coming, dropped and caught the fighter's right foot as it sailed above his head, and drove his own right foot out in a low side kick. It slammed into Prasong's left knee side on and blew through it, ripping the knee apart and bringing a sharp cry of pain.

He held on tight to the right foot, braced himself and caught the back of Prasong's hair as the man fell backwards. Travis' right knee was hard and rock steady on the ground, and he added his own strength to Prasong's weight in its downward fall.

Prasong landed square on the knee in the centre of his back, the impact fracturing his spine with a loud crack. He kicked and flopped and Travis withdrew his knee, rolling him face down and dropping on him again with a bent knee.

Despite his crippling injury Prasong snatched hold of Travis' left wrist in his own and tried to bite down on it.

Travis ripped his hand free and locked it under Prasong's chin, the other hand on the crown of his head. Knowing what was coming, Prasong let out an animal screech and tried to buck his opponent off his broken back.

Travis ignored the resistance and finished it. He wrenched hard and snapped Prasong's neck then let him drop to the ground.

He pushed himself up and stood over the dead fighter, breathing hard. He checked Stephenson, who was stirring back to consciousness. His left knee was bent at an unnatural angle and he was weakly trying to reach for it.

Travis crossed to him, lifted his head by the hair, and drove a fist into his jaw. The jaw cracked and The Pastor slumped into unconsciousness again.

Travis straightened and looked up at Chambers, who was leaning forward in his throne and peering down into the pit.

'Is he dead?' the Englishman called down.

Travis put his hands on his hips and sucked in some deep breaths. 'It's over,' he managed.

'Is he dead?' Chambers repeated, louder this time. His face was getting pinker.

'It's over,' Travis repeated. 'Let her go.'

Chambers leaped to his feet. 'It's over when I say it's over!' he screeched, his robes flying around him as his arms thrashed. 'Kill him!'

Travis spat on the ground. 'I'm happy to kill him,' he said coldly. 'Release her first.'

'You don't make the rules,' Chambers bellowed, drawing his Browning from under his robes and taking aim at Travis. 'I am the King, and I make the rules!'

He fired a shot, the echo loud in the enclosed space, and dirt kicked up a metre from Travis' feet.

'I said kill him!'

Travis' lip curled with disdain. 'I can't kill him if you shoot me, can I?' he pointed out.

Chambers waved the gun angrily, his face a mask of frustrated rage, before he let out an angry *'Aaaaagghh!'* and stomped out of sight.

**34**

―――――

itchell unlocked the cell door, his Beretta casually aimed at Brad's gut.

'Out.' He moved back and gestured with the gun barrel towards the door to the pit.

Brad came out and paused, eyeing him carefully.

'It'd be the last move you ever made,' Mitchell told him softly.

Brad turned his back and made his way back into the pit. He saw Jack there, now shirtless and grimy, bleeding from the nose, cheek and knuckles. Prasong lay dead with his head rolled at a strange angle. Stephenson lay unmoving, his chest gently rising.

The two men looked at each other.

'I heard a shot,' Brad said.

'I think Chambers has flipped completely,' Travis replied. 'Don't know where he's gone now.'

The answer came a second later, when Mitchell appeared over the lip of the pit. He was holding a chain and dragging something heavy. He got to the edge and jerked on the chain, then leaned down and heaved something over to the edge.

It was Susie, her hands tied behind her and the chain secured around her neck like a noose.

She was conscious and her face was grimy and sweat stained.

Chambers stepped up to the side of the pit, a triumphant look on his face. 'Now,' he smiled, 'let us stop the schoolyard nonsense and get down to business.' He looked down pointedly at Susie's prone form. 'This is a business arrangement, Mr Travis. You kill him,' he jabbed a finger towards Stephenson, 'or we kill her.'

He smiled like it was an every-day agreement. 'Quite simple, wouldn't you say?'

'He'll kill you anyway, Jack!' Susie shouted. 'He's bloody mad!'

'Shut up.' Mitchell jerked on the chain like she was a dog.

'Fuck you,' she snarled back.

Chambers spread his hands and gave them a questioning look. 'Do we have a deal?'

Travis and Brad looked at each other. An unspoken agreement passed between them.

'Well,' Travis said aloud. 'Looks like we're a bit fucked, doesn't it?'

Chambers smiled down at them benevolently. Gone was the raging psycho now, replaced by the kindly monarch.

'A somewhat crude description,' he purred, 'but it does sum the situation up nicely.'

'Send down your boy first,' Travis called up, nodding his head towards Mitchell.

'If he can beat me, I'll kill Stephenson.' He spread his hands, mirroring Chambers.

Mitchell glanced at his boss. 'It's a trick,' he said.

Chambers sneered. 'Come now, Johnny, surely you can beat him?' He smiled indulgently. 'You are a SEAL, after all...'

Mitchell hesitated, torn between common sense and his professional pride. For the second time that night pride won out and he handed the chain to Chambers. 'Keep a gun on them until I get the big one locked up,' he warned.

Chambers took the chain and drew his Browning again, training it on Travis.

Mitchell moved out of sight and Brad moved too, wind milling his arms as if warming up. Travis backed up to the wall facing Chambers, making eye contact with Susie as he did so. He flicked his eyebrows and got the tiniest of nods in return.

It was three seconds since Mitchell had disappeared from view. Brad linked his fingers into a stirrup and quickly backed up to the opposite wall. Travis moved.

Chambers realised something was up and yelled a warning, unleashing a shot into the pit and kicking at Susie.

Travis bolted across the pit and brought his foot up into Brad's hands.

Susie was powerless to fight Chambers' foot shove and rolled over the edge of the pit with a sharp gasp. She dropped down until the chain ended and nearly ripped her head off. She began to swing like a pendulum, held by the chain round her throat.

Travis pushed off and Brad heaved upwards, the joint effort sending him hurtling up the face of the pit wall.

A second shot cracked and he felt the wind of it passing above his head. Susie swung back to her right, the chain tight around her throat.

The door was flung open and Mitchell burst through, staying wide and keeping his Beretta tucked close to his body.

Brad landed a thunderous right cross to the side of the ex-SEAL's head and grabbed for the Beretta as it fired.

Chambers' third shot was deafeningly loud as he fired from only a metre away, but Travis was so focussed on his purpose that he barely acknowledged it. He cleared the lip of the pit by a good foot, and threw himself at the criminal mastermind as he landed.

The Browning fired again and he felt a tweak at his left shoulder. He grabbed Chambers by the front of his robes and yanked him off-balance, snatching at the gun hand.

Mitchell recovered quickly and fought to retain his weapon, jabbing at Brad's face with his left while he did so. Brad had his right wrist and was holding the Beretta away at arm's length. He swatted Mitchell's hand away and grabbed him by the throat. The Beretta fired into the dirt as they wrestled together. Mitchell craned his neck and latched onto Brad's hand, biting hard onto a knuckle.

Travis got hold of the Browning by the barrel and pushed it away to the side, then smashed his head forward in a brutal head butt.

Chambers' head flicked back with the impact and the skin above his nose split. Travis went for a second head strike but Chambers threw a desperate knee at him, caught up in his flowing robes. Travis took it on the thigh and snapped an elbow to Chambers' temple, stunning him.

The pressure was building on Susie's head and throat and she couldn't breathe. Dangling by her neck from the chain noose, she knew it was only a matter of time before she choked to death.

Despite the size difference, Mitchell was extremely strong and Brad had his hands full containing him. The ex-SEAL ripped the knuckle open and threw knee strikes and kicks at him. The pain in Brad's hand was excruciating but he held on, locked tight on the man's throat. He dug his fingers in around the windpipe and squeezed hard.

Mitchell twisted his right wrist free from Brad's big paw and started to bring the Beretta pistol up. His vision was blurring and the pressure was building in his head. Brad saw the pistol coming round and squeezed harder on his opponent's throat, forcing his fingers together through the skin and gristle. Mitchell gaped like a fish, his eyes bugging wildly.

Travis hooked Chambers to the head, and a second, and a third, pushing him away and ripping the Browning from his grasp.

Brad snatched the Beretta out of the air in his left and plucked it from Mitchell's hand. His right arm strained under the effort as he lifted the mercenary onto his toes and throttled him. Mitchell kicked frantically and thrashed with his arms, slapping wildly as the life slipped out of him. His eyes rolled in his head and Brad dropped him in a heap. He swapped the Beretta to his right hand and fired a single shot, straight between Mitchell's eyes. Blood and grey-pink brain matter splattered across the dirt.

He heard a shot from above the pit and whirled, bringing the pistol up.

Travis triggered a single shot into Chambers' chest, seeing the stain of red blood spread across the front of the man's robes. Chambers clutched at his chest and gasped.

Travis dropped the Browning and seized him by the shoulder and the back of his robes, running him forward a few steps before hurling him over the edge.

Brad saw the robed man fly through the air above him, crash into the opposite wall head first with a loud crunch, and drop to the ground.

He hit the dirt and lay still.

'Susie!' Travis shouted, scrabbling for the Browning again. If he was lucky, she was still alive. If not...

He found it and scanned for the chain's anchor. He spotted a large bolt at the base of the wall, the chain secured to it with a D-ring. He fired once, bending the steel but not breaking it. He fired again, hearing his nephew shouting 'Hurry up, Jack!'

Travis fired again, moving closer, and got to a metre away from the D-ring. He ripped off two more shots and the ring snapped. The chain pulled away and snaked rapidly across the floor.

Susie dropped like a stone and Brad caught her at the bottom, getting his fingers under the chain and yanking the noose open, unhooking it over her head.

She gasped for breath, her chest heaving as her starved lungs sought oxygen.

Brad freed her hands and she rubbed tenderly at her throat.

Travis appeared through the door and came to her, scooping her into his arms and pulling her close, shushing her and touching her face softly.

Brad backed away and checked Stephenson; still out cold. He checked Mitchell next; brain matter still leaked out the back of his head. Brad figured it was safe to rule him out as a threat. He started to move towards Chambers.

Travis felt relief flooding through him as he held Susie against his chest. It was only early days and who knew what lay ahead of them, but he didn't want to contemplate the idea of being without her.

He heard a shuffle of movement behind him and a shout from Brad.

Travis whirled, bringing the Browning around. Brad was off to his right with the Beretta up.

Chambers had pushed himself into a sitting position, a wide red stain over his chest, his left shoulder hanging limply at his side. In his right hand was a stubby-barrelled pistol, coming on line with Travis.

Both men opened fire with their captured pistols. The volley of shots blasted across the pit and peppered Chambers' torso, causing him to jump like some sick marionette.

Travis' slide locked open as the magazine went empty and he lowered his gun. Brad stopped shooting as Chambers' body collapsed backwards, leaking blood from numerous new wounds. He glanced over at Travis and Susie.

'Everyone okay?'

'Yep,' Travis replied, helping Susie to her feet.

'Yeah,' she croaked, a reluctant smile breaking across her dirty face. 'Just bloody peachy.'

## 35

A quick search of the island premises had recovered not only their own weapons-Travis' Python and Susie's Glock 26 had been retained by Dang and Mookjai respectively, as well as Brad's Smith and Wesson and the Glock 17s that Travis and Brad had carried-but also uncovered a pair of Russian-made Kedr PP-91 machine pistols.

Travis had heard of them but never seen one in the flesh before, and Susie stood waiting impatiently while he and Brad took a couple of minutes to examine them. Finally she'd had enough and snatched the two weapons from them.

'You do realise we have a building full of dead guys here, don't you?' she snapped. 'Enough jerking off over the guns, okay? Let's get our collective arse in gear.'

Brad cocked an eyebrow at his uncle. 'Fiesty,' he said.

'Fair point though,' Travis conceded. 'Let's go.'

Travis had guided one of the boats back to the resort and they had found their rooms secured by Police tape but no guards in place. Within five minutes they had recovered all their gear and legged it to the car park, where they found the two white Land Cruisers used by Dang and his crew.

Travis' hot wiring skills had been put to use and they arrived at the Koh Samui airport as dawn broke over the island paradise, following directions from Stephenson to the right hangar.

Neither of the pilots were to be seen and they went unhindered.

The DC-3 had certainly seen better days, but the old crate was built to last and appeared to have been well maintained. It was soon winging its way south with a full tank and only a handful of passengers. Susie was at the controls, happy to be taking the bird up and making for home. It had been a while since she'd flown but she was comfortable with it and glanced at Travis in the co-pilot's seat.

'Go and take a breather,' she said through his headset, her voice raspy. 'I've got this.'

He nodded and took off his headset, moving out of the cockpit.

He stopped and came back, leaning over to kiss her on the cheek. 'Thanks, Cap'n.'

She grinned and he moved back into the hold.

Ingoe had been alerted and would have a reception party waiting for them at Whenuapai military base when they landed, including medical staff and intelligence officers.

'How was he?' Brad asked, speaking loudly over the roar of the engines. The aircraft had a few drop down seats for passengers and crew but the hold was basically empty, due to its main function as a cargo plane.

Travis crooked a smile. 'He's a hard man to read sometimes,' he said, 'but he was okay.'

'Did you tell him we shot everything to shit and just got out by the skin of our teeth?' Brad watched as Travis eased himself into one of the seats opposite him.

'I did. He didn't sound too surprised.'

Brad grinned and jerked a thumb to the stretcher on the floor where Stephenson lay, securely strapped in and sedated. 'I bet he's happy to be getting this little present, though.'

Travis nodded, looking thoughtfully at the prisoner. They had given basic medical attention to Stephenson, and Travis figured he was in for a long recovery. 'He is. Reckons the Director will be particularly pleased.' He turned and his eyes met those of his nephew. 'We don't get many traitors in NZ; I'd say people will be chomping at the bit for a crack at this guy.'

Brad nodded, holding his gaze for a moment before looking away. His expression gradually changed from excitement to contemplation. Travis watched him, knowing what he was thinking. He'd been there himself.

'We did good,' he said.

Brad looked up but said nothing.

'These are real bad guys, Brad. The hurt and chaos they cause...' Travis shook his head. 'There's only one way to deal with them, and that's to put a bullet in their fucken heads. It's all they understand.'

Brad nodded slowly. 'I got no problem with that,' he rasped. 'I'm just thinking about my boys, that's all.' He rubbed the stubble on his jaw. 'I've done what I can with these shit kickers, but I still need to make peace with the families.'

Travis nodded. He stayed silent and let the younger man get it off his chest. Travis was no tree-hugging head-shrinker, but he knew what made fighting men tick. Sometimes, after the dust had settled and physical wounds had been patched up, they needed to clear their heads in a safe environment.

'I can't hide,' Brad said softly. 'Those boys all signed up for a job, but their families never did. I need them to know what it meant to be alongside their husbands and fathers, what it meant to be there at the end.' He nodded, dropping his head and looking away.

'That's important,' Travis told him. 'For them, and for you.' He paused, and waited until his nephew looked up again. 'And when that's done, you have a decision to make.'

Brad looked at him quizzically.

'I spoke to Ingoe about it. After this, and with your face having been all over the media, it would be hard to go back to STG. If you want it, there's a spot for you at the Division.'

Brad flicked his eyebrows and nodded. 'What about you? What're you going to do? Go back to prepping for the end of the world?'

Travis gave a small smile. 'I prepare for the unexpected and unwanted. Always have. Being a soldier is an extension of that.'

'Nice diversion,' Brad noted, 'but are you going to stay on with this outfit?'

'Would it make a difference to you either way?'

Brad shrugged. 'Probably not. Doesn't seem like I have too many options really. And besides...' He gave a grin. 'It seems like it's in my blood to be a gunslinger.'

Travis smiled. 'You've been in my study.'

Brad nodded. 'A lot of family history there I didn't know.'

'No reason for you to have known; your mother wanted no part of that world and had other things on her plate.' There was sadness in his smile now. 'If you want to know, I'm happy to tell you.'

Brad nodded. 'That'd be good.' He looked around him at the battered aircraft, the weapons and the incapacitated prisoner. 'This is me.' He thumped his chest with a fist. 'In here, this is me.'

Travis leaned forward and looked him in the eye. His tone was soft but firm. 'It's what we do, Brad. Men in our family have always been fighters.' He paused and set his jaw. 'Warriors.'

Looking at his uncle across the width of the aircraft, a battle-hardened Special Forces operator, a relentless fighter and professional soldier, a specialist in every sense of the word, Brad knew he was right, and he felt it within himself. A surge of pride, of wanting to be one of them, to be the best of the best, to take the fight to the terrorists and tyrants of the world, to take them down and move on to the next battle. He didn't know what the future held, but he knew the path he would take.

Travis saw the change in his nephew's demeanour and felt himself smile inwardly. He knew the decision had been made for the younger man, and equally he knew it had been made for himself.

The request to become involved, what seemed so long ago, had nothing to do with fate or the Gods. It was just how it was; the way of the world. Despite retiring from Special Forces, the war was not over for him. Maybe it never would be. But he had been asked to do a job and he had done it. He had no doubt there would be another job after this, another mission requiring men like him. Men who did the dirty work so others could sleep peacefully at night.

It was a calling, an instinctive drive he had no control over.

It was a call to arms, and he knew within himself, he would answer that call.

# BONUS CHAPTERS

# THE DIVISION SERIES #3
THE SHADOW DANCERS

*London*
*May*

The hotel room was small but adequate and smelt of sex in the mid afternoon. Moore rolled onto his side and propped his head up so he could see into the bathroom.

The woman in the shower was tall and curvy, with shoulder length blonde hair and heavy breasts. She had a pale birth mark shaped like a speech bubble on her inner left thigh. He watched as she turned the water off and stepped out, grabbing a towel from the rack. She dried herself quickly and caught him watching.

'Didn't you see enough before?' she enquired with a cheeky grin.

Moore pushed up and swung his legs over the side of the bed. His feet touched the worn carpet.

'I saw plenty,' he said. 'Doesn't mean it's enough.'

She finished drying herself and applied deodorant and perfume from her handbag. She stepped back into the room and found her knickers on the armchair by the window. They were flimsy pale blue satin.

The woman's name was Michelle McGregor, and she was thirty

eight years old. She was also Alan McGregor's wife, which for Moore added a thrilling extra dimension to their affair. Any chance to get one over that brown-nosing prick was an opportunity that had to be taken. He knew the consequences of being caught would probably derail his career, but at the moment he really didn't care.

Moore watched her get dressed before standing himself, naked before her. He was an even six feet with a thick dark rug on his strong chest. He was greying at the temples, his dark hair cut short. His torso was lean and hard.

Michelle secured her gold necklace and tossed her hair. She straightened her red sundress before grabbing her handbag.

'Best I get a move on, lover,' she smiled, and kissed him hard on the lips.

Moore kissed her back, touching her hips and pulling her to him. She pulled back momentarily before he felt her relent. His tongue found hers and he pressed harder against her, hoping she would respond, eager for more. He started to ease backwards towards the rumpled bed, but she put a hand firmly on his chest and pushed away.

'No,' she said, 'I can't. I need to go.'

'Come on,' he said, trying his best boyish smile. 'You don't need to go just yet...'

'I do.' She was definite now, and he knew there would be no changing her mind.

He sat down on the edge of the bed anyway, watching as she checked she had everything. He wanted to say something but didn't know what. He wanted her to stay but knew she wouldn't, and couldn't.

'Happy birthday, big boy,' Michelle smiled, leaning down and giving him another quick kiss on the lips. 'Hope you're having a good day.'

Moore gave a small smile in return. 'So far, so great. Thank you.'

She tapped his nose with a painted nail and moved to the door.

'I'll be in touch,' she said as she opened the door. She checked the corridor outside before turning and blowing him a kiss. 'See ya.'

Moore nodded and watched the door close. The lock clicked into place and silence fell on the room.

He was alone again.

He hadn't seen her for three weeks, what with her own commitments and him in Singapore for half that time. Far from being an R&R trip, it had been an annual exercise with other operators from The Division. It had been wet and exhausting, and had ended with an Anzac Day dawn service and too much rum.

Now here he was in a budget London hotel, celebrating his birthday by screwing the wife of a colleague.

Moore shook off the gloom that threatened to descend. It didn't matter. She was someone else's wife; no point mooching around like a love struck school kid.

He checked the G-Shock on the bedside table. 11am. Time to get back to work.

He headed for the shower.

The depot was quiet and still at 1am on a Monday, a light breeze flicking the odd leaf or piece of rubbish across the forecourt where the trucks came in and turned round to be loaded.

A row of semis lined one side of the compound, big and dark and empty, all emblazoned with Marcus Haulage markings. A security light flickered weakly and cast only a slight glow through the darkness. The chain link fence rattled and the gate squeaked as it was pushed open.

The man at the gate checked his watch nervously for the fourth time in as many minutes. He shivered even though it wasn't cold.

An engine could be heard and a second later bright headlights swept round the corner into the street and approached the end of the cul-de-sac where the man waited on the footpath by the open gate. It was an industrial area populated by trade centres and auto businesses and nobody was around at this time of night.

The lights blinded him as the truck swung easily through the gate and entered the depot, making a wide half circle before smoothly backing up to the loading bay. This wasn't a semi-truck like the ones parked up in a row at the side of the depot, but a smaller delivery truck with no markings. The man shut the gates and looped the chain through without locking it. He hurried over to the truck and met the driver and his passenger as they jumped down.

'Good work,' the driver told him with a smirk, 'let's get to it.'

He was a burly man with greasy hair showing under his cap. He had the strong forearms built from years of guiding 18-wheelers down the highways and the red nose of a hardened drinker. His companion was of a similar build but taller, with tattoos discolouring his own forearms. He also had a spider's web tattooed on the left side of his neck and several tear drops inked into the skin by his right eye. He was harder looking than the driver and didn't speak.

'Hurry,' the man who'd opened the gate said, checking his watch again, and the driver sneered at him with contempt.

'Just open up, fella,' he replied, hitching his jeans up, 'let us do our job.'

The first man unlocked the door beside the loading bay then lifted the roller door. He stood and watched as the other two men entered the warehouse, turned a couple of lights on and got to work. Within twenty minutes they had loaded the back of the truck with several pallets of boxes, replaced the forklift, turned out the lights and locked up again. It was a smooth, efficient operation, done with minimal fuss.

The driver and his companion climbed back into the truck and the nervous man went to the gate to let them out. The truck paused in the gateway and the driver wound down the window, leaning casually out.

'Cheers buddy,' he smirked, 'see ya next time. We'll be in touch, aye?'

The passenger stared at the nervous man with a blank expression, and the nervous man nodded glumly.

'Okay, okay,' he replied, 'just go. Just go.'

The driver laughed and the truck moved away up the road. The nervous man wiped his brow on the sleeve of his jacket, locked the gate again and hurried away into the darkness.

Silence returned to the depot.

The lady sitting on the red fabric sofa in the corner of the office was well dressed and smelt of expensive perfume. She appeared uncomfortable, as if she were waiting for the dentist or a mammogram. She was middle aged and had perfectly styled hair and flawless make up.

The man sitting on the matching chair at right angles to her was twenty years younger, with broad shoulders and a confident air about him. He had dark eyes and dark hair with a hint of grey at the temples, a full moustache, and was dressed in casual chinos and an open necked shirt.

He looked up from the notes he'd made on the pad on his knee and smiled at her. It was a calm reassuring smile, and it eased her discomfort a degree or two. He had a direct gaze and intelligent eyes, the sort of face that was more interesting than handsome. A faint scar showed at his chin, a patch where no stubble could grow.

'Okay Mrs MacNamara,' he said, 'is there anything else you can tell me that may help? Any particular routine that your husband follows that may help me narrow it down a bit?'

She thought for a moment.

'He plays squash every Monday and Thursday night right after work. He always starts work by seven and usually gets home about six.' She frowned. 'That's it I'm afraid. I can't think of anything else.'

'No problem.' He jotted it down, got the name of the squash club from her, and smiled again. 'That's it, Mrs MacNamara. We'll get onto it right away, and give you an update as soon as we know anything, okay?'

'How long will it take?' she asked, and for the first time her voice quavered. She paused to re-gather herself before continuing. 'I mean, will I hear from you this week?'

'It really depends on what your husband does and what we find, Mrs MacNamara.'

He stood and she followed suit, allowing herself to be ushered over to the desk by the door. 'We'll be in touch as soon as we can, hopefully in the next few days.'

She nodded and he gave her that reassuring smile again.

'If you can give your deposit to Molly I'll quickly print off a contract for you.'

He moved to the second desk in the office, which faced the first one across the floor space. Mrs MacNamara turned to the woman at the first desk-Molly-and passed her a gold Visa.

Molly took it and used it to take an electronic deposit of ten hours work. She was a striking woman of classical beauty, with wavy dark hair and sparkling, friendly green eyes. She had full red lips and wore little make up-mainly because she didn't need to. She had the sort of look that defied pigeonholing. She could pass for a European or a country girl, depending on what she wore. Today she wore a simple black skirt and silver blouse, elegant and understated.

Mrs MacNamara cast a furtive look at the man as he printed out a contract for her. He seemed like a nice person but she sensed he was not the sort to mess with. She glanced back at Molly, who was smiling at her and holding her card and receipt out for her. Her eyes smiled as well as her mouth, and Mrs MacNamara felt herself smile in return.

The man came over and gave her a copy of the contract and had her sign his copy. She folded it and put it in her bag with her card and receipt. Then he handed her a business card and smiled again. Molly smiled again too, and Mrs MacNamara felt a little better. She thanked them and allowed him to hold the door for her.

'We'll be in touch,' he told her, and closed the door behind her.

Mrs MacNamara walked towards the stairs down to the street. She could hear the motorway behind her on the other side of the building, and the main street of Ellerslie village was in front of her. She looked at the card in her hand.

Chase Investigations, it said. Dan Crowley, Director. It was a plain white card with blue lettering, the company's name in italicised lettering across the top as if it really was chasing something, his name and title below it in smaller letters. Address and contact details at the bottom.

She tucked it into her bag with the rest of the stuff, and checked her watch. It was 930am. Nearly time for her manicure.

Dan Crowley passed the notes and contract to his wife and went to the kitchenette off the office.

'What do you think?' he asked as he poured a coffee for himself and a green tea for her. 'If we could get a few more Mrs MacNamaras in here with their Remuera cheque books, I'd be happy.'

'If we get a few more Mrs MacNamaras in here, 'Molly replied, 'there won't be room to move. You've got a full week already, honey, and now this as well.'

'I'll give it to old Neil,' he told her, handing her a tea cup and perching on the corner of her desk.

'He's already got a full week as well.' She clicked open the weekly planner on her desktop and opened up the tab for Neil. 'He's in court for the Shelby theft case today, he's got the Parker and Philips fraud, four accident reports due in and he's got five processes.' She took a sip of tea and gave him a plaintive look. 'What, no biscuits this morning?'

Dan went to the kitchenette and brought back the cookie jar.

'How about you, could you squeeze it in?' He bit into a ginger crunch and showered crumbs down his front. He didn't seem to notice.

'I'll have to, won't I?' Molly sighed and frowned at him. He didn't seem to notice that either.

'We need to take someone else on though, honey. Neil's as slow as a wet week.'

'He is officially retired.'

'So he should retire properly then. I'm supposed to be part time but I'm practically full time and you did sixty hours last week.' She pouted at him. 'You need to get someone in.'

He sipped his coffee and nodded.

'You're right.' He smiled at her and patted her cheek affection- ately. 'No worries gorgeous, I'll sort it out. I'll talk to Buck and see if he knows of anyone wanting to get out.'

The door opened and an elderly man with grey hair and a beer pot entered, a battered briefcase in one hand and a copy of the Racing Times in the other.

'Morning all,' he said cordially, kicking the door closed behind him, 'how are we?'

'We be fine,' Dan replied with an amused smile. 'How are ye?'

'Ye be good,' Neil replied, taking a seat at the third desk, the one in the corner with the empty file tray. He opened his briefcase and removed a thick manila folder. He carried it over to Molly's desk and put it down with a flourish.

'Here you go, my dear lady,' he said grandly, shooting the cuffs of his dark suit and smoothing his tie. 'All my files, up to date and complete.'

He looked across at Dan, who was coming from the kitchenette with a coffee for him.

'I'm retiring,' he announced, drinking in their surprised looks. 'Yep, I thought it was about time. I don't need to work; I've got my pension and not long left to spend it. June's found a place in Tauranga and put an offer in, it got accepted over the weekend and we move this week.'

'That soon?' Molly looked stunned.

'That soon,' he said. 'I'm sorry to drop it on you like this, but we got the word on Friday night. I cleaned up my files over the weekend, all the documents are served, the crash reports are done and photos on the disk, and I've done the preliminary work on the Parker and Philips job.' He glanced back to Dan. 'You'll just need to finish it off, Daniel.'

'Uh-huh.' Dan nodded and went to his desk. 'You're still in court today, I take it?'

'Indeed, indeed. The last time I'll be giving evidence, I should imagine.' He nodded solemnly. 'No more running round playing private eye for old Neil, it's time for fishing and golf.'

'And spending quality time with June,' Molly reminded him.

'Yeah, that too,' he conceded.

There was an awkward silence for a moment. Nobody seemed to

know what to say. Molly looked to her husband, but he remained silent. She felt her cheeks flush.

'Anyway, I better get to court,' Neil said eventually, 'justice waits for no man.'

'I think you mean time,' Dan told him.

'Don't I know it.'

Neil grabbed his briefcase, took a quick slurp of coffee and was gone, banging the door behind him again as he left.

Dan and Molly looked across the office at each other.

'Be careful what you wish for,' he said.

'D'you think he heard me?' she frowned.

'Probably.' He groaned and rubbed his face. 'Now we really need someone. Better book dinner for four at Luigi's, I guess.'

'Ooh, are you taking your wife out for dinner?' she cooed, making eyes at him across the room.

'Hmm, something like that.' He grinned. 'In company, of course, so you don't get any fancy ideas.'

'Typical. Where's the romance gone?'

'He could've given us more notice than a day,' Dan grumbled. He leaned back in his chair and put his feet up on the edge of the desk.

'That's what you get for taking on a contractor,' she told him, 'all care, no responsibility. I think we should take on a permanent employee this time.'

'Then I'd have to pay them holidays and sick and whatever else they can think of.' He shook his head in despair. 'Just can't get the staff.'

'You've gotta try first. What about Buck?'

'What, Buck himself? Na, he's got it too cushy where he is, why would he give that up?'

'Being the Ellerslie community cop can hardly be stimulating,' Molly opined.

'Not too taxing either, though. He hasn't got himself in trouble since...well...'

'Since he stopped working with you?'

'Exactly.'

His mobile bleeped on the desk with an incoming message. He smiled as he checked it.

'Mike,' he said, 'wants to meet for a coffee urgently.'

'Wonder who he's in love with now?' Molly speculated.

'You're such a cynic.'

'You know it's true. Ten to one it's a drama about some woman.' She gave him a challenging look. 'Go on, bet against me.'

Dan shook his head and got up.

'That's a sucker's bet.' He bent over her desk and kissed her softly on the cheek. 'And I'm no sucker.'

'No, you're a hot shot private eye.' Her eyes twinkled at him. 'But you know what it'll be.'

'Maybe.' He kissed her firmly on the mouth now. 'I'll shoot down and see Buck first, then go see him then head off and do the Parker and Philips case.'

'Hey.' Molly caught him by the sleeve. 'Maybe Mike wants a job?'

'You think?' He considered it for a second then shook his head. 'Na, can you really see him as a PI? Doubt it. We don't do debt collection.'

'You used to,' she reminded him, and he shrugged.

'Yeah, but now we're chasing better money than that. Any port in a storm I guess, but I'd rather Mrs MacNamara brought her friends to see us. At least you know you won't get your head stoved in investigating a cheating husband or corporate fraud.'

He leaned down and kissed her again.

'I'll call you later.'

He left the office, wondering what it was that Mike had got himself into now.

# MESSAGE FROM THE AUTHOR

Thanks for taking the time to read *Call To Arms*. I hope you enjoyed the second book in the **Division** series. The third book in the series is *The Shadow Dancers* - A politician's daughter is missing in Turkey, just as Russia is bombing Syria and the Middle East powder keg is about to explode. Someone else is pulling the strings and Moore is forced to dance to a tune he doesn't know. One wrong step and he's dead.

I'd love it if you could please take the time to leave an online review of *Call To Arms* with your favourite book retailer.

If you'd like to know about new releases and receive a free book, sign up to my **Hitlist** on Facebook -

https://www.facebook.com/writer-angus-mclean

Cheers,
   *Angus McLean*

# ACKNOWLEDGMENTS

The author would like to thank the advisers who have assisted with the writing of this book. They must remain anonymous for security reasons, but they (and only they) know who they are.

They are the true heroes who put their lives on the line to protect our freedoms. My sincerest gratitude goes out to them.

And once again, huge thanks to "Tori" who does my covers and provides great advice. You rock.

This is a work of fiction, and all errors are the responsibility of the author.

# ABOUT THE AUTHOR

Angus McLean is a South Auckland Police officer.

His experience as a cop and a private investigator give his writing a touch of realism. He believes reading should be escapist entertainment and is inspired by the TV shows he watched as a youngster.

His real identity remains a secret.

www.writerangusmclean.com